One Night, Two Babies
by Kathie DeNosky

From the desk of Emerald Larson, owner and CEO of Emerald, Inc

To: My personal assistant, Luther Freemont
Re: My granddaughter, Arielle Garnier

My granddaughter, Arielle, has moved to Dallas, Texas, and successfully taken over Premier Academy for Pre-schoolers. But during my recent investigation to find her and her brothers, it was brought to my attention that she's pregnant and has been unable to locate the baby's father. I've been advised by the lead investigator that he's Zach Forsythe, whose nephew attends Premier Academy. I have every reason to believe they will come face to face in the very near future. That said, I expect you to arrange whatever you deem necessary to accomplish my goal of bringing them together. Keep me informed of the progress.

As always, I am relying on your complete discretion in this matter.

Emerald Larson

Valente's Baby
by Maxine Sullivan

"Maybe you could have handled this differently, *figlio mio*."

"You were the one who told me to marry her, Dad."

"Megan needed the Valente name. If you hadn't, I would have found a way to force you."

"Yeah, like you did with Alex and Nick."

"Naturally." There was a lengthy pause before Cesare spoke again. "What are you going to do now?"

"I'm not sure," Matt murmured, sounding distracted.

Lana, standing in the doorway, felt as though her breath had been cut off. They were talking about *her*.

And what was this about Alex and Nick? Cesare had forced them to marry their wives? He would have forced Nick to marry, too?

God, how many lives were the Valentes prepared to wreck for the sake of the family name?

ONE NIGHT, TWO BABIES

BY
KATHIE DeNOSKY

VALENTE'S BABY

BY
MAXINE SULLIVAN

First published in Great Britain 2010
Harlequin Mills & Boon Limited,
Eton House, 18-24 Paradise Road, Richmond, Surrey TW9 1SR

The publisher acknowledges the copyright holders of the individual works as follows:

One Night, Two Babies © Kathie DeNosky 2009
Valente's Baby © Maxine Sullivan 2009

ISBN: 978 0 263 88177 6

51-0810

Harlequin Mills & Boon policy is to use papers that are natural, renewable and recyclable products and made from wood grown in sustainable forests. The logging and manufacturing processes conform to the legal environmental regulations of the country of origin.

Printed and bound in Spain
by Litografia Rosés S.A., Barcelona

ONE NIGHT,
TWO BABIES

BY
KATHIE DeNOSKY

Dear Reader,

Last month you met the Garnier siblings, three more of Emerald Larson's ILLEGITIMATE HEIRS, and with her help, watched Luke find true happiness with his executive assistant, Haley Rollins. This month, Emerald turns her unwavering determination and full attention to setting things right for Luke's sister, Arielle.

After spending the most exciting week of her life in the arms of Zach Forsythe, Arielle Garnier finds herself alone and facing the challenge of single motherhood. But when she unexpectedly comes face to face with Zach and he learns she's pregnant with twins, he's determined to do "the right thing" and make Arielle his wife.

So please sit back and enjoy the ride as, once again, Emerald Larson helps one of her illegitimate heirs find true love in *One Night, Two Babies*.

All the best,

Kathie DeNosky

Kathie DeNosky lives in her native southern Illinois with her big, lovable Bernese mountain dog, Nemo. Writing highly sensual stories with a generous amount of humour, Kathie's books have appeared on bestseller lists and received the Write Touch Readers' Award and the National Readers' Choice Award. Kathie enjoys going to rodeos, travelling to research settings for her books and listening to country music. Readers may contact Kathie at PO Box 2064, Herrin, Illinois 62948-5264, USA or e-mail her at kathie@kathiedenosky.com. They can also visit her website at www.kathiedenosky.com.

This series is dedicated to Charlie, the love of my life.

A special thank-you to Donna Swan, Carolyn Jordan and Lisa Swan for the Saturday Night Girls' Club. You're the best.

One

"Mrs. Montrose, I know what Derek did was wrong, but you have to give him another chance."

When Arielle Garnier looked up from her computer screen at the sound of the male voice, her heart came to a screeching halt. The man who just stopped inside her office doorway was the last person she ever expected to see again. And if the look on his handsome face was any indication, he was just as surprised to be coming face-to-face with her, as well.

His vivid green eyes pinned her to the chair. He stared at her for several uncomfortable seconds before he finally spoke again. "I need to talk to the preschool's administrator, Mrs. Montrose, about an incident involving Derek Forsythe. Could you please tell me where I could find her?"

"Helen Montrose is no longer in charge here. She sold the school and retired a couple of weeks ago." Arielle tried desperately to keep her voice even in spite of her jangled nerves. "I'm the new owner and administrator of Premier Academy for Preschoolers."

She took a deep breath and reminded herself to remain outwardly calm, even if his reappearance in her life did shake her all the way to the core. This was her territory and he was the one intruding. Besides, she'd rather walk barefoot across hot coals than allow him to think he still had any effect on her.

When he continued to stare at her, she forced herself to ask, "Was there something you needed?"

He finally shook his head. "I don't have time to play games, Arielle. I need to speak with Helen Montrose as soon as possible."

The shock of seeing him again quickly gave way to anger that he didn't believe she was the new owner. "I told you, Mrs. Montrose retired. And if you have business here at the school, you will have to deal with me."

He didn't look at all pleased with the situation, but that was just too bad. She certainly wasn't excited to be seated before the man who, three and a half months earlier, had spent a week loving her like she was the most desirable woman alive, then disappeared without so much as a backward glance. He hadn't even had the decency to call or leave her a note.

"All right," he eventually said. She could tell he wasn't happy, but instead of pressing the issue any further, he took a deep breath. "I suppose this would be a good time to reintroduce myself. My real name is Zach Forsythe."

Arielle's heart felt as if it had fallen to her feet. Among his other transgressions, he'd lied to her about his name? He was really Zachary Forsythe, owner of the Forsythe resort and hotel empire? And if he was here to discuss Derek Forsythe, did that mean he was the little boy's father? Was he *married?*

Bile rose in her throat and she desperately tried to think if she'd heard or read anything about him recently. But all she could remember for certain was that Zach Forsythe was reputed to prefer a quiet lifestyle out of the spotlight and guarded his privacy as if it were the gold in Fort Knox. Unfortunately, she didn't know anything at all about his marital status.

But the very thought that she might have spent a week in the arms of a married man sent a cold chill slithering down her spine. "Correct me if I'm wrong, but a few months ago I distinctly knew you by the name of Tom Zacharias."

He ran an impatient hand through his thick dark brown hair. "About that—"

"Save it," she interrupted, holding up her hand. "I don't particularly care to hear whatever explanation you're about to fabricate. I believe you wanted to talk about Derek Forsythe?" When he nodded, she went on. "And I assume you wish to discuss his pending suspension for biting another little boy?"

His mouth thinned into a grim line before he gave her a short nod. "Yes. You have to give him one more chance."

"I haven't been here long enough to be familiar with his past behavioral patterns, but your son's teacher said he's—"

"Nephew." Frowning, he then flashed her the same smile that he'd used to seduce her almost four months earlier. "Derek is my sister's little boy," he corrected. "I'm not now, nor have I ever been, married, Arielle."

She was relieved to hear that she hadn't done the unthinkable. But his devastating smile and the intimate tone he used to say her name made it hard to think.

"You don't have to be married to have a child," she countered, doing her best to regain a bit of her equilibrium.

"I suppose it's a personal choice," he observed, shrugging. "But I, for one, won't have a child outside of marriage."

"Whether you do or not isn't the issue here, Mr. Forsythe."

"Call me Zach."

"I don't think…"

Before she could go on, he took a step closer.

"And marriage may not be the issue, but I can't have you thinking—"

"What I think is irrelevant." Desperate to change the subject, she tried to concentrate on the matter at hand. "Derek's teacher said this is the third time he's bitten another child in the past week." She glanced at the teacher's recommendation for suspension on top of a stack of papers on her desk. "And the school has a strict three-strikes policy when it comes to this kind of behavior."

"I understand that. But he's only four and a half years old. Can't you make an exception this one time?" he asked, turning up the wattage on his cajoling smile. "If you haven't been told about my sister's accident by some of the other teachers, I won't bore you with the details, but Derek's experienced quite an upset in his life in the past few months and I'm sure that's the reason he's been acting out. Things are getting back to normal now and I'm sure he'll settle down. Believe me, he really is a good kid."

Zach or Tom or whatever he was calling himself these days was putting her in a very awkward position. On one hand, rules were rules and had been put into place to discourage students' undesirable behavior. If she made an exception for one child, she'd have to make it for all of the children. But on the other hand, if she didn't give the little boy another chance, it might appear that she was punishing him for the actions of his nefarious uncle.

"Would it help sway you if I promise to have a long talk with Derek and make him understand that it's unacceptable to bite other children?" he asked. Apparently sensing her indecision, he walked to her desk and, propping his fists on the edge, leaned forward until their faces were only inches apart. "Come on, darlin'. Everyone deserves a second chance."

After the way he'd lied to her about his name, then disappeared without a word of explanation, she would debate that issue. But his close proximity and hearing him call her "darlin'" with his rich Texas drawl caused her to shiver.

"A-all right," she finally replied, forcing herself not to lean away from him, even though it made her extremely nervous being so near.

She was willing to say just about anything to get him to turn off the charm and get out of her office so that she could draw a decent breath. Besides, the longer he stayed the greater the possibility he'd find out why she'd spent several weeks desperately trying to reach him. And at the moment, that was something she just wasn't ready to address, nor was her office the place to do it.

"If you'll explain to Derek that it's wrong to behave that way toward other children, I'll let him off with a warning this time," she decided firmly. "But if it happens again, he will have to serve the suspension."

"Fair enough." He straightened to his full height, then, stuffing his hands in the pockets of his suit pants, rocked back on his heels. "Now that we have that settled, I'll let you get back to whatever it was you were doing." Walking toward the door, he stopped and turned to give her another one of his charming smiles. "By the way, it was a very pleasant surprise running into you again, Arielle."

And jackasses have sprouted wings and learned to fly, she thought, barely resisting the urge to convey her sarcasm aloud. But before she could comment on his obvious lie, he exited her office as quickly as he'd barged in.

Sinking back into the plush leather of her desk chair, Arielle tried to think. What on earth was she going to do now?

She'd given up all attempts to find him months ago when every one of her efforts met with a dead end. Of course, now she knew why. The man she'd been looking for didn't even exist. It had been Zachary Forsythe, hotel and resort magnate, who had held her, made love to her and…lied to her. And here he was living in the city she'd recently moved to, with a nephew in her preschool.

"How did my life get so out of control?"

Burying her head in her shaking hands, she did her best to organize her scattered thoughts. She had no idea what to do, *if* she should do anything. Clearly he'd never expected to see her again, and wasn't overjoyed that he had. And she certainly wasn't thrilled with the situation, either.

Her stomach did a fluttery lurch and, placing a calming hand over it, she tightly closed her eyes as she fought to keep her emotions in check. First and foremost, she'd made a huge mistake falling for his charismatic charm. And second, she'd wasted count-less hours trying to find a man who'd just proved he wasn't worth finding.

But she'd foolishly held out hope that he'd have a plausible explanation for leaving her to wake up alone all those months ago. Deep down she'd known she was deluding herself, but it was easier than acknowledging how gullible and utterly foolish she'd been. Now there was no denying that he was every bit the jerk she'd feared him to be.

She swallowed hard and, opening her eyes, reached for a tissue to dab at the moisture threaten-ing to spill down her cheeks. Her move to Dallas was supposed to be a good thing—a symbolic gesture of leaving the past behind and making a fresh start. But he'd just ruined that. There was no way she could forget about him and move on with her life if he showed up at the school from time to time.

Sniffling, she reached for another tissue. She hated being so darned weepy all of the time, but then, that was his fault, too.

Her stomach clenched again and she automatically opened her desk drawer, reaching for the bag of crackers she kept for just such occasions. Yes, Zachary Forsythe was to blame for her hormones making her emotional, as well as her other current problems. And the most pressing problem of all was figuring out how and when to tell the biggest jerk in the entire state of Texas that even though he wasn't married as he said he would be, in about five and a half months, he was indeed going to have a child of his own.

Zach entered his executive office at the Forsythe Hotel and Resort Group corporate headquarters still thinking about his unexpected run-in with Arielle Garnier. He'd thought about her a lot since their time together in Aspen, but he'd never expected to see her again. And certainly not at the same preschool where his nephew was enrolled. But thanks to the little boy's latest antics, Zach had been put in the awkward position of pleading Derek's case to the woman he'd, for lack of a better word, *dumped* a few months ago.

Walking over to his desk, Zach sank into the high-backed chair. Swiveling around, he gazed blindly at the framed aerial photograph of his luxury resort in Aspen. He distinctly recalled Arielle telling him that she was a teacher at some nursery school in San Francisco. So why had she relocated to Texas? And where had she come up with the money to buy the most prestigious preschool in the Dallas area?

He supposed that her older twin brothers might have had something to do with that. If he remembered correctly, she'd told him that one was a highly successful divorce attorney in Los Angeles and the other owned the largest construction and development company in the south. They certainly could have afforded to front her the money to buy the school. In fact, they'd been the ones who'd given her the week's ski trip, complete with deluxe accommodations at the Aspen Forsythe Resort and Spa for her twenty-sixth birthday.

Focusing his attention on the photograph of the luxury mountain resort, Zach couldn't help but grin when he thought about the first time he'd met Arielle. It had been her engaging smile and flawless beauty that had first attracted him. Her silky, dark auburn hair had complimented her porcelain skin to perfection and she had the prettiest hazel eyes he'd ever seen. But as the evening wore on, it had been her sense of humor and obvious intelligence that had him thoroughly captivated. By the following morning, they had become lovers.

As he sat there thinking about what had been the most exciting, memorable week of his life, his office door opened. His sister slowly walked across the room to lower herself into the chair in front of his desk.

"Did you speak with Mrs. Montrose about Derek?" she asked, propping her cane against the edge of his desk. "She's always been extremely fair and since the accident, she's been very understanding about his uncharacteristic behavior."

Zach shook his head. "Helen Montrose is no longer in charge at Premier Academy, Lana."

"She's not?" There was a hint of panic in his sister's voice. "Who's taken over for her? Is he going to have to serve the suspension? Did you explain to whomever's in charge now that Derek's normally a very well-behaved little boy?"

"Arielle Garnier is the new owner and administrator," he answered, searching his younger sister's pretty face. To the outward eye Lana looked the picture of health. But she still had days when the fatigue of recovering from her horrific accident was overwhelming. "I don't want you to worry about it. I've taken care of everything and promised to have a talk with Derek about what's acceptable and what isn't. He won't have to serve the suspension, unless he bites the other children."

"That's a relief," Lana replied, finally smiling as she sat back in the chair. "He's settled down quite a bit now that I've had the casts taken off and we've moved back into the condo. And as our lives get back to normal, I'm sure his behavior will continue to improve."

With Lana having two badly broken legs, internal injuries and a couple cracked ribs, Zach had insisted that his sister and nephew move into his place during her recovery. And it was a damned good thing that he had. After her release from the hospital, Lana couldn't take care of herself, let alone see to the needs of an extremely active four-and-a-half-year-old boy.

"How did your physical therapy session go?"

Zach inquired, noticing Lana wince as she shifted to a more comfortable position. "You seem to be having a little trouble."

"I'm ahead of where the therapist expected at this stage, but it's not the exercises I'm doing that's causing my soreness today." She pointed to the floor-to-ceiling glass behind him. "It's this dumb weather. Since the accident I'm better at predicting a rainstorm than a barometer."

He glanced over his shoulder at the bright sunlight and brilliant blue sky just beyond the window. "It looks fine out there to me."

"I don't care," she objected, shaking her head. "My knees are telling me it's going to rain buckets sometime today, so grab an umbrella when you go out."

"I'll keep that in mind." When he watched her shift again, he offered, "If you'd like to go home and get some rest, I can have Mike pick up Derek from school in the limo."

Lana nodded as she levered herself out of the chair, waving Zach back down in his seat, and reached for her cane. "That might not be a bad idea. I promised him I'd bake some chocolate chip cookies for his afternoon snack. And a nap before I get started would be nice."

"Just don't overdo things."

She laughed as she made her way to the door. "No danger in that."

"By the way, I'm heading up to the ranch this

weekend. Would you and Derek like to go along?" he asked, thinking they might like to get out of town for a while. Located just north of the city, the ranch where he and Lana had grown up had become a peaceful weekend getaway.

Turning, she shook her head. "Thanks, but now that I'm doing better, I think Derek needs some uninterrupted mommy time. Besides, you know how it floods up there when it rains. I don't want to be stranded for the next few days while we wait for the water to recede. But please, give Mattie my love and tell her that Derek and I will be up to visit in the next couple of weeks."

"I'll drive myself and leave Mike here to take you wherever you need to go. If you change your mind, have him drive the two of you up to the ranch."

"I will, but don't count on us," she suggested, smiling.

After his sister left, Zach returned to work. But soon his thoughts were straying to Arielle Garnier and how absolutely amazing she'd appeared that morning. There had been a glow about her that he found completely fascinating.

He frowned. As unbelievable as it seemed, she was even prettier now than she had been when they'd first met.

But he wondered what brought her to Dallas. When they first met, she'd told him that she'd been born and raised in San Francisco and how much she loved it there. Had something happened to change her feelings? And why hadn't she moved to Los Angeles or Nashville to be closer to one of her brothers?

By the time he left the office for the day, Zach was filled with far more questions than he had answers. Something just didn't add up. And even though where Arielle lived or what she did was none of his concern, he decided to stop by the school on his way out of town. He had every intention of finding out why a woman who had been perfectly content with her life a few months ago would make such a drastic change.

"Thank God it's Friday," Arielle muttered as she pulled her raincoat close and splashed through the ankle-deep water covering the school's parking lot on her way to her red Mustang. "The whole day has been one big royal pain in the neck."

The gentle spring rain that had started shortly before lunch had quickly turned into a torrential downpour and had continued throughout the afternoon, causing the pre-K field trip to the petting zoo to be canceled. Then, if thirty extremely disappointed four-year-olds hadn't been enough to contend with, one of the little girls in the three-year-olds' class stuffed a bean up her nose during craft time and had to be taken to the urgent care facility around the corner to have it removed.

Opening the car door, she quickly closed her umbrella, threw it into the backseat and slid in behind the steering wheel. She couldn't wait to get home to her new apartment, slip into a baggy pair of sweats and forget the entire day ever happened. Since becoming pregnant, she'd started taking a nap when the children took theirs. Having missed hers this afternoon, she was not only tired, she was cranky, as well.

But her well-laid-out plan to spend a quiet weekend at her new home came to a swift end when she backed the low-slung car from her reserved space, drove halfway across the parking lot and listened to the motor sputter twice, then die. When all of her attempts to get the car going again failed, she closed her eyes and barely resisted the urge to scream. She should have known when Zach Forsythe showed up first thing this morning that it was going to be one of those days.

She sighed heavily and, reaching for her cell phone, quickly dialed the number for roadside assistance to send a tow truck. But her already low spirits took a nosedive when, after holding for ten minutes, a representative came on the line to inform her that due to the high number of calls from motorists with stalled-out cars, it would be several hours before one of their drivers could come to her aid.

As she ended the call, she glanced at the water covering the parking lot, then at the school's front entrance. She couldn't just sit in the car until they arrived and trudging back into the school through inches of water wasn't appealing, either.

But her mood lightened considerably when the reflection of car lights in her rearview mirror drew her attention. A Lincoln Navigator pulled to a stop beside her. She briefly wondered if she should err on the side of caution and refuse any offer of help from a stranger. But she instantly dismissed the thought. They were in an exclusive, very affluent area of the city, it was still daylight and how many criminals drove luxury SUVs?

But when the driver got out, opened the passenger door of her car and Zach Forsythe got in, Arielle's gratitude died in her throat. "What do you think you're doing?" she demanded.

His knowing grin caused her heart to flutter like a trapped butterfly. "It would appear that I'm going to be rescuing you."

She shook her head. "No, I don't need help." Especially from you, she added silently.

"Then why are you sitting here in your car in the middle of a flooded parking lot?"

"Maybe I just want to."

"Start the car, Arielle."

"No." Why couldn't he just go away and leave her alone?

His grin widened. "Is it because you don't want to or that you can't start the car?"

She glared at him before she finally conceded, "I can't."

He nodded. "That's what I thought. It's stalled out, isn't it?"

"Yes."

"Well, that tells me you *are* in need of my help."

"Thanks for the offer, but I'm sure you'll understand why I have to decline," she said stubbornly. If he was her only alternative, she'd just as soon fend for herself.

"Don't be ridiculous, Arielle."

"I'm not. I've already called my auto service."

"Really?" He didn't look at all convinced. "And just when is it supposed to arrive?"

"I'm sure it will be here any minute," she lied, staring at the street. Maybe if she wished long and hard enough, a tow truck would miraculously appear and Zach would disappear.

"Nice try, darlin'. But I'm not buying it." He leaned close as if he was about to share a secret. "Remember, I'm from Dallas. I know how it is around here in the spring and how long the auto club will take to get to you at this time of day. I also know that calling a cab would take just as long."

"I don't mind waiting," she repeated.

Why did he have to be so darned good-looking?

"In case you haven't noticed, it's pouring and doesn't look like it's going to let up anytime soon. You'll be lucky if anyone can get here until this time tomorrow."

"Surely it won't take that long."

"Trust me, it could be even longer. And there's no way in hell I'm going to leave you sitting here in your car all night."

"I'll just go back inside the school until they get here," she decided, thinking quickly. Sleeping on the narrow couch in her office held very little appeal, but it would be a lot better than accepting aid from a lying snake like Zach Forsythe.

After a long staring match, he finally insisted, "Let me make this clear for you, darlin'. Either you get in my SUV and let me take you home or I'm going to stay right here with you for as long as it takes to get your car towed."

"You can't do that."

He folded his arms across his broad chest and settled back in the bucket seat. "Watch me."

His overly confident smile and arrogant manner grated on her nerves. "I'm sure you have more interesting things to do with your time than sit here with me all evening, so I suggest you go do them."

"Actually, I don't."

"Then why don't you go hunt for something to do and leave me alone?"

A tiny ache began to settle in her stomach and she wished he'd leave so she could go inside and find something to eat in the cafeteria before she got sick. Her morning sickness had mostly disappeared a few weeks ago, but she still became queasy if she let her stomach get empty.

Besides, the longer she was around Zach, the greater the chance he would discover that she was pregnant. And although she would tell him that he was going to be a father, she wasn't prepared to do so at this moment. She was still coming to terms with the shock of running into him again.

Shrugging, he shook his head. "I'm not leaving until I'm certain you're okay."

"Why not? If you'll recall, you didn't seem to have that problem almost four months ago," she retorted before she could stop herself.

His smile fading, he uncrossed his arms and reached out to lightly trace his index finger along her jaw. "The circumstances are entirely different than they were then. Now, if you don't get out of this car and into mine voluntarily, I swear I'll pick you up and put you there myself."

A shivering thrill raced up her spine at his touch. "Is that a threat, Mr. Forsythe?"

"No, darlin'. That's a promise."

Two

Zach steered his SUV out of the school parking lot and onto the street. After giving him her address, Arielle plastered herself to the passenger-side door and clutched the front of her oversize raincoat like a security blanket. He'd also noticed she'd become quite pale.

His earlier irritation with her stubbornness quickly turned to concern. The woman he'd known in Aspen had been vibrant, outgoing and exuded good health. But Arielle's demeanor and the disturbing pallor of her complexion gave him every reason to believe that she was coming down with something.

"Are you all right?" he asked, glancing over at her again.

"I'm fine."

Stopping at the red light on the corner, he turned to face her. "I don't think so. You make a ghost look colorful."

She shook her head. "I'll be a lot better if you'll just take me home. Once I have something to eat, I'll be okay."

When the light changed, he gave serious consideration to taking her to her apartment, bidding her farewell, then leaving town as he'd planned. But his conscience nagged at him and he just couldn't do it.

Arielle was new to town, had no family in the area that he knew of and he'd bet his last dime that her only acquaintances were the people she worked with. How could he possibly leave her to fend for herself when she was obviously ill?

Making a snap decision, he headed straight for the interstate. She might not like it, but she needed someone with her until her illness passed. And the way he saw it, he was about the only choice she had.

"What are you doing?" she asked, raising her head from where it had rested against the passenger window. "Why did you pass up my street?"

"It's obvious you're sick and I don't think you need to be left alone."

"I told you, I'm fine," she insisted. "Now turn this truck around and take me home."

"No." He changed lanes to avoid a huge amount

of water covering the road ahead. "I'm taking you to my weekend place north of the city."

"I'm not going anywhere with…you." Her voice sounded a bit shaky and her pale complexion had taken on a sickly, greenish hue. "All I need is some-thing to…eat and I'll be…good as new."

"I'll let my housekeeper, Mattie, be the judge of that." He'd feel a lot better having her oversee Arielle's care. Mattie had been like a grandmother to him and Lana and nursed them through every one of their childhood illnesses with a jar of VapoRub in one hand and a bowl of homemade chicken soup in the other. "Her home remedies are as effective as any prescription medication."

"I'm sure they are. But my apartment is a lot closer and…I told you, I'll be fine as soon as I—" She stopped suddenly. "Pull over. I think…I'm going to be…sick."

Zach had the SUV stopped before she could finish the thought. Throwing open the driver's door, he rushed around the front of the truck to help her out. Putting his arm around her shoulders, he supported her while she was sick, and if he wasn't sure before that he'd made the right decision, he was now. The last thing she needed was to be left alone to contend with a very bad case of the flu.

"I think I'll be…all right now," she finally said, raising her head.

After helping her back into the truck, Zach got in

behind the steering wheel and turned on the heater. "Let's get you out of your raincoat," he proposed, reaching over to help her. The garment was completely soaked. "I'm sure you're cold and uncomfortable in that thing."

"I'd rather keep it on," she objected, shaking her head as she clutched the folds of the coat. "It's water-resistant and the inside is still warm and dry."

Had that been a flash of panic he'd seen in her expressive hazel eyes? Why the hell would she be afraid to take off her wet coat?

"I'm not absolutely certain that's a good idea, darlin'."

"I am." As she leaned her head back against the headrest, he watched her close her eyes as if it was too much of an effort to keep them open. "Now, will you please stop telling me what to do and listen to me? I want to go home to my apartment."

"I'm sorry, Arielle, but I just can't do that. Try to rest. We'll be at my ranch before you know it."

"This could easily be considered a kidnapping," she relayed, sounding extremely tired.

"Not if the alleged kidnapper is only trying to do what's best for the alleged kidnappee," he elaborated, shifting the SUV into gear and merging back into the busy rush-hour traffic.

"Best in…whose opinion?" she argued, delicately hiding a yawn behind her hand.

"The only one that counts right now—mine." He

smiled at the long-suffering expression on her pretty face. "Now, try to take a little nap. I'll wake you once we get to the ranch."

When she felt herself being gathered into strong, capable arms, Arielle's eyes snapped open. "Wh-what on earth do you think you're doing, Zach?"

Lifting her to him, he gave her a grin that curled her toes inside her soggy shoes. "You're not feeling well, so I'm helping you—"

"Just because I'm not one hundred percent doesn't mean I can't get out of the truck on my own," she interrupted, desperate to put some distance between them. What if he felt the bulge of her stomach?

"You need to conserve your energy to fight whatever bug you have," he explained, setting her on her feet. When he shut the SUV's door, he placed his arm around her shoulders, tucked her to his side and guided her from the garage across the covered breezeway into the house. "Besides, I'm not running the risk of you passing out and possibly adding a concussion to your other ailments."

His secure hold caused her heart to thump even harder. "H-how many times do I have to tell you? All I need is something to eat and I'll be fine."

He stopped ushering her along when they entered the kitchen. "Mattie?"

"Stop your hollerin', Zachary. I'm old, but I ain't deaf." A gray-haired woman in her late sixties walked out of a pantry and stopped short at the sight of Zach holding her. "Did I forget about you bringin' company for the weekend?"

He shook his head. "No, but Arielle's sick and can't be left alone. Probably coming down with a bad cold or maybe even the flu and requires your expert care."

Arielle tried to push away from him. "I don't have the—"

"Hush, darlin'," he said close to her ear, causing a shiver to course through her. "Mattie Carnahan, this is Arielle Garnier. She's in need of some dry clothes. See if you can find something of Lana's for her to put on while I take her to the guest room."

He led her down a hall and opened the door to a beautifully decorated room. When he reached to help her out of her coat, Arielle shook her head and took a step back. "I don't need your help."

"You need to take that coat off," he insisted, moving toward her. "It's soaked."

She took a few steps backward. "The only thing I want from you is to be left alone. But if you feel you have to do something, find me something to eat and then take me back to my apartment. What part of that don't you understand? And exactly how can I make it any clearer for you?"

As they stood glaring at each other, Mattie walked into the room to place a set of gray sweats and a heavy pair of socks on the bed. "Honey, he can be as stubborn as a jackass when he gets something in his head." She motioned for Zach to leave. "You go get your things out of the car and I'll have supper on the table by the time you get unpacked."

Zach didn't appear to be all that happy with his housekeeper taking over the situation. "I can do that later. I need to make sure Arielle is—"

"Go," Arielle and the older woman both said at the same time.

Muttering a curse, he finally turned and walked from the room.

Mattie started to follow him. "If there's anything else you need, just let me know."

"Thank you," Arielle said, meaning it. At least the housekeeper had given her a bit of a reprieve from Zach's overpowering masculinity. "And for the record, I don't have the flu."

Mattie nodded as she stepped back into the room and closed the door. "Zachary means well, but he doesn't have any idea you're pregnant, does he?"

A cold sense of dread spread throughout Arielle's body. "I… Uh, no, he doesn't."

"How far along are you, child?" Mattie asked, her voice so kind and understanding it chased away some of Arielle's apprehension.

There was no use denying what the housekeeper had guessed, although Arielle didn't have any idea how the woman could have possibly figured it out.

"I'm only three and a half months pregnant, but I'm already starting to get a nice little bulge."

Mattie nodded. "I thought you must be showing some since you were so determined to keep your coat on and kept holding it together. That's why I brought some of Zachary's sweatshirts and pants, instead of his sister's. You'll have to roll up the legs and push up the sleeves, but I thought you might need the extra room."

"But how did you know?" Arielle was thoroughly amazed by the woman's intuitiveness.

"Some women have a look about them when they're pregnant and if ever a woman had that glow, you do," Mattie revealed, shrugging. "And if that wasn't enough, Zachary telling me that you got sick on the drive up here and your insistence that all you needed was something to eat was. I always had to keep something on my stomach when I was carrying both of my boys." She smiled. "Now, get changed and come to the kitchen. I'll make sure you get something to eat before you get sick again. Then I'm going home so that you and Zachary can talk things over in private."

When Mattie closed the door behind her, Arielle at last took off her soggy raincoat and sank down on the bed. There hadn't been the slightest bit of condemnation in the older woman's voice, but she had to have strong suspicions that Zach was the baby's father. Why else would she leave them alone?

As Arielle started taking off her damp clothes to put on the dry fleece, she sighed heavily. It appeared that the time had come to tell Zach about the baby and discuss how they would handle the issues of custody and visitation.

She wasn't looking forward to it, but it would almost be a relief to finally have her pregnancy out in the open. Other than her new sister-in-law, Haley, and her newfound grandmother, no one—not even her brothers, Jake and Luke—had a clue that she was going to have a baby.

And although she loved her brothers with all of her heart, just the thought of telling them about her pregnancy made her want to take off for parts unknown. She was no longer the ten-year-old girl they'd raised after their mother's death, but they still insisted on meddling in her life. Although she'd learned to stand up to them, if they knew, they would tell her what they thought was best for her and the baby. No doubt they'd even convince her to move closer to one of them.

But thankfully they wouldn't have the opportunity to once again play the overly protective older brothers. Now that she'd found Zach, she fully intended to handle things on her own terms. By the time she told Jake and Luke about her pregnancy, she and Zach would have hopefully made all of the important decisions.

She finished pulling the thick, warm socks on her feet then stood to go into the kitchen. In theory, her plan sounded logical and should work out. But something told her that if telling Zach he was going to be a father went like the rest of her day, she'd better brace herself for life to become more complicated instead of simpler.

When Zach walked into the kitchen, Arielle was already seated at the table with a plate in front of her piled high with mashed potatoes, vegetables and a country-fried steak smothered in milk gravy. "Shouldn't you be eating something a little lighter than that?" He frowned when he watched her take a big bite of the steak. "Chicken soup would be a much better choice for someone with the flu."

He watched her close her eyes for a moment, obviously savoring the taste of the beef. For someone with an upset stomach, she certainly had a hearty enough appetite.

"We'll talk about the reason I got sick after we eat," she replied, reaching for a slice of homemade bread. "But maybe now you'll believe me when I say I don't have the flu."

"Leave her be and have a seat, Zachary." Mattie had always called him by his given name, and although he preferred the shortened version, he'd long ago stopped trying to get her to change. "That little gal is going to be just fine."

"If Arielle doesn't have the flu, what's wrong with her?" he demanded, getting the distinct impression that the two women knew something he didn't.

Ignoring his question, Mattie set a plate of food at his usual place at the big, round oak table. "I'm gonna cross the yard to my house before the ground gets so mushy I end up sinkin' to my knees in mud. And if you need me for anything, it had better involve somebody bleedin' or somethin' bein' on fire before you call me to come back over here."

"Is it still raining hard?" Arielle asked a moment before he watched a forkful of mashed potatoes disappear into her mouth.

He couldn't get over the change in her. The more she ate, the less sickly she appeared.

"It's supposed to keep rainin' like this all weekend," Mattie informed, nodding. "And if it does, y'all will be on your own tomorrow and Sunday because I'm too old to be gettin' out in weather like this."

"Don't worry about me," Arielle responded, taking a big drink of milk. "I won't be here. I'm going to have Zach take me back to the city after dinner. But it was very nice meeting you, Mattie." When neither he nor Mattie commented, she frowned. "Is there something I should know?"

"Do you want to tell her or should I?" Mattie offered, turning her full attention on him.

"I will," he conceded, seating himself at the table.

When his gaze clashed with hers, he watched Arielle slowly put her fork on the edge of her plate, her expression guarded. "Tell me what?"

"We probably won't be going back to Dallas before the middle of next week at the earliest."

She didn't look as if she believed him. "You're joking, right?"

"I'll let you kids work this out," Mattie remarked, quickly removing her jacket from a peg by the door. "I'm goin' home before all hell breaks loose."

He heard the back door close as he and Arielle sat, staring at each other over the table. "When it rains like this, the Elm Fork of the Trinity River backs up into the tributaries and the creek between here and the main road floods out," he described. "You were asleep when we drove over the bridge, but we barely made it across. By now I'm sure it and the road are under several feet of water."

"In other words, you're telling me we're trapped?" She made it sound more like an accusation than a question.

"You could look at it as being on a minivacation," he suggested, turning his attention to his own plate.

"But I have things at school to take care of and an important appointment to keep."

He nodded. "I've got things I need to do, too. But that doesn't change the fact that I can't drive you back to Dallas until the water recedes."

Arielle's ravenous appetite suddenly disappeared. "Isn't there another road that's not flooded?"

"Not really." He shifted in his seat. "The way the creek winds around, it makes this part of the ranch a peninsula. Then, when rains are heavy, like now, the dry wash cutting through the middle of the property floods and this section becomes an island."

"That's kind of poor planning, don't you think?" she asked, raising one perfectly shaped eyebrow.

Laughing, he shrugged. "I suppose it seems that way now, but when my great-great-grandfather settled here over a hundred years ago, it wasn't. Back then, a natural water source was essential to a ranch's survival. Besides, we're two miles from the creek and there's a couple hundred acres between here and the dry wash. Not exactly a threat of being flooded out here on higher ground."

"But you knew this would happen and you still insisted on bringing me here?" If the heightened color on her face was any indication, Arielle was more than a little upset with him. "Why, Zach? Why did you do that when you knew full well how much I wanted to go home?"

"You were ill and needed someone to watch over you," he noted, stating what he saw to be obvious. "And since you don't have family close by, I was the only available choice."

She shook her head. "You're unbelievable. If I had been sick and did need someone to care for me, it would have made more sense to take me to my apartment. It was closer to the school and at least in the city, there are doctors and hospitals close by. And none of this was necessary because I'm not ill."

Truthfully, he wasn't entirely certain why he'd brought her to the ranch. Maybe it had been a way to make things up to her for leaving her in Aspen without so much as a simple goodbye. But whatever the reason, when he'd seen she was in need, he just hadn't been able to walk away.

"If you weren't sick, then why did you look like you were at death's door?" he observed, his own irritation beginning to rise. "And why did we have to stop on the way here for you to throw up?"

He watched her take a deep breath, then, as if coming to a decision, meet his questioning gaze head-on. "Do you know why I get sick if I don't eat? Or when I do eat, why I put food away like a starving lumberjack?"

The back of his neck began to tingle the longer they stared at each other. He had a feeling he was about to learn something that he wasn't prepared to hear and might not like.

"No."

"Because that's what happens to some women when they become pregnant," she said defiantly.

Silence reigned while he tried to process what she'd said. "You're pregnant?"

"Yes."

"Just how far along are you?" he prompted, his heart beginning to thump inside his chest like an out-of-control jackhammer.

Her gaze never wavered from his when she answered. "Three and a half months."

He immediately glanced at the front of the sweatshirt she wore, but it was big on her and a little too early to notice any telltale thickening of her stomach. Unable to sit still, Zach rose to his feet and began to pace the length of the kitchen. It didn't take a math degree to figure out that the baby she was carrying was most likely his.

"And before you ask, yes, I'm pregnant with your baby," she stated, confirming his suspicions.

His stomach twisted into a painful knot as he recalled another time a woman was carrying his child. "We used protection."

"Yes, but one of the condoms broke," she reminded him.

He'd figured the chances of making her pregnant from that one time had to be fairly remote. Apparently he'd been wrong.

Nodding, he rubbed the tension building at the back of his neck. "I remember. But why didn't you tell me sooner?" Her desire to be left alone to deal with the flooded-out car and her refusal to take off her bulky raincoat suddenly made perfect sense. She'd been trying to hide the pregnancy from him. With his jaw clenched so tight it felt welded shut, he asked, "Didn't you think I had the right to know?"

He watched her expression turn from defiant to righteously indignant. "Oh, no you don't, buster."

She stood to face him. "I'm not letting you get away with playing the victim here. You *lied* to me about who you were. And up until this morning, when you barged into my office and told me your *real* name, I thought I was having Tom Zacharias's baby." She started to walk away, then, turning back, added, "And just for the record, I searched desperately to find a man who didn't even exist because I thought he needed to know that he was going to be a father." She swiped away the tears suddenly spilling from her eyes. "When all of my efforts proved useless…you can't even begin to imagine…how much of a fool I felt or…the emotional pain I went through. So don't… even go there."

Zach stood in the middle of the kitchen long after he watched Arielle rush down the hall toward the guest room. Stunned, he had a hard time believing how rapidly his life had changed in the past twelve hours. When he'd gone to the school this morning, he'd had nothing more on his mind than sweet-talking Helen Montrose into going easy on his mischievous nephew, then heading to the office to go over the contracts and blueprints for his newest resort. But along with his discovery that the old gal was no longer in charge at Premier Academy, the only woman he'd been tempted to have a relationship with since his ill-fated engagement had reappeared in his life and was pregnant with his baby.

Just the thought that he was going to be a father

caused a myriad of feelings to course through him. Had it not been for his ex-fiancée, he might have felt pride and excitement about the baby Arielle carried. But thanks to Gretchen Hayden and her duplicity, he was filled with a deep sense of apprehension that he just couldn't shake.

Five years ago, he'd thought he had it all—a thriving business, a devoted bride-to-be and a baby on the way. But all that had changed when Gretchen decided that motherhood would be detrimental to her figure and seriously limit her options should something better than being the wife of a hotel entrepreneur come along.

He took a deep breath in an effort to chase away the ugly memory of the day he'd discovered the woman he'd thought he loved had deliberately ended the life of their unborn child. All of his focus now needed to be on Arielle and protecting the baby they'd created together. And this time the outcome was going to be different than it had been five years ago. *This time,* he wasn't going to take it on faith that Arielle truly wanted his baby. He was going to make certain his child was protected.

Most of his anger dissipated as he thought about her trying to tell him about the baby and how hurt she'd been when she couldn't. But not all of it.

He understood her inability to find him after they parted in Aspen. In order to be completely anonymous, he always registered under an assumed name when he checked into one of his hotels. It was the only way to get an accurate idea of the quality of guest services and the efficiency and courtesy of the resort management. Besides, it was standard practice that guest information was kept in the strictest of confidence. If Arielle had inquired about him, and he had every reason to believe that she had, the management at the resort wouldn't have given her anything. And even if they had broken protocol and given her the name and address he'd registered under, the information would have proven completely worthless.

But that didn't explain why she hadn't told him about the pregnancy when they were in her office this morning. And she'd had ample opportunity to tell him this afternoon when he'd discovered her sitting in her car in the school's parking lot. And why hadn't she told him the real reason that she had become sick on the drive to the ranch?

His appetite deserting him, Zach removed their plates from the table, scraped the food into the garbage disposal and put the dishes in the dishwasher. He'd give her time to calm down, then he wanted answers. And he wasn't going to bed without them.

With her emotions once again under control, Arielle wiped away the last traces of her tears and sat up on the side of the bed to look around the guest room. It was decorated in shades of peach and antique white and at any other time, she would have loved staying in such a beautiful room. But at the moment, it felt like a prison cell, albeit a very pretty one.

She was stranded on a remote ranch with the man who had lied to her about his identity, abandoned her without a word, broken her heart and made her pregnant. And if all that wasn't enough, he was blaming her for not telling him about the pregnancy.

"Unreal," she said aloud.

But even more incredible was that her life was paralleling her mother's. Francesca Garnier had fallen in love with a man who had impregnated her with a set of twin boys and simply walked away. Then, ten years later, the man had shown up long enough to rekindle their romance, which led to the birth of Arielle, and once again disappeared. And when Arielle and her brothers first met their paternal grandmother a few months ago, they'd learned their father had used an assumed name.

Instead of Neil Owens, the starving artist their mother knew, their father was the infamous playboy Owen Larson, the only offspring of Emerald Larson, one of the richest, most successful businesswomen in the modern corporate world. During the ten years away from their mother, Owen Larson had fathered three other children—all boys and all with different women.

It was so bizarre, she even had a hard time believing it. But when Emerald Larson had contacted them Arielle had gained three more brothers. And Emerald had embraced the Garnier siblings as part of her family, giving each a multimillion-dollar trust fund and one of the many companies within the Emerald, Inc. empire. Arielle became the new owner of Premier Academy and moved to Dallas.

But that was immaterial. What was extremely disconcerting was, as her mother had done with her father, Arielle had fallen for a man she'd thought to be as honest and forthright as she'd been with him. But just like her father had done to her mother, Zach had deliberately lied to her to keep her from finding him.

She shook her head to chase away her disturbing thoughts and concentrated on forgetting what she couldn't change and focusing on her present dilemma. In spite of the stress and tension she had experienced or because she hadn't finished her dinner, her hunger had returned full force.

Unfortunately, if she went to find something for herself in the kitchen, she'd likely run into Zach. Though they had several things to discuss and decisions to make, she wasn't ready for that just yet. She'd already had an extremely upsetting day.

But the decision was taken out of her hands when her stomach rumbled. If she waited much longer she'd become sick again and since they were flooded in, she didn't have much choice.

Sighing, she rose from the bed, opened the door and walked right into Zach's broad chest. "Oh, I…um, didn't know you were there. Excuse me."

He placed his hands on her shoulders in a steadying gesture and she noticed his gaze immediately settled on her stomach. "Are you all right?"

Even though his touch through the thick fleece sweatshirt and the low timbre of his voice sent shivers straight up her spine, she forced herself to remain motionless. "I need something else to eat," she said, nodding.

"Yeah, that probably wouldn't be a bad idea." He released her, running a hand through his thick hair. She could tell by the action that he wasn't comfortable with the situation, either. "Neither of us finished dinner."

They stared at each other as if thinking of something to say when her stomach rumbled again. "I'd better find something in the fridge or I'm going to be sorry."

"Oh, yeah, sure," he agreed, standing back for her to precede him down the hall.

When they entered the kitchen, Zach walked to the refrigerator and opened the door. "Do you want a sandwich or would you prefer something else?"

"A sandwich and a glass of milk would be nice," she answered, trying not to think about how handsome he was.

He'd changed into a pair of worn jeans and a black T-shirt that emphasized every well-defined muscle of his upper body. Dear Lord, he was without a doubt the best-looking man she'd ever seen. She'd thought so in Aspen and she thought so now. But thinking along those lines was what had landed her in his bed and ultimately led to her current predicament. She'd do well to remember that and concentrate on their upcoming conversation about the baby and what role, if any, he intended to take as the baby's father.

"If you'll tell me which cabinet the glasses are in, I'll pour the milk," she offered, forcing herself to look away from the play of his biceps as he lifted a gallon jug from inside the refrigerator door.

"I'll take care of that." He motioned toward the pantry. "Why don't you get a loaf of bread and see if you can find a bag of chips."

As he poured two glasses of milk, she retrieved the bread and a bag of pretzels and by the time everything was on the table, her nerves were stretched to the breaking point. They were both being overly congenial and polite, but there was an underlying current of tension that was so strong, it could have been cut with a knife.

"We have to stop this, Zach," she declared, seating herself at the table.

To his credit, he didn't feign ignorance and act unaware of what she was referring to. "I don't want to upset you any more than I already have," he began, setting a couple of plates on the table. "But I'd bet my next resort project that our discussions are going to be tense at best."

"I'm sure they will be," she concurred, reaching for a package of sliced turkey. If she'd thought their talk was going to be unpleasant, the strained atmosphere now was far worse and she'd just as soon get it over with. "But putting it off isn't going to make it any easier." She nibbled on a pretzel. "Where would you like to start?"

He held up his hand. "We'll go into my study after we finish eating. I don't think it would be a good idea for you to have another meal interrupted, do you?"

"Probably not," she agreed, taking a bite of her sandwich.

They both fell silent as they ate and by the time they'd cleared the table, Arielle found herself actually looking forward to the confrontation she knew would follow. It would be a relief to get it over with so they could move forward. Zach was a highly successful businessman, much like her brothers, and she had no doubt he'd start by making demands and telling her what he expected her to do. But thanks to dealing with her brothers, years ago she'd learned to stand up for herself and she knew exactly how much she was willing to give and what she intended to get in return. And the sooner Zach came to that realization, the better.

Several minutes later, he showed her into his study. Arielle glanced around, then seated herself in one of the plush chairs in front of the stone fireplace. She wasn't about to sit in the chair in front of his desk. He would have no doubt sat behind the desk, giving him a huge psychological advantage, much like a boss talking to his employee. And she wasn't allowing him any kind of edge.

"How has the pregnancy gone so far?" Zach asked, walking over to stand by the fireplace. Once again his gaze came to rest on her belly. "Have you experienced any problems other than having to eat frequently?"

"Not really." She shrugged. "Aside from a couple of weeks of intense morning sickness, everything has gone quite well."

"As long as you eat frequently?"

"Correct."

When she'd first discovered she was pregnant, she'd hoped that once she found him, the man who had made love to her with such tender care would be, if not happy, at least interested in their child. It appeared that Zach was very interested. But she couldn't ignore how he'd lied to her. Trusting him now would be foolish.

"When do you learn the sex of the baby?" he inquired, finally raising his eyes to meet hers.

"I'm not sure. On Monday, my obstetrician planned an ultrasound to make sure everything is going well, but I don't know if the sex can be determined this early. But now I'll have to reschedule the appointment," she decided, it being pointless to remind him why.

To her surprise, he shook his head. "You won't have to reschedule. I'll call my pilot to bring the helicopter up from Dallas."

"But I thought you said we were stranded here until the water went down."

He again shook his head. "I told you I couldn't drive you back to the city, but I never said we were completely stranded. Besides, that was before I knew about the baby and the ultrasound." He gave her a determined smile. "Don't worry, I'll make sure that we keep this appointment and every other one until you give birth."

"We?"

"You didn't think I wouldn't be involved once I knew I had a baby on the way, did you?" There was an underlying edge of challenge in his tone and they were quickly approaching the more stressful phase of their discussion.

"To be perfectly honest, I didn't know if you would care one way or the other." She met his accusing gaze head-on. "If you'll remember, the man I thought I knew doesn't even exist."

The intense light in his dark green eyes stole her breath. "Darlin', the only difference between me and the man who made love to you in Aspen is the name."

"Really?" she dared, ignoring the swirl of heat the memory created and concentrating on the hurt and disillusionment of discovering she'd been abandoned. "So when you're not using an alias, you habitually use women, leaving them behind, without waking them to say goodbye?"

"No, and that's not what happened," he retorted, shaking his head. "That morning, I had to get back to Dallas—"

"To tell the truth, it doesn't really matter, Zach."

She could see that he was angry she'd cut him off, but that was his problem, not hers. She had her pride and didn't particularly care to hear that he'd left because he'd grown tired of her or that things between them had moved way too fast and he'd wanted to avoid an uncomfortable scene.

"The only thing we need to talk over now is where we go from here," she stated determinedly. "I'm perfectly capable of taking care of the baby's needs, so I don't want, nor do I need, monetary help from you. What I want to know is how involved you want to be in the baby's life. And will you want visitation rights every other weekend, once a month or not at all?"

His eyes narrowed as he took a step toward her. "Oh, I intend to be completely involved in every aspect of my child's life, Arielle. And as far as shared custody, visitation rights and child support are concerned, there is no need to work out any agreement."

"What do you mean?" Surely he didn't expect her to hand over full custody of her baby. If he did, he was in for the biggest, nastiest fight of his life. "I love this baby and I'm not giving it up to you or anyone else."

Closing the distance between them, he stood over her much like her older brothers used to when she'd been called on the carpet for doing something they had disapproved of. "I'm not telling you I want full custody, darlin'. But spending time with my baby and supporting him won't be an issue because once we get back to Dallas, you and I are getting married."

Three

Zach watched Arielle open and close her mouth several times before she finally said, "You can't possibly be serious."

If ever a woman had the deer-in-the-headlights look about her, it was Arielle. Good. Now that he had her attention, maybe she'd start listening to him.

"Rest assured, I'm very serious." He folded his arms across his chest as he gazed down at the woman he had every intention of making his wife. "I don't joke about something as important as taking a trip down the aisle, darlin'. If *you'll* remember, I told you this morning that I wouldn't have a child out of wedlock. And I meant every word of it."

Anger sparkled in the depths of her hazel eyes. "And as I told *you* this morning, you don't have to be married to have a baby."

"That might work for some people, but not for me. I'm of the opinion that when a man makes a woman pregnant, he stands by her and does the right thing. We will be married as soon as possible."

"Oh, no, we won't." She rose to her feet, then poked the middle of his chest with her index finger. "Let me tell you something, Mr. High-and-Mighty. You're going to have to get used to the idea of being a single father because I would never marry you even if you got down on your knees and begged me."

Zach wasn't used to having anyone openly defy him—not in the business world, not in his personal life. And if anyone did have the courage to cross him, they found themselves embroiled in a battle of wits they were most assuredly going to lose. But for reasons he couldn't quite put his finger on, he found Arielle's defiance mildly amusing, if not downright cute.

Maybe it was because of their considerable height difference. At six feet four inches, he towered over her. But that didn't seem to intimidate her one damned bit. Or it could have been the fact that he'd never had a pregnant woman get in his face and poke him in the chest to make her point the way Arielle had just done. Either way, he barely resisted the urge to smile. Their marriage was going to be anything but dull.

"Never say 'never,' darlin'."

"I'm telling you right now, it's not going to happen," she declared, shaking her head. "Being married isn't a requirement to have a baby. Other arrangements can be made for you to play an equal role in the baby's life, so you might as well start thinking along those lines and stop insisting on a marriage that is never going to happen."

Without giving it a second thought, he reached out and took her into his arms. "First and foremost, calm down. Getting upset is not good for you or the baby." Pulling her against him, he finally smiled. "And second, it *is* going to happen. So I would suggest that you get used to the idea pretty quick and start thinking about what you're going to wear and whether or not you want your brothers to give you away during the ceremony. I'm willing to wait until next weekend if you want them in attendance, but no longer than that."

Before she could protest further, Zach lowered his head to silence her with a kiss. As he covered her mouth with his, the memories of what they'd shared in Aspen came rushing back full force. From the moment he'd seen her that morning, he'd wondered if her perfect lips were still as soft and if her response to him would be as passionate and unbridled as his memories.

At first she remained motionless in his arms. But as he reacquainted himself with her sweetness, Zach felt some of her tension drain away and he seized the opportunity to deepen the kiss. To his immense satisfaction she finally parted her lips on a soft sigh and allowed him entry to her tender inner recesses. At the same time she wrapped her arms around his waist.

The signs of her acceptance encouraged him to explore her with a thoroughness that immediately had his body reminding him that several long months had passed since he'd held her, kissed her, made love to her. Stroking her tongue with his, his lower body tightened and his heart took off at a gallop. His faulty memory forgot how intoxicating her kisses were and how perfect she felt in his arms.

Unable to resist, he moved his hands to her sides and slowly slid them beneath the bottom of her sweatshirt, up along her ribs to the swell of her breasts. He realized she wasn't wearing a bra and without a moment's hesitation, he cupped the weight of her with his palms. The soft mounds were larger, most likely due to her pregnancy, and when he lightly brushed the pebbled tips with his thumbs, her tiny moan of pleasure indicated they were highly sensitive, as well.

But as he continued to reacquaint himself with her body, Zach pressed himself closer and the slight bulge of her stomach reminded him of their current situation and the raw feelings still churning inside him. Arielle said she loved and wanted his baby, but he'd heard that from another woman just before she deliberately caused herself to miscarry.

Suddenly needing to put distance between them, he broke the kiss and, removing his hands from her breasts, pulled the sweatshirt down and took a step back. Gratified by the dazed expression on her face, he could tell that Arielle had been as shaken by the kiss as he had. But if past experience had taught him anything, he would not allow his judgment to be clouded by the haze of desire. Besides, they had more than enough to deal with at the moment without adding another complication to the mix.

"Why did you do that?" she asked, sounding delightfully breathless.

Her cheeks had turned a rosy pink and he wasn't certain whether the heightened color was due to rising passion or embarrassment at her eager response. It was probably a combination of both, he decided as they stood staring at each other.

"Kissing you was the only way I knew to stop you from arguing with me."

She swiped at her mouth with the back of her hand as if trying to wipe away his kiss. "Well, don't do it again."

"You used to like it when I kissed you," he reminisced, stuffing his hands into the front pockets of his jeans to keep from reaching for her again.

"That was before I discovered how deceptive you are." If looks could kill, hers was sure to finish him off in about two seconds flat.

"What time is your appointment for the ultrasound?"

"Monday afternoon at three." She gave him a confused look. "Why?"

"I'll arrange for my pilot to pick us up before noon on Monday," he said, quickly calculating how long the helicopter flight would take to get back to the city. "I have clothes here, but that should give us more than enough time to go by your place so that you can get ready and still make the appointment."

She shook her head. "I'm sure you have another resort to build or some corporate thing that needs your full attention. You don't have to go with me. I'll be fine without you."

Yes, he did have to accompany her. But he wasn't about to tell her that he felt an obligation to protect his unborn child, even though she'd given him no good reason for concern.

"Clearing my calendar for the day won't be a big deal." He shrugged. "I'd already counted on spending a few extra days here because of the flooding. Besides, that's the beauty of being the sole owner. You can do what you want, when you want and nobody says a word unless they don't care about being fired."

"Let me put it this way, Zach." He watched as she clenched both fists at her sides and he could tell her frustration level was close to the boiling point. "I don't *want* you to go to the doctor with me."

"Why? You said you spent several weeks trying to find me. Now you're telling me you don't want me around?"

"I searched for you because I thought you might want to know that you'd fathered a child," she said tightly. "Not because I wanted you to go with me to doctor appointments or 'do the right thing.'"

"That's too bad, darlin'." He rocked back on his heels. "I'm going to the doctor with you and there isn't a damned thing you can do to stop me." Smiling, he added, "And I will be doing the *right thing* and making you my wife."

"I don't understand why you're being so stubborn about this, Zach," she grumbled.

"I could say the same thing about you."

Closing her eyes for a second as if trying to keep from belting him one, when she opened them, they sparkled with anger. "I give you my word that I'll tell you everything the doctor says and even make an extra copy of the picture from the ultrasound for you."

"I'm sure you would." He'd like to believe Arielle would be completely honest with him, but he couldn't be one hundred percent certain. After all, he'd trusted his former fiancée and that had ended in absolute tragedy. "But I'm a hands-on kind of guy, darlin'. I never rely on secondhand information and I want to hear for myself what the man has—"

"Woman," she corrected him. "My obstetrician is a woman."

"Okay. I want to hear what the *woman* has to say." He smiled as he reached forward and placed his hand on her pregnant stomach. "I'm the daddy. I'm entitled to know what's going on, as well as finding out whether we're having a boy or girl at the same time you do."

She shook her head and removed his hand from her stomach. "I didn't say you weren't. But did it ever occur to you that it might make me uncomfortable to have you in the room during an examination?"

Her revelation was unexpected. Before he could stop himself, he reached out to run his index finger along her creamy cheek. "Why, Arielle? It's not like I haven't been intimately acquainted with your body before."

"That was several months ago and a lot of things have changed since then," she said, looking away.

"Like what?" he asked, fighting the urge to take her back into his arms. "We're still the same two people who spent an entire week together."

As he watched, the color on her cheeks deepened. "I didn't mean *that*."

"Then what?"

"After waking up alone to find that I meant absolutely nothing to you, I don't particularly care to be around you," she declared flatly. "Nor do I care to hear the reason you left."

He regretted the emotional pain he'd caused her. But that couldn't be changed now. "I'm sorry you feel that way, darlin'. But it's something that's going to have to change, and damned quick." He caught her chin between his thumb and forefinger and, tipping it up, forced her to look him straight in the eye. "Once we get married, we'll be together all of the time. We're going to live together, go to all your prenatal appointments together and…we'll be sharing a bed."

He heard a hitch in her breathing a moment before she backed away from his touch. "I don't think so." As she turned to leave, she added, "It's not going to happen and you might as well get used to that fact just as quick."

Watching Arielle storm from the room, Zach straightened his stance. Oh, it was going to happen, all right. They would be married as soon as he could get a marriage license. When he wanted something, he went after it with a single-minded determination that never failed to net him the desired results. And that was something else *she* was going to have to get used to.

From everything she'd said and the way she acted, she was happy and looked forward to having his child. But he would not take it on faith that was the case here. That's why he fully intended to make her Mrs. Zach Forsythe and ensure his right to monitor everything that took place for the rest of the pregnancy.

Abandoning the book she'd been reading, Arielle shifted to a more comfortable position on the window seat and watched the pouring rain. She had successfully avoided Zach at breakfast by getting up around dawn and bringing a couple of muffins and a glass of milk back to the guest room. But she wasn't naive enough to think she could do the same thing for lunch.

In fact, she was surprised that Zach hadn't looked for her when she remained in her room all morning.

Sighing heavily, she lovingly placed her hand on her stomach. She could understand Zach's desire to be with his child, but it didn't have to be a package deal. Surely they could work out something that was acceptable for both of them without entering into a marriage for all of the wrong reasons.

When she finally did get married, she wanted it all—a home, a family and a husband who loved her. Not the loveless marriage she would be getting if she went along with Zach's plan.

Lost in thought, she jumped at the sudden rap on the door. Before she had the chance to answer, Zach walked in.

"Are you all right, Arielle?"

"I'm fine." At least she had been before he entered the room.

Good Lord, if she'd thought he had looked good last night, it couldn't hold a candle to the way he looked now. Zach wasn't just attractive, he was drop-dead gorgeous.

The pair of jeans he wore today were faded and rode lower on his lean hips than the ones from the night before. And he hadn't bothered buttoning his light blue chambray shirt, giving her a very enticing view of his chest and ripped abdominal muscles. Memories of him holding her to that chest as they made love, feeling every perfectly defined muscle pressed against her, caused her heart to skip several beats and her breathing to become shallow.

"Arielle, are you sure you're okay?" he repeated, frowning.

"Oh…um, sure." When she started to get up, he shook his head. "Stay right where you are. I know how hard it was for my sister to find a comfortable position, even in the early stages of her pregnancy."

"Some of the teachers at school said that being comfortable will become a very big issue the further along I get," she agreed, nodding.

Walking over to the window seat, he lifted her outstretched legs and sat down, lowering them to his lap. "Lana had a lot of trouble with her feet and legs getting tired," he said, gently massaging her foot. "Does that feel good?"

She could lie and tell him it didn't, but what was the point? He could tell from her serene expression that it did.

"Actually, it feels like heaven," she admitted, closing her eyes as he skillfully rubbed her arch.

"Have you had problems with muscle cramps?" he asked as his hands continued to work their magic.

"Not many." Enjoying his relaxing touch, she'd never realized that a foot rub could chase away tension throughout the rest of her body. "My legs cramped up a few times while I was sleeping, but that's about it."

He shoved one leg of her sweatpants up and began

to gently move his hands over her calf. "How did your brothers take the news about the baby?" he continued conversationally.

His touch caused a sense of euphoria to sweep over her and it took a moment to realize what he'd asked. Opening her eyes, she shook her head. "I haven't told them yet."

"Why not?" He moved to massage her other leg. "I was under the impression that you had a good relationship with them."

"We are very close." His hands moving over her leg made it hard to think and she paused to collect her thoughts. "But I'm almost sure they won't be happy with the decisions I've made lately."

Zach stopped his tender ministrations and a protective sparkle appeared in his dark green eyes. "They wouldn't talk you into terminating the pregnancy, would they?"

"Oh, no. Not that." She knew for certain her brothers would never do something like that. "They'll both be absolute fools over their niece or nephew."

"Then what's the problem?" he prodded, his hands once again moving over her legs with care.

"Instead of moving to Dallas, they'd want me to live with one of them." She sighed. "And as much as I adore both of them, I'd rather eat a big ugly bug than do that."

Zach threw back his head and laughed. "I see you still express yourself in a way that leaves no doubt what you mean."

The sound of his rich laughter sent a tingling sensation skipping over every nerve in her body. His sense of humor was one of many things about him that she'd found irresistible.

Shrugging one shoulder, she smiled. "Well, it's the truth. Luke would want me with him and his new wife, Haley, in Nashville. And Jake would insist that I move into his condo in Los Angeles."

"In other words, you'd have to choose between them?" Zach summarized.

"Not exactly. Either would be fine with me living with the other." She tried to concentrate on what she was about to say, but the feel of his hands smoothing over the sensitized skin at the back of her knee made that very hard to do. "For one thing, Luke and Haley have only been married a couple of months and they need their alone time. Plus they have a baby on the way and I don't think Luke could survive living with two women experiencing mood swings and emotional meltdowns at the same time."

"Oh God, no." Zach gave an exaggerated shudder. "One hormonal woman is enough to contend with, but two would send a man running like hell." He shook his head. "My sister moved in with me for a short time when she was pregnant. Her apartment was being painted. I never knew if what I said would make her angry enough to bite my head off or cause sobbing like her heart was broken." He lowered his head. "It was like living with Dr. Jekyll and Ms. Hyde."

"Your sister is single?" If his sister could be a single mother, why was Zach so insistent that they had to be married?

He nodded. "Lana wanted a child, but after several failed relationships, she decided a visit to the sperm bank was the answer for her." He stopped massaging her legs, but continued to hold them on his lap. "And before you ask, I failed to talk her out of it. But I supported her decision and help out with Derek whenever she needs me."

"Jake and Luke will be the same way with me."

"They won't have to be," he said, giving her a meaningful look. "I'll be with you every step of the way." Before she could comment, he went on, "But what about your brother in L.A.? Why wouldn't you want to live closer to him?"

"Don't get me wrong, Jake is a wonderful guy and I love him with all my heart. But living with him would drive me over the edge." Just the thought was almost laughable. "Besides, I prefer a much quieter lifestyle and I couldn't have kept up with which one of his women was the flavor of the moment."

"Moment?" He sounded surprised.

"Jake's fascination with a woman has never lasted longer than a couple of weeks," she explained.

"That could present a problem."

She nodded. "Plus the fact that they still think of me as a child."

"Hey, give them a break, darlin'." He grinned. "I

pretty much think along the same line when it comes to my sister."

She sighed. "Your sister has my heartfelt sympathy."

"So why did you decide to move to Texas?"

Gazing into his questioning green eyes, she wondered how much she should tell him. She'd been cautious about revealing her relationship with Emerald Larson to anyone. Who would believe she'd gone from a struggling preschool teacher, barely making ends meet, to an heiress with a bottomless bank account and a thriving business? She had never openly discussed her financial affairs with anyone but her brothers.

"I was presented with an opportunity to run my own preschool and I took it," she responded, settling on an honest but sketchy answer to his question. "And Premier Academy just happened to be in Dallas."

Zach stared at her wanting to ask more about her acquisition, but thankfully her stomach chose to rumble, reminding both of them that it was lunchtime.

"Uh-oh, we'd better get you something to eat before you get sick again," he stated, lifting her legs from his lap and rising to his feet. He held his hand out to help her up from the window seat. "What would you like me to make? Pasta or hamburgers?"

"You're going to cook?"

"I can handle things," he said, nodding his head. "Mattie's stocked the kitchen for my visit."

"Why don't we have something easy for lunch,"

she suggested when her stomach made its presence known again. "A sandwich would work."

"Need something pretty quick, huh?"

"I'm hungry enough to gnaw the legs off the table," she detailed as she walked into the kitchen and went straight to the refrigerator for a package of roast beef and some cheese.

"My cook in Dallas is going to love having you around," he said, laughing as he handed her a loaf of bread from the pantry. "Nothing makes her happier than feeding people."

Arielle stopped piling the sliced meat on two pieces of bread. "I won't be around for her to feed."

"Sure you will." She watched him remove the milk from the fridge, then reach into the cabinet for a couple of glasses. "Once we're married, you'll be living there, remember?"

She shook her head. "It's never going to happen, *remember?*"

His low masculine chuckle caused her heart to skip several beats. "Like I told you last night, never say 'never,' darlin'."

Four

On Monday afternoon, Zach sat beside Arielle in the obstetrician's waiting room, thumbing through a magazine. He wasn't the least bit interested in reading about or looking at pictures of maternity clothes. But since Arielle had been giving him the silent treatment ever since their helicopter flight to Dallas, it gave him something to do while they waited for her to be called to see the doctor.

Over the weekend, they seemed to have reached a truce of sorts and instead of arguing about their upcoming marriage, they had—as if by unspoken agreement—stopped talking about it completely. He still had every intention of making her his wife as soon as possible. Nothing she could say or do was going to change that.

"Arielle Garnier?"

Zach glanced up to see a nurse standing at the door leading back to the examination rooms. "Looks like it's our turn, darlin'," he said, rising to his feet, then offering his hand to help Arielle out of her chair.

Frowning, she placed her hand in his, stood and turned to face him. "It's my turn, not *ours,* and I'd rather you stay here while I'm with the doctor."

"You've made that very clear, darlin'. And I've made it just as clear that I'm going with you." He placed his hand to the small of her back and started guiding her across the waiting room.

Her body language and stormy expression indicated that he would hear all about this once they left the doctor's office. But if she thought that was enough to intimidate him, she was sadly mistaken. Nothing was going to keep him from seeing the first images of his child.

The nurse motioned for them to enter a small room at the back of the office. There she recorded Arielle's weight, then took her temperature and blood pressure. "The doctor will be in shortly," she estimated, smiling as she walked to the door. "If you'd like, you can have 'Dad' help you onto the examination table. Then go ahead and pull your top up to just below your breasts and your pants down to just below your tummy."

As the woman closed the door behind her, an odd feeling spread throughout Zach's chest. Although he'd thought of little else since learning that Arielle was carrying his child, something about the nurse calling him "Dad" made it a reality.

"For the last time, I would prefer to see the doctor without an audience," Arielle protested, her tone reflecting her outrage.

Turning to face her, he cupped her soft cheeks with his hands. "It's all right, darlin'. I know you're probably self-conscious about your stomach," he said, making certain his tone was sympathetic, even if he didn't quite understand why she was uncomfortable about it. "But that's to be expected. You're pregnant. And there's nothing I'm going to see now that I haven't already." Kissing the tip of her nose, he smiled. "Now, let's get you on that table, ready to find out what we're having—a bouncing baby boy or a sweet baby girl."

She gave him one last belligerent glare, before allowing him to help her up onto the examination table.

"Didn't the nurse tell you to expose your stomach for this?" he asked, reaching for the bottom of her maternity top.

To his surprise, she slapped the back of his hand. "I'll wait until the doctor comes in."

"Okay," he uttered, quickly releasing the hem of the garment. Zach knew better than to press the issue if he wanted to keep his head resting comfortably between his shoulders.

"My nurse told me you brought the baby's father with you for the ultrasound, Arielle," a woman wearing a white lab coat announced when she walked into the room. Closing the door behind her, she smiled and stuck out her hand. "Good afternoon, I'm Dr. Jensen."

He shook her hand. "Zach Forsythe."

"Nice to meet you, Zach." She walked to the other side of the examining table and, looking down at Arielle's rounded stomach, shook her head. "My goodness, I think you've blossomed even more since last week at your regular appointment." Gathering an instrument that looked a lot like a microphone, she reached for a tube of clear gel. "If either of you have any questions during the procedure, please don't hesitate to speak up. I like for the dad to be just as involved as the mom throughout the pregnancy and delivery."

There was something about Dr. Jensen that instilled confidence and he could understand why Arielle had chosen the woman to deliver their baby. "At the moment, I can't think of anything. But I'm betting that changes, real quick," he said, smiling.

Dr. Jensen nodded and, turning her attention to Arielle, asked, "How have you been feeling? Anything we need to address before we get started?"

Zach watched Arielle shake her head as she lifted her maternity top, then hooked her thumbs in the elastic waistband of her slacks and lowered them below her slightly rounded stomach. "I still have to make sure I eat something when my stomach gets empty, but otherwise, I've felt pretty good."

"That's not all that unusual," the doctor assured her, squeezing a generous amount of the gel onto Arielle's stomach. She held the instrument poised over the clear blob. "Are you both ready to see your little one for the first time?"

"Y-yes," Arielle answered, her voice reflecting an anticipation as strong as his own.

"Will we be able to find out whether to decorate the nursery in pink or blue?" Zach asked.

The doctor smiled. "Probably not this time, but it won't be too much longer."

Nodding, Zach reached out and took Arielle's hand in his. When she gripped his hand tightly, he knew she appreciated his support.

"Ready whenever you are," he said, his gaze never wavering from Arielle.

When the doctor began moving the scope around Arielle's stomach, a fuzzy, twitching image immediately popped up on the monitor. Zach wondered what the hell he was supposed to be looking at. But the more Dr. Jensen moved the wand around, he noticed what might possibly be an arm or a leg.

The woman pointed to the screen. "See, there's your baby's head and back." She moved the instrument to the other side of Arielle's stomach. "Let's see if we can detect the sex from this angle." Her sudden frown caused Zach's heart to grind to a halt. "What's this?" she asked, adding to his anxiety. "It certainly explains why you're a bit larger than normal."

"I-Is something wrong?" Arielle murmured, sounding as if she might burst into tears.

Zach lightly squeezed her hand in an effort to lend her every ounce of strength he possessed. "I'm sure everything is fine, darlin'."

"Oh, there's nothing wrong," Dr. Jensen confirmed, turning to them with a wide grin. "I'm just wondering how you will keep up with two toddlers when they start walking."

"Two?" Arielle echoed, her eyes round with shock.

"Twins?" Zach croaked at the same time.

Dr. Jensen laughed as she pushed the print button on the side of the monitor. "The way the first baby was lying, I couldn't see the second one until I changed sides. But yes, you're definitely having twins."

At that moment, Zach couldn't have forced words past the lump clogging his throat if his life depended on it. He was not only going to have a child, he was going to have two. Unbelievable.

His chest felt as if it had swelled to twice its normal size. Words couldn't express what he was feeling, and, leaning down, he covered Arielle's parted lips with his for a brief but intense kiss.

"Do twins run in either of your families?" the doctor inquired as she wiped the excess gel from Arielle's stomach with a handful of tissues. She didn't comment that both of them were breathing as if they'd run a marathon by the time he lifted his head and Zach figured the woman was used to displays of emotion after learning the results of an ultrasound.

Clearly in a state of shock, Arielle stared at him as if urging him to answer Dr. Jensen's question. "Arielle has twin brothers," he responded, finally getting his vocal cords to work. "But to my knowledge there aren't any twins in my family."

The doctor tilted her head. "Well, there are now." She picked up Arielle's chart and made a notation. "I see neither of you anticipated a multiple birth."

"I…uh, suppose I knew it was a possibility, but…" Looking utterly stunned, Arielle's voice trailed off as she rearranged her clothes and sat up on the side of the exam table.

"Are both of the babies okay?" Zach thought to ask as his brain began to function again.

"Actually, everything looks very good." Dr. Jensen smiled. "Both fetuses appear to be a good size and I'd estimate the right weight for this stage of their development."

Helping Arielle down from the table, he asked the doctor, "Is there anything special that we should or shouldn't be doing?"

Dr. Jensen shook her head. "As long as you feel like it, Arielle, there's no reason you can't enjoy your normal activities, including sexual relations."

He caught Arielle's warning glare and wisely

refrained from commenting on the doctor's stamp of approval for their making love. But he didn't even try to stop his wide grin.

Dr. Jensen started for the door. "I'll see you in three weeks for your regular appointment and of course, if you have any problems or questions before then, don't hesitate to give me a call."

Zach and Arielle walked together down the hall to the elevator. They remained silent on the ride to the lobby and he figured she was coming to terms with the idea of having twins.

"How long will it take you to pack an overnight bag?" he asked as he helped her into the back of his limousine.

"Why would I need to pack?" she questioned, when he slid into the seat beside her.

"Because I'm moving you into my place." It was more important now than ever that Arielle took good care of herself.

"No, you're not." She shook her head. "I'm going to go home, change into a circus tent and call my brothers to tell them the news about the baby… babies." She suddenly emitted a nervous giggle. "Oh my God, I'm having twins."

"Yes, you are, darlin'." Giving instructions to his driver to take them to her apartment, he put his arm around her shoulders. He could tell she was still over-whelmed by the news and now wasn't a good time to press her on the issue of moving in with him.

"We'll spend the night at your apartment and move you into my home tomorrow morning."

"No, we won't. You're going to drop me off at my place and then go home to yours while I call my brothers. End of discussion." She sounded quite adamant, but he noticed that she wasn't scooting away from him, was allowing him to hold her close to his side.

"Sorry, darlin', but I told you that I would be with you every step of the way." He kissed the top of her head. "And that means from here on out, we'll be doing whatever needs to be done together. Everything from doctor appointments to breaking the news to your brothers that we're going to have twins."

By the time they arrived at her apartment, the fact that she was going to be the mother of twins had sunk in and she was regaining some perspective. "I think it might be better if I'm the one to break the news to my brothers." Removing her cardigan sweater, she walked over to hang it in the entryway closet, hoping Zach would take the hint that she needed a little time alone. "While I make the call from my bedroom, please make yourself comfortable. I'll only be a few minutes." She'd given up on him going home.

"I'd rather you stay right here and make the call on the speakerphone." He shrugged out of his suit coat, loosened his tie and released the button at the neck of his white oxford cloth shirt, then walked over to place his hands on her shoulders. "I promise I'll keep quiet as long as they don't give you too much flak." He used his index finger to raise her chin until their gazes met. "But I reserve the right to break my silence at any time if I think they're upsetting you."

Where was all this concern almost four months ago when she discovered he was gone and cried for days feeling like such a fool? Or a few weeks later when she realized she was pregnant with no way of contacting her baby's father?

The heat from his hands permeated her shirt and sent an excited little shiver up her spine. Trying to ignore the way his touch made her feel, she advised, "I'm a big girl, Zach. I can take care of myself."

"You don't have to, Arielle. Not anymore." Her breath caught when he took her in his arms, but it was the look on his handsome face that sent her heart racing. "From here on out, that's my job. And believe me, I have every intention of taking it very seriously. I give you my word that I'll do everything in my power to protect you and our babies. And if I have to, I'll have no problem taking on both of your brothers to keep that promise."

She could have asked him who was going to protect her from him, but he chose that moment to lower his head and cover her mouth with a kiss so poignant it brought tears to her eyes. At first, it seemed just a kiss to seal his vow to take care of her and their babies, but as his lips moved over hers, it quickly evolved into so much more.

As Zach tasted and teased, she tried her best to suppress her reaction to him. She started to push against his chest, but just like the first night at his ranch, her will to resist evaporated like morning mist on a hot summer day and she melted against him.

She briefly wondered how she could succumb to his charm after all that had happened. But as he parted her lips with his tongue and began a tender exploration, she quickly forgot the past and lost herself to the mastery of his caress.

Heat coursed through her at the speed of light as he coaxed and demanded that she respond, drawing her into his sensual web. A tingling sensation spread throughout her entire body as he slowly moved his hands down her back to the tail of her oversize shirt.

He slipped his hands beneath the gauzy lavender fabric, then up along her ribs to cup her breasts. She knew she should call a halt to things right away and regain her senses. Nothing had changed between them. She still wouldn't complicate matters by agreeing to get married, or moving into his home. But when Zach rubbed her overly sensitive nipples through the satin and lace of her bra, all rational thought deserted her and she leaned into his embrace.

"I think before this goes any further, we'd better make that call to your brothers," Zach said, nibbling tiny kisses along her jaw to the hollow just beneath her ear. "Otherwise, there's no telling when we'll get around to it."

He continued to tease her with his thumbs. When she realized what he'd said, her cheeks heated and she started to back away from his electrifying touch. But to her dismay, he slipped his hands from her breasts and around to her back to hold her to him.

"We'll pick up where we left off after we make the call," he whispered, sending a wave of goose bumps sliding over her body.

She shook her head. "That wouldn't…be a…good idea."

"Sure it would, darlin'." He nuzzled his cheek against her hair then took a step back. "Now, why don't we make this a conference call and tell them at the same time?"

Still feeling a bit lightheaded from Zach's drugging kiss, Arielle nodded and, dialing Jake's number first, put him on hold while she called Luke. When she had both of her brothers on the line, she switched the phone to speaker, sank down onto the couch beside Zach and took a deep breath.

"I have some news to share and I decided to tell you both at the same time."

"Will this explain why you cry every time I've talked to you for the past few months?" Jake asked, sounding uncharacteristically serious.

"And the reason you've avoided talking to me?" Luke added, his tone stern.

"I'm sorry, Luke," she apologized, feeling guilty. She'd known how concerned her brothers were, but she wasn't sure how to tell them that she was in the same predicament as their mother all those years ago. "You know how much I love both of you. I just had some things that I needed to work out."

"You know we'd have done everything in our power to help," Jake reminded her.

From the corner of her eye, she noticed Zach nodding his approval, feeling the same way about his own sister. "I know you would have, but this was something I had to work through on my own."

"So you've done that and you are ready to tell us what's been going on?" The more serious of the two men, Luke never wasted time getting to the heart of the matter.

"Yeah, don't keep us in suspense," Jake urged.

Taking another deep breath, she asked, "How do you feel about being uncles to twins in about six months?"

The silence that followed proved that this was not what her brothers had expected.

"I know this comes as a—"

The first to recover, Jake interrupted her. "You're pregnant…"

"With twins," Luke finished, sounding more formidable than she'd heard in a long time.

"Who's the father?" Jake demanded.

"And how do we contact him?" Luke asked, sounding just as determined as his twin.

"Yeah, we'd like to have a little talk with the bastard," Jake spat, going into "big brother" mode.

Before she could answer, Zach took her hand in his and gave it a gentle squeeze of support. "I'm right here with your sister. The name's Zach Forsythe. Arielle and I are getting married as soon as I get the arrangements made."

"No, we're not," she contradicted, glaring at Zach. She tried to pull her hand from his, but Zach held it firmly in his much larger one. "I told you that marriage isn't required to have a child."

"And as I have told *you,* it is for me," he vowed stubbornly.

"Sounds to me like things aren't completely settled after all," Luke spoke up.

"Don't do anything until I get there, Arielle," Jake advised quickly. "And for God's sake, don't sign any legal documents until I look at them." The sudden sound of pages being shuffled came across the line and she knew her brother was checking his schedule. "I have a couple of discoveries to get through and a court date scheduled for Friday, but I'll be there first thing Saturday morning."

"Good idea," Luke agreed. "Haley and I will be there, too. And it might not be a bad idea for you to draw up a prenuptial agreement and bring it with you, Jake."

"I was thinking the same thing, bro," Jake acknowledged.

"None of this is necessary," Arielle insisted, wondering how something as simple as a phone call to tell her brothers she was pregnant had gotten so out of hand. "I'm not getting married and even if I was, I'm perfectly capable of making my own decisions."

"I think it's great you are coming to Dallas," Zach interjected as if she hadn't said a word. "I'd like to meet my future brothers-in-law. After all, we'll be family soon." He gave her an *I told you so* grin as he added, "And since I have more than enough room, I'd like to invite everyone to stay at my place." He gave her brothers his cell-phone number. "Let me know your arrival times and I'll have my driver pick you up at the airport."

"Sounds like an excellent plan," Luke affirmed as if everything was settled. "And in the meantime, give him a chance, Arielle. Seems he wants to do the right thing."

"We'll see you on Saturday, little sister," Jake added before he and Luke both hung up, ending the call.

"That went pretty well," Zach announced, sitting back and looking so darned satisfied with himself she wanted to bop him. "I think your brothers and I are going to get along just fine."

She stood up to glare down at him. "At the moment, I'd like to take all three of you and clunk your heads together."

He looked taken aback. "Why? What did we do?"

"You're all just alike. There wasn't one of you who paid the least bit of attention to what *I* want." She shook her head. "I told them I had everything under control. I even told them that I had no intention of marrying you. But did they listen? No. They'll be here on Saturday in full 'big brother' mode, ready to tell me what they think is best and expect me to go along with it." She wiped at the tears of frustration threatening to spill down her cheeks. "And you, you're too stubborn to give up on your harebrained notion that we *have* to get married."

"You're getting way too upset about this, Arielle," he noted, rising to his feet.

When he reached for her, she shook her head and, backing away, pointed toward the hall. "I'm going into my bedroom to lie down and try to forget that phone call ever happened. When I get up, I expect you to be gone. Please lock the door when you leave."

Without waiting for him to respond, she spun around and marched into her bedroom, slamming the door as hard as she could. She should have known better than to call while Zach was with her, she thought as she kicked off her shoes and stretched out on her bed. He and her brothers were so much alike it was uncanny. All three were highly successful self-made men with take-charge personalities and it really shouldn't have surprised her that they'd controlled the entire conversation.

Jake and Luke, she could understand. It had been an overwhelming responsibility for two twenty-year-old young men to finish raising their ten-year-old sister. And after all those years of making every decision for her, it had to be hard for them to admit that she'd grown up and could take control of her own life.

But Zach was an entirely different story. His insistence that they get married was just plain ludicrous. He didn't love her and the way he'd left her behind in Aspen, it was a safe bet that he'd grown tired of her, just the way her father had grown tired of her mother all those years ago.

She turned on her side and hugged one of her pillows. Three and a half months ago, she'd wanted Zach to ask her to be his bride. And if circumstances were different now, nothing could stop her from committing herself to him for the rest of her life. But it was his desire to be a full-time father that was fueling his demand, not the fact that he cared about her. And that wasn't enough.

A fresh wave of tears coursed down her cheeks. Closing her eyes, she vowed to remain true to her heart. For the first time in her life, she understood why her mother had fallen into Owen Larson's web of deceit the second time. But she was going to be wiser, stronger, than her mother had been.

Unfortunately, Zach was a powerful force and one she was finding almost impossible to resist. Each time he touched her, held her, kissed her, she lost every ounce of sense she possessed. And it was becoming increasingly more difficult not to fall hopelessly in love with him all over again.

* * *

Turning on the television but lowering the volume, Zach propped his feet on the coffee table and settled back to wait for Arielle to wake up from her nap. The phone call with her brothers had gone well for him, but she'd become upset with all of them and he intended to put a stop to it right away.

It had occurred to him after Arielle stormed into her bedroom that he should adjust his tactics with her. In Aspen, things between them had progressed way too fast and had actually been based on deception. Then, before he could tell her who he really was, he'd returned to Dallas because of Lana's accident and in the weeks that followed, had no time to follow up and explain. And when he finally did have the time, it had already been so long that he'd figured it was too late to set things straight with her. But he'd been wrong. They had a set of twins on the way and that changed everything.

He thought about the obstacles he'd have to overcome to get Arielle to agree to marry him. He'd hurt her deeply with his unexplained disappearance and the use of his alias had destroyed any trust she'd had in him. That was definitely something they would straighten out. Pressing her to get married before he explained why he'd left that morning in Aspen would be a study in futility. But he did have a fairly good idea how to get her in a more receptive mood to hear him out and he had every intention of putting his theory into action immediately.

Taking his cell from the clip on his belt, he dialed his home number and when his housekeeper answered, had her put him through to the kitchen. Telling his cook what he wanted, he instructed her to have his driver bring the special dinner over to Arielle's apartment as soon as it was ready.

Given her recent appetite, a scrumptious meal was definitely going to make points with her and hopefully put her in the mood to listen to his explanation. Satisfied with his plan, he waited for Arielle to wake, certain they'd soon be a step or two closer to a weekend wedding.

Five

She awoke to the tantalizing aroma of food. Getting out of bed, Arielle walked into her bathroom and washed the evidence of tears from her face. Zach obviously hadn't paid a bit of attention to her request for him to leave, but given his bullheaded tenacity, she really hadn't expected him to. And although she was frustrated beyond words by his dogged determination that they marry, she wasn't about to send him away until she'd sampled some of whatever smelled absolutely wonderful.

When she walked into the dining area, Zach had just lit the wicks on a couple of long white tapers in beautiful silver candlesticks. "Hey there, sleepyhead.

I was just about to wake you," he revealed, giving her a smile that warmed her all over. "How was your nap? Did you sleep well?"

"As far as naps go, it was okay," she said.

She was supposed to be angry with him, but that emotion was decreasing with each passing second. He looked so darned handsome in the glow of the candlelight and the way he'd rolled up the sleeves of his dress shirt was just plain sexy.

She swallowed hard. Her pregnancy hormones had to be completely out of whack if just the sight of his tanned forearms was enough to send her temperature soaring.

Deciding to concentrate on something besides the sexiest man she'd ever known, she pointed to the two elegant place settings filled with delicious-looking food. "What is all this?"

He pulled out one of the chairs for her. "I thought you might need something to eat when you woke up."

"I appreciate your thoughtfulness, but something to eat is soup or a sandwich," she pointed out, sitting in the chair he held. "This is a feast."

He shrugged as he lowered himself into the chair at the head of the table. "A light meal is good once in a while, but it doesn't provide enough of the vitamins and minerals you and the babies need to stay healthy."

"When did you become a nutritionist?" she quipped, picking up her napkin to place it on her lap.

"Actually, I was relying more on common sense

than knowledge," he confessed, grinning. "But it sounded pretty impressive, don't you think?"

"Yes, but you'd better be careful." She couldn't help but laugh at his smug expression. "Don't break your arm patting yourself on the back for being so clever."

The easy camaraderie continued throughout the most sinfully delicious meal she'd had in a long time. By the time they finished dessert, Arielle felt positively stuffed. "The chocolate mousse was scrumptious and, hands down, the best I've ever tasted."

Zach nodded. "I'm convinced that Maria Lopez is, without question, the best cook in the whole state of Texas."

"After that meal, she certainly has my vote," Arielle agreed, rising to her feet.

When she started to take their plates, he caught her hand in his and pulled her down to sit on his lap. "I'll take care of clearing the dishes in a few minutes."

"But—"

"Arielle, we need to talk about Aspen."

"Zach, I—"

"I've tried to tell you before and you haven't wanted to hear it, but this time, I'm not taking no for an answer," he interrupted, determined to have his say. "I'm going to tell you exactly what happened—from using another name to the reason I left that morning."

Whether she liked what he had to say or not, the time had come to hear him out. If she didn't, they'd never work out an amicable agreement to share the raising of their children.

"All right," she concurred cautiously. "I'm listening."

She felt his chest rise and fall against her side as he took a deep breath. "First of all, it's a habit of mine to use another name when I check into one of my resorts to observe how my employees interact with our guests."

"And no one has figured out who you are?" she ventured, unable to believe he'd maintained his anonymity. "Surely there are people at your hotels who have met and recognize you."

He nodded. "Of course there are. But besides arranging my visits while the resort manager is on vacation or away for a training seminar, my hotels are large enough that I can avoid being recognized by posing as—"

"Tom Zacharias, skiing enthusiast," she interjected, beginning to understand.

"That's right, darlin'. When I check in as someone else, I'm treated like any other guest." He shrugged. "And you'd be amazed at how much more I learn about guest services, maintenance and customer satisfaction than if I had made an announced visit."

"I would assume everyone would be on their best behavior if they knew who you were."

"And I wouldn't know a damned thing about the areas that need improvement."

What he said made sense, but that didn't explain why he couldn't have told her who he was. "But what about me, Zach? Why couldn't you have been honest with me about your real identity? Or do you also make a habit of having a fling with one of your female guests every time you visit one of your resorts?"

"No, Arielle, I don't." He leaned back until their gazes met. "Until you, I had never even asked another guest out to dinner."

She could tell by the light in his dark green eyes that he was telling the truth. "What made me different?"

"Besides being the sexiest, most beautiful woman on the mountain, you were funny, intelligent and when you found yourself on the expert run instead of the beginner slope, you were so damned determined to get yourself out of a bad situation, I couldn't resist." His easy smile warmed her. "When I came across you making your way down that section of the Silver Queen run, you were scared to death, but you weren't about to throw up your hands and wait for someone to find you. You had the courage to get yourself down the mountain. I admired that, darlin'."

"All right, but that doesn't explain why you didn't tell me who you really were sometime later during the week," she countered, refusing to let him off that easily.

"You're right, Arielle. I should have told you my real name." He touched her cheek with his index finger. "But you took me by surprise, darlin'. I wasn't expecting you or how fast things developed between us." His expression turned serious. "And the reason I left that morning without waking you or leaving a note was because of an emergency about my sister. If I had been thinking clearly, I swear I'd have never left without at least telling you goodbye."

"What happened?" She hadn't considered that he'd been called away because of an emergency.

"Lana was almost killed in a head-on car crash. All I could think about was getting back to Dallas to see her."

"Oh my God, Zach. Is she all right?" He'd mentioned his sister several times, but Arielle couldn't remember him speaking about her in the present tense.

"She's doing well now, but for several days after the accident, the doctors weren't sure she would pull through." He took a deep breath. "It's been a long, hard recovery for her and she's just recently started walking again."

Without a moment's hesitation, she wrapped her arms around him. She couldn't even imagine how frightening the ordeal had to have been for him. If something like that had happened to one of her brothers and she thought there was a possibility she might lose one of them, she doubted that she would have had the presence of mind to do any differently.

"And for the record, I thought about contacting you after I knew Lana was out of danger. But so much time had passed, I decided it was best just to leave things the way they were because you probably wouldn't want to hear from me, anyway," he explained, his strong arms tightening around her. "I know that's a poor excuse, darlin'. No matter how long it had been, I owed it to you to pick up the phone and let you know what happened."

"The accident was the upheaval in your nephew's life that you referred to Friday morning, wasn't it?" she concluded with sudden insight.

Zach nodded. "Derek really is a good kid. He's just had a hard time understanding what was going on and why Lana couldn't give him the attention he's used to getting from her."

"And it resulted in behavior problems," she guessed, having seen children react like that when something upsetting happened in their young lives.

Zach squeezed her slightly. "But now that he and Lana have moved back into her condo and things have settled down, he'll do a lot better."

"I'm sure he will." She smiled. "Children always do better in a familiar environment. It gives them a sense of much-needed security."

"And are you feeling a little more secure about me now?" he asked, nuzzling the side of her neck.

She fully understood why he'd left, and, to a point, why he hadn't contacted her. As time passed, it was always easier to let things be. But even if he had called her, it would only have been to explain his disappearance, not because he wanted to rekindle the relationship they'd shared in Aspen.

"Give it some thought, darlin'," he whispered. "Why don't you go into the living room and put your feet up."

Heat streaked straight through her and she had to remind herself to breathe when he brushed her lips with his. "You arranged for the meal. The least I can do is clear the table."

He shook his head. "I told you, I fully intend to take care of you and our babies and that includes making sure you don't overdo things."

"I don't think there's any danger of doing more than I should," she declared, feeling more breathless with each passing second. "I'd have to actually *do* something before I could overdo it."

"Hey, you're going to be the mother of twins in a few months. Take it easy while you can." His lips skimmed the side of her neck, sending shivers throughout her body. "Besides, I like pampering you."

A honeyed warmth began to flow through her veins and she had to remind herself that although he'd explained what happened, she wasn't entirely certain she could trust him not to disappear all over again. Their current circumstances were a direct result of her falling for Zach's line of sensuous persuasion once before and doing so again could very well be disastrous for her. But heaven help her, it certainly was tempting.

"I think I'll take you up on that offer," she decided suddenly, getting to her feet.

"I'll join you in a few minutes." He walked into

the kitchen and when he returned, he held a small cardboard box. As she watched, he started placing their plates, silverware and glasses inside.

"Aren't you going to put them in the dishwasher?" she chided, frowning.

He shook his head as he grabbed his cell phone and dialed a number. "Not when I have a driver waiting outside to take these back to my place."

"Oh, good Lord," she began, rolling her eyes as she walked over to the sitting area of the room. "Don't tell me you're going to make the poor man drive all the way to your house, then come back to get you later."

"Nope." He paused long enough to tell the chauffeur to come to the door for the box, then, ending the call, he smiled. "Remember, I told you we'd spend the night here, then go to my place tomorrow before we go in to work."

Why wasn't she surprised that he hadn't given up on that?

"After that wonderful meal, I really don't feel like arguing with you, Zach," she conceded, lowering herself onto the couch.

"Then don't." When the doorbell rang, he handed the box of dishes to his driver, closed and locked the door, then walked over to where she sat on the couch. "Let's just watch a movie and relax. It's been a big day and I think we could both use a little downtime, don't you?"

"That's about the first thing you've said today that

I agree with." She started to settle against the cushions, but he took her hand and pulled her back to her feet. "Now what?"

Before she could stop him, he sat in the corner of the couch, stretched out one long leg against the back cushions, then pulled her down to sit between his thighs. "Lean back against my chest and relax, darlin'," he ordered, kissing the back of her neck.

The sensations he evoked in her rendered her utterly speechless and without a thought to the danger he posed to her heart, she did as he instructed. The feel of his warm, solid chest against her back caused her heart to beat double-time, but when he wrapped her in his arms and splayed his hands on her stomach, her heart felt as if it might jump right out of her chest.

"What are you trying to do to me, Zach?" She didn't for a single minute believe that relaxation was all he had on his mind.

His hands glided over her stomach in a soothing manner. "I'm doing what I told you I was going to do—take care of you and make sure you take the time to unwind."

She shook her head. "You know what I mean."

He kissed her shoulder and the column of her neck. "Hopefully, I'm reminding you of how good we were together and how good we can be again."

"Zach, this isn't going to change my mind about—"

"Hush, darlin'." He picked up the remote control from the end table and turned on the DVD player. "We can talk about all of that later. Let's watch the movie."

As the opening credits of the romantic comedy he'd selected appeared on her television screen, Arielle tried to concentrate on watching the show and forget about the man holding her so snugly. But the feel of his strength surrounding her and the sexy scent of his woodsy aftershave assailing her senses made it hard to think of anything else.

The way he gently massaged her stomach, she could almost believe he was trying to release the tension that had built up over the day. But she'd learned the hard way not to allow his tender touch and charming words to cloud her judgment. And she wasn't naive enough to think his consideration had anything whatsoever to do with her. Everything he'd done, everything he'd said, had been for the welfare of the babies. Even his insistence that they had to get married was because she was pregnant, not because he cared deeply for her.

But her disturbing introspection was suddenly cut short at the feel of Zach's rapidly hardening body pressing insistently against her backside. The longing that followed the realization that he'd become aroused was staggering and had her struggling to sit up.

"I think it would be a good idea if I changed positions."

Holding her firmly against him, he nuzzled the side of her neck. "Are you comfortable, Arielle?"

Shivers of desire made it difficult to form a rational thought, let alone an answer. "Y-yes…I mean, no."

His deep chuckle vibrated against her back. "Do you want to know what I think?"

"Not really." She didn't need for him to point out the obvious.

"I'm fairly certain that my becoming hard is reminding you of how good it felt to have me inside you," he whispered. "And I'm betting that you're disturbed that you're as turned on as I am."

The feel of his warm breath feathering over her skin and the memory of the sultry passion they'd shared in Aspen had her catching her breath. "Not even close," she lied.

He had the audacity to laugh out loud. "Whatever you say, darlin'. Now settle back and enjoy the movie."

That was going to be easier said than done with his hard body touching every part of her back. Eventually she did become intrigued by the story line and before she knew it, the film had ended.

"The meal was beyond delicious and the show was very entertaining, but I'm exhausted," she recapped, yawning as she sat up. Turning to face him, she added, "I think it's time you called your driver to take you home."

"I gave Mike the rest of the night off," Zach reported, stretching his arms.

"Then I suggest you call a taxi."

He shook his head. "I don't use public transportation."

"There's a first time for everything, Mr. Forsythe. Now go home."

"Why would I want to do that, darlin'?" He lazily stroked her shoulders. "We're staying here tonight and going to my place tomorrow."

"You're unbelievable." She stared at him for several long seconds. Then, needing to put distance between them, got to her feet. "This apartment only has one bedroom and I'm not sharing."

He rose to stand in front of her. "I'll be fine right here on the couch."

Reaching out, he took her into his arms and before she could stop him, he lowered his head to press his lips to hers. A jolt of longing so intense it caused her head to spin surged through her veins and she had to put her arms around him to keep her suddenly rubbery knees from giving way.

Caressing her mouth with his, he quickly had her conforming to his demand to deepen the kiss. She reveled in the game of advance and retreat that followed. He seemed to be challenging her to explore him as he explored her and without hesitation, Arielle complied.

As she stroked his tongue with hers, she delighted in his deep shuddering groan and the immediate tightening of his embrace. Feminine power filled her, and if she hadn't been lost in the moment, she might have been shocked by her own boldness.

As the passion within her began to build, so did the realization that she was about to be swept up into Zach's sensual trap again. She wasn't stupid. The delicious candlelight dinner, the romantic movie and his refusal to go back to his own place meant he was trying a different tactic in his bid to get her to marry him. No matter how wonderful it felt to be in his arms again, to have him kiss her and know that he wanted her, she couldn't let down her guard. She'd barely survived his leaving her once; she'd never get through it if he left her a second time.

Breaking the kiss, she stepped back on wobbly legs. "Goodbye, Zach."

His expression gave nothing away as he paused for a moment before leading her by the hand to her bedroom door. "Good night, darlin'," he murmured, lightly brushing her lips with his. "If you need me, I'll be right out there on the couch."

As she watched him walk down the hall, she wondered what she was supposed to do now. She wouldn't be able to get a wink of sleep just knowing he was on her couch. Possibly in his boxer shorts. Possibly wearing nothing at all.

"Oh, dear Lord."

Hurrying into her bedroom, she closed the door then leaned back against it. She was in deep, deep trouble and it was going to be a very long night if just the thought of Zach being nude could send fire streaking through her veins and cause her pulse to pound so hard she could feel it in every cell of her body.

Zach stared at the ceiling of Arielle's living room long after he heard her close her bedroom door. If he wasn't so damned uncomfortable, the situation would be downright laughable. Hell, he'd single-handedly built and maintained a thriving empire of luxury resorts. He had several billion dollars in assets. He had a mansion with eight bedrooms, all with very comfortable king-size beds. And here he was, on a couch that was too short, his head resting on a throw pillow hard as a chunk of concrete and covered up with a stadium blanket that needed three more feet.

But other than his back was going to kill him in the morning and he was in one room while Arielle was in another, the evening had gone rather well. After her nap, he'd finally explained about Aspen, hadn't pushed the marriage issue and his body let her know in no uncertain terms how he still desired her as much now as he had then.

Now he had to convince her that getting married was in the best interest of their babies and by the time her brothers and sister-in-law arrived on Saturday, everything should be set for a weekend wedding. Granted it would be a small, family-only affair, since they didn't have time to make a lot of arrangements.

But later, if Arielle wanted something larger, they could plan a lavish wedding and reception.

Extremely satisfied with the way he was handling everything, he'd just drifted off to sleep when a woman's keening wail caused the hair on the back of his neck to stand straight up and had him bolting off the couch in less than a heartbeat. His heart hammered hard against his ribs as he made his way across the dark room and when he stubbed his toe on the armchair, he muttered a curse that would have had Mattie washing his mouth out with soap when he'd been younger. But ignoring the throbbing pain that followed, he rushed down the hall and flung open Arielle's bedroom door.

Relieved to see there wasn't someone in the room trying to hurt her, he then realized she was writhing under the duvet as if in extreme discomfort. Rushing to her, he turned the bedside light on, pushed the covers away and noticed she was desperately trying to rub her left calf.

"Arielle, what's wrong?"

"L-leg…cramp," she moaned, her normally melodic voice tight with pain.

Kneeling on the bed, he brushed her hands aside and immediately massaged her left calf as he loosened up the muscle. "Hang on, darlin'. It should start feeling better in just a minute or two."

In a matter of seconds, her expression told him the

pain was lessening. Now sitting beside her, he continued to gently rub her calf.

"That feels…much better," she admitted. "Thank you."

During the ordeal with the muscle cramp, her thin yellow gown had ridden up well above her knees and he noticed that although her stomach had rounded slightly from being pregnant, the rest of her body was every bit as shapely as in Aspen. Just the memory of having her long slender legs wrapped around him as they made love caused his body to harden so fast, it left him feeling light-headed and made him damned glad that he had on a pair of loose boxers.

Without a thought to the damage he might do to his well-crafted plan not to push Arielle too far, Zach stretched out beside her. Then, gathering her to him, he pulled the sheet over them.

"What do you think you're doing?" she demanded, her eyes wide.

He wasn't entirely sure why, but he did know it felt completely right. "The couch is too short. Besides, you might have another leg cramp and I'd rather not risk breaking my neck getting to you the next time."

"That's about the most contrived excuse I think I've ever heard," she protested, turning on her side to face him. At least she was still talking to him and not ordering him out of the room.

He laughed. "It was pretty weak, wasn't it?"

Nodding, she asked, "Seriously, what are you doing in my bed and why?"

"I wasn't exaggerating about the couch. It's about a foot and a half too short to be comfortable for a man of my height."

"I'm sure your own bed is long enough to accommodate you. You could go home."

"No, I couldn't." He brushed a strand of silky auburn hair from her cheek. "I told you I'd be here for you, no matter what. And I'll keep that promise or die trying." He paused, then, deciding to lay it on the line, added, "And the biggest reason I'm in bed with you is because I want to hold you while you sleep and wake up with you in my arms."

He could tell by the look on her pretty face that she had serious doubts about his motives. "Zach, I—"

"I'm not going to lie to you, darlin'. I want to make love to you. I want to be buried so deep inside you that you forget where you end and I begin." He kissed the tip of her nose. "But I give you my word, I'm not going to press you for more than you're ready to give. When the time is right, we'll know and nothing will stop me from giving you so much pleasure that we both collapse from exhaustion."

She finally nodded. "I truly appreciate your consideration. Unfortunately, I don't trust myself any more than I trust you."

"I can understand having a doubt or two about me,

but why can't you trust yourself?" he inquired, enjoying the feel of her soft body against his much harder one.

"My judgment isn't at its best when I'm around you." She closed her eyes, debating with herself about how much she wanted to say. When she opened them, she found him intently watching her face. "I let myself throw caution to the wind with you once before and although I want and love these babies more than life itself, I would have preferred we were…" She stopped for a moment, trying to find the right words. "That things between us had gone a little more conventionally."

He knew exactly what she meant. She'd wanted a relationship that progressed into a commitment before she had become pregnant. But that hadn't happened and there was no way to go back and change things. The way he saw it, they should move forward and make the best of the situation.

"Let's just take it one day at a time and see where it takes us." He slid his hand over her side, then around to her back to pull her closer. "But I'd like for you to promise me that you'll at least give me—give us—a chance. Can you do that, Arielle?"

He could see the uncertainty in the depths of her hazel eyes before she finally spoke. "I'll think about it."

Immense relief washed over him at her concession. If she was willing to give the matter some thought, he was wearing her down and that's all the opening he needed to achieve his ultimate goal.

Giving her a little more encouragement, he covered her mouth with his, and at the first touch, he felt a spark light his lower belly. But when she put her arms around his neck and eagerly accepted his kiss, the spark quickly turned into flames.

As he deepened the kiss, he reached down to lift the hem of her gown. Sliding his hand underneath, he caressed her leg from knee to thigh. Fire immediately streaked through his veins at the feel of her satiny skin beneath his palm and her eager response to his tongue teasing hers.

He slid his hand up her side to the swell of her breast, then took the weight of her in his hand. When he teased the tip with the pad of his thumb, his blood pressure went through the roof at the sound of her soft whimper. But it was the feel of her warm touch when she placed her hand on his bare chest, doing a little exploring of her own, that caused his body to tighten almost painfully.

He wanted her with a fierceness that defied every good intention about waiting until she was ready. And when she moved her hand to his abdomen to trace her finger down toward his navel, he was pretty sure she wanted him just as much. But he had to know for certain.

"Darlin', we've reached a line here and once crossed, there won't be any turning back," he implored, kissing his way to the hollow of her throat. "At least not without a cold shower and a lot of suffering on my part." Raising his head, he caught her gaze with his. "So if this isn't what you want, too, you'd better tell me right now and show me where you keep your bath towels."

Just when he thought she was going to tell him to take that cold shower and go back to the couch, she took a deep breath. "There are a lot things about us that I'm unsure of. But the one thing that hasn't changed is how much I want you."

"Are you…sure, Arielle?" he persisted, finding it hard to draw in his next breath.

"No. But where you're concerned, being certain doesn't seem to matter." The look in her eyes robbed him of air and caused the flames in his belly to burn out of control. "Please make love to me, Zach."

Six

As Zach brought his mouth down to cover hers, Arielle wondered if she'd lost the last traces of her sanity. Not once since their unexpected reunion had he apologized for what had taken place in Aspen. He'd explained using an alias and leaving without telling her goodbye, but hadn't said he was sorry. That didn't change the fact that with one kiss, one touch of his hand on her body, she was completely lost. It had been that way almost four months ago and it was that way now.

Wrapping her arms around him, she briefly considered how she would survive if she found him gone the following morning—or any other morning for that matter. But as he kissed and teased her with such infinite care, she quickly abandoned her disturbing thoughts and gave in to her feelings.

Heat shimmered behind her closed eyes and a tingling excitement skipped over every nerve in her body as he caressed his way to her panties, then eased them down and with her help, took them off. But when he moved to lift her gown out of the way, her heart skipped several beats and she suddenly wished for darkness.

"Zach, would you…please do something for me?" she asked, easing her lips from his.

"What's that…darlin'?" He sounded as if he had as much trouble breathing as she did.

"Would you please turn off the light?"

Leaning back, he propped himself up on one elbow. "If you're worried about what I think of your figure now that you're pregnant, don't." He shoved the sheet to the end of the bed. Then, grasping her nightgown, slid his hands up her sides and along the undersides of her arms, raising them over her head as he went. He lifted her slightly as he whisked her gown away in one smooth motion. His eyes never leaving hers, he eased her back down on the bed. "You've always been beautiful, Arielle."

It wasn't until his survey drifted ever so slowly along the length of her body that she truly believed he meant what he'd said. It almost felt as if he had physically caressed her.

"I was wrong," he amended, gently placing his hand on her tummy. He leaned down to press a kiss just above her navel. When he raised his head to look at her, the light shining in his dark green gaze stole her breath and erased every one of her reservations. "You're more gorgeous today than you were in Aspen and I have no doubt you'll be even more beautiful tomorrow."

Keeping his eyes locked to hers, he got out of bed. Hooking his thumbs in the waistband of his boxer shorts, he slowly lowered them down his long muscular legs. His sculpted physique was every bit as breathtaking as she remembered. As Zach revealed himself to her, her eyes widened when she noticed the strength of his thick arousal rising proudly from the patch of dark hair at his groin.

But it was the heated look he gave her when he got back into bed that rendered her utterly speechless. "I've wanted you from the moment I saw you again," he confessed, gathering her to him.

The feel of hard masculine flesh pressed against her softer feminine skin, the scent of his woodsy cologne and the sound of his harsh breathing sent sparks skipping along every nerve in her body. But when he caressed her back, then traced his hands the length of her spine to cup her bottom and pull her forward, his groan mingled with her moan and she instinctively knew that he was experiencing the same intense pleasure she was.

Heat thrummed through her veins as he covered her mouth with his. When he deepened the kiss, she threaded her fingers through his thick hair and boldly met his tongue with her own. She wanted him to know the degree of passion he instilled in her, the urgent hunger that only he could create and quench.

She felt his body pulse with need and her own body responded with a tightening deep in the most feminine part of her. It had been a long time since she'd been held by him this way and she felt as if she'd finally come home. Never had she felt such intimacy, such safety as she felt in Zack's arms.

He broke their kiss to nibble his way down the base of her throat, past her collarbone, to the slope of her breast. She held him to her as he took the hardened peak into his mouth, and the intensity of sensations coursing through her at the feel of his lips on her body sent a need racing through her entire being so strong it threatened to consume her.

"Please," she whimpered. "It's been...so long."

"Easy, darlin'," he warned as he trailed his hand down her side to her hip, then lower still. "I want you, too. But I want to make sure this is as good for you as I know it's going to be for me."

He parted her then and at the first stroke of his fingers, waves of exquisite delight flowed through her. His intimate touch was driving her absolutely crazy and caused an ache she knew only he could ease.

"I...need...you, Zach," she whispered, surprised

that she formed a coherent thought, let alone words. "Now."

"We're going…to do this…a little differently this time," he said, sounding winded as he sat up.

He lifted her to straddle his lap and held her gaze as he slowly, carefully, lowered her onto him. Arielle felt complete for the first time in months. As her body consumed his, she placed her hands on his wide shoulders and, closing her eyes, melted around him, reveling in the feelings of becoming one with the man who had stolen her heart all those months ago.

"You feel so…damned good," he groaned through gritted teeth.

When he was completely buried within her, he crushed her lips to his. In spite of the problems they had yet to address, she knew for certain she was in danger of falling in love with him.

"We're going to take…this slow," he described when he finally broke the kiss. "And I want you to tell me if you have the slightest bit of discomfort."

She could have told him that being with him again was the most comfort she'd had in the past few months, but the words died in her throat when he placed his hands on her hips and began to guide her in a slow rocking motion against him. Closing her eyes, heat filling every cell of her being, she knew as surely as she knew her own name that she'd never feel even a fraction of the emotions she felt for Zach for any other man.

As they moved together, his lips skimmed over the sensitive skin of her throat, accelerating the delicious tightening in her feminine core. Her mind closed to anything but the urgent need to find completion. She desperately tried to prolong the swirling sensations building inside her, but the hunger he created became a force she couldn't resist and she gave herself up to the power of his lovemaking. Clinging to him, she moaned his name as the hot tide of passion washed over her and she found release. She heard Zach groan, then felt his much larger body go completely still a moment before he found his own shuddering reprieve.

As the intensity subsided and they drifted back to reality, he asked, "Are you all right?"

Arielle sighed contentedly. "That was amazing."

"I couldn't agree more." He eased her down beside him, then collapsed back against the pillow. "But are you all right?"

"I'm wonderful."

"I know the doctor said it would be okay for us to make love, but—"

"Don't worry," she stressed, yawning. She knew he was overly concerned because of the pregnancy. "I'm just fine."

He chuckled as he pulled the sheet over their rapidly cooling bodies. Turning on his side, he then wrapped his arms around her and drew her close. "You do seem a lot more relaxed than when I first walked in here."

"Barged."

"What?"

She yawned again. "You didn't walk in here, you barged your way in."

"Whatever. I don't think you'll have any more problems with muscle cramps tonight." Zach kissed her soft cheek. "Can I ask you to do something else, darlin'?"

"What?"

"Would you take the rest of the week off?"

She looked questioningly at him. "Why would I want to do that?"

"I'd like for us to spend some quality time together, instead of a few hours here and there before or after you go to the school and I head to my office."

In Aspen they'd had an uninterrupted week of getting to know each other and that was exactly what they needed now. He needed to gain her trust.

"I just took over the school," she protested.

"That's true, but you're also the administrator now," he reminded. "You can take off any time you please."

"Can *you* take time away from your business?" she asked pointedly.

He smiled. "Of course. I'm the boss, remember?"

When she nibbled her lower lip, he could tell she was contemplating his request. "If I did take the time off, you'd have to promise me something."

"What's that, darlin'?"

"I'd need your assurance that you wouldn't bring

up the subject of marriage one time during the next four days." She raised her eyebrows. "Do you think you could manage that?"

He'd promise just about anything to get her to agree. Grinning, he nodded. "I'm pretty sure I can, provided you know I haven't given up on that particular issue."

"It never occurred to me that you would, Mr. Forsythe," she commented, hiding another huge yawn behind her hand.

"Good. Now that we have that settled, you need to get some sleep, darlin'."

When he realized that Arielle had already nodded off, Zach smiled as he reached to turn off the bedside lamp. Getting enough sleep was not going to be a problem for Arielle and one less thing he needed to worry about. Unless he missed his guess, Arielle could drift off to sleep anywhere, at any time.

As he lay there contemplating other ways to ensure she was taking good care of herself, he compared the differences between her and his ex-fiancée. Although Gretchen had told him how much she looked forward to having a baby, it hadn't taken long for her to change her tune. Within a few days of learning she was expecting, Gretchen started acting as if she thought eating was the ultimate sin and became obsessed about gaining weight. And that was just the tip of the iceberg when it came to her irrational reaction to the pregnancy.

She had complained that it wasn't a good time to have a baby and she was too tired to get out of bed. Then one morning, she'd surprised him when she got up and began an exhaustive schedule of physical exercises that he'd later realized was a desperate attempt to end the pregnancy. And in less than two weeks of nonstop exertion, sleeping very little and eating less than a bird, she'd succeeded in causing herself to miscarry.

Zach took a deep shuddering breath. He still carried a lot of guilt over not recognizing what Gretchen had been up to and his failure to protect that baby. He should have paid more attention.

But it wasn't going to happen again. The babies Arielle carried were depending on him and Zach wasn't about to let them down.

Fortunately, Arielle seemed to view her pregnancy in an entirely different way than Gretchen. Arielle indulged her hearty appetite, took it in stride that she was going to gain weight and got plenty of rest. And not one time since they'd reunited had he heard her express anything but pure joy over the prospect of becoming a mother.

Kissing the top of her head, he closed his eyes. Although he'd never intended to marry or trust another woman to have his child, he anticipated everything working out this time around. There was every indication that Arielle was not only going to be a good, loving mother to their twins, she was the most exciting, intoxicating woman he'd ever met and having her in his bed every night was definitely going to be a huge benefit of marriage.

Oh, he knew that Arielle wanted the whole package—marriage, children and an enduring love that would see them through whatever life sent their way. But caring that much for a woman put a man at risk of losing his perspective and set him up to make a fool of himself. And that was one chance Zach just wasn't willing to take again. As long as he didn't allow love to enter into the picture, he'd not only be able to keep his children safe, he wouldn't have to worry about losing his pride or his heart.

Satisfied that everything would work out, sleep began to overtake him. Although he couldn't give Arielle the love she wanted, theirs would be a good marriage based on mutual respect and a sincere fondness for each other. As far as he was concerned, that should be enough to make them both happy.

After taking her shower and calling the preschool to arrange for her assistant administrator to take over for the rest of the week, Arielle waited until she heard Zach go into the bathroom and turn on the shower before reaching for the phone again. Deciding it was probably the only time she'd have to call her newfound grandmother without him overhearing the conversation, she sat down on the end of the couch and dialed Emerald, Inc. headquarters in Wichita.

She'd been thinking quite a bit about her unexpected run-in with Zach and the fact that it had been just a little too convenient to be a coincidence. She wasn't sure how, but she'd bet Emerald Larson had had a big hand in the reunion.

Of course, she wouldn't be surprised if it turned out Emerald *had* discovered Zach was the father of her babies. Arielle wasn't quite sure how Emerald had managed it, but when she contacted her and her brothers to tell them who their father was, Emerald had admitted to Arielle that she knew all about her pregnancy and her inability to find the baby's father.

"Good morning, Mrs. Larson's office. How may I help you?" Luther Freemont answered in his usual dry monotone. Over the past few months, she'd spoken with him several times and if Emerald's personal assistant ever put any kind of inflection in his voice, she hadn't heard it.

"Hello, Luther, this is Arielle. I'd like to speak to Emerald for a few minutes. Is she available now or should I call back at another time?"

"Of course she's in for you, Miss Garnier. Please hold while I put your call through to your grandmother's private line."

Within seconds, Emerald came on the line. "Arielle, darling, what a pleasant surprise," she greeted, sounding truly happy to hear from her only granddaughter. "To what do I owe the pleasure of your call?"

"Hello, Emerald." Considering that she'd only recently learned about the woman, Arielle wasn't comfortable calling her "grandmother." But they had formed a friendly, pleasant relationship and Emerald had made it clear that she was always available whenever Arielle needed to talk. "I hope I'm not interrupting anything."

"No, dear. In fact, I was thinking about giving you a call to see how you're doing with Premier Academy. Has the transition of ownership gone smoothly?"

"Oh, yes. It's actually been easier than I anticipated," Arielle confessed, smiling. "The entire staff has been very welcoming and helpful."

"Good." Emerald paused. "And how are *you* doing, darling? I trust everything is going well with your pregnancy?"

"That's one of the reasons I called," Arielle informed. "I had the ultrasound yesterday."

"And what is my next great-grandchild going to be—a boy or a girl?"

"It's still a little too early to tell yet, but how do you feel about having another set of twins in the family?"

There was stunned silence before Emerald spoke again. "Twins? Oh, how marvelous. Have you told Luke and Jake yet? I'm sure they're overjoyed for you."

"I called them yesterday after I returned from the doctor."

"How did they take the news, dear?"

"To say they were shocked is an understatement," Arielle revealed, laughing. Now she could find the humor in her normally verbal brothers being struck speechless. "At first they were both a bit miffed that I'd waited so long to tell them, but they let that go in favor of wanting to know who the father was and how they could find him."

"Oh, I'm sure they were ready to take the young man to task. What did you tell them, dear?"

"I didn't have to tell them anything." Arielle sighed. "I made the mistake of making the call with Zach sitting right beside me. He spoke up and admitted he's the babies' father. He told them we would be getting married this coming weekend."

"You're going to marry Zachary Forsythe, the hotel and resort tycoon?"

"No, I'm not."

"I see." Emerald paused, as if she knew she'd revealed a bit more than she should have. "However did you find him, darling?"

"You tell me," Arielle prodded, knowing for certain that her grandmother had orchestrated their reunion. She hadn't told her Zach's last name.

"Me? Why, I have no idea what you're talking about."

"Oh, I think you do, Emerald. You knew I was pregnant, and it's my guess that your team of private investigators discovered who the father was and where he lived." She sighed. "Why didn't you just tell me instead of buying the preschool his nephew attends and waiting for us to run into each other?"

To her credit, Emerald didn't deny that she'd been behind the setup. "I didn't want to meddle, darling."

"You're absolutely priceless." Arielle rolled her eyes and shook her head. "I've already heard the stories of my half brothers and their spouses being brought together by your matchmaking efforts."

"That worked out quite well." Emerald didn't sound the least bit repentant. "Caleb, Nick and Hunter are all very happy now and have since thanked me for intervening."

"Is that what you're doing?" Arielle asked. "Do you think that bringing Zach and me back together is going to result in another of your heirs finding their soul mate?"

"There is that possibility, Arielle."

Deciding it would be futile to get her grandmother to admit to any wrongdoing, she took a deep breath. "I'm not sure I'll ever be able to trust him."

"Oh, darling, I know it has to be difficult after what happened in Aspen," Emerald concluded, her voice genuinely sympathetic. "But give the man a chance. I'm sure there's a reasonable explanation for his disappearance." She paused before adding, "Your and Zachary's situation is nothing like your mother and father's."

"You knew why he left that morning, too, didn't you?" Arielle was certain Emerald had uncovered everything about Zach, including why he'd deserted her. "Why didn't you tell me?"

"I have to go now, dear," Emerald declared suddenly. "Please give me a call to let me know how everything goes with you and your young man."

Before Arielle said another word, Emerald ended the connection, leaving Arielle frustrated and wondering how much more her grandmother knew about her life. And why was everyone so sure that she should give Zach another chance?

First her brothers and now Emerald had encouraged her to give him the opportunity to prove himself. But they'd forgotten one extremely important factor. They weren't the ones in danger of getting their hearts broken all over again.

"What's wrong, Arielle?" Zach asked, walking into the room wearing nothing but a towel wrapped around his trim waist.

The sight of all that bare, masculine skin stole her breath. Zach was without a shadow of doubt the sexiest man she'd ever had the pleasure of meeting.

"N-nothing is wrong. Why do you ask?"

"You've got a frown that tells me otherwise, darlin'."

"I was just thinking about something," she mused, hoping he'd let the matter drop.

Zach walked over to stand in front of her and an excited little thrill raced up her spine knowing that he was naked under the towel. "Was there a problem getting someone to cover for you at the school?"

She shook her head as she tried to forget how wonderful his nude body had felt against hers. "No problem at all. Marylou was quite willing to take over in my absence."

"Good." He reached down to hold her hands and pulled her to her feet. "There's something I want us to do today and it doesn't include either of us going anywhere near work."

When he wrapped his arms around her and drew her close, she braced her hands on his bare chest. "What did you have in mind, Zach?"

"You'll see," he promised.

He nipped at her lower lip a moment before he traced it with his tongue. His actions quickly had her feeling as if she might melt into a puddle. But when he dipped his tongue inside her mouth, she couldn't stop her frustrated moan from escaping when he stopped and stepped back.

Taking a deep breath, he shook his head as if trying to clear it. "Go get dressed while I call my driver and have him bring me a change of clothes. Otherwise, we'll end up making love all day and miss out on what I have planned."

While he called his chauffeur, she tried to remember why she had to be cautious. The more he held her, kissed her, touched her, the easier it would be to forget all about the past and the danger he still posed to her heart. But that was something she just couldn't afford to do. No matter how many family members told her to give him a second chance, there were no assurances that their situation wouldn't parallel her parents'.

When Zach's private jet landed at the San Antonio airport, he released his seat belt, then reached over to unfasten Arielle's. He would remind her how much they'd enjoyed each other's company in Aspen. He wanted to make her forget all about the doubts she still had about him.

He stood and held out his hand to help her to her feet. "Are you ready to have some fun?" he asked, grinning.

Giving him a cautious smile, she placed her hand in his. "I've never been to San Antonio."

She gazed up at him and he thought she looked absolutely radiant. She wore a mint-green sundress that complimented her hazel eyes and peaches-and-cream complexion, and she'd drawn her hair into a sleek ponytail, exposing her slender shoulders and delicate neck.

He swallowed hard against his suddenly dry throat. It was going to take everything he had in him not to spend the day in a perpetual state of arousal. All he wanted, all he could think about, was exploring every inch of her satiny skin and spending the day making love with her.

"I thought we'd have lunch along the River Walk and visit a few of the shops, then maybe take a carriage ride," he relayed, bringing his wayward thoughts back under control. He'd considered renting a boat and taking her for a ride down the river, but decided against it. The boat might have swayed and caused her to take a fall. And that was one risk he wasn't willing to take.

"That sounds nice."

He preceded her to the exit of the plane, then reached up to place his hands on her waist to steady her for the descent down the jet's small steps. "After that we'll have to get back to Dallas to change for dinner."

"I was hoping to see the Alamo," she mentioned as they crossed the tarmac to a waiting limo. "I've heard it's a must-see."

Zach nodded. "I wouldn't think of bringing you to San Antonio without taking you to visit the Alamo. That would be downright sacrilegious."

"Is that your Texas pride talking, Mr. Forsythe?" she hinted, her tone sounding a little more relaxed.

Grinning, he gave her a quick kiss that left him hungering for more. But he ignored the urge to ravish her right there in the backseat. The day was all about having fun and keeping things light between them.

"Once a Texan, always a Texan," he finally murmured.

They rode the distance to the River Walk in companionable silence and by the time they reached the quaint outdoor café he'd selected for lunch, a modicum of his control had been restored.

"This is wonderful," she remarked, looking around.

Her eyes were wide with wonder and he was going to enjoy seeing the historic city from her perspective. She pointed to one of the shops down the way. "If we don't go anywhere else, we have to go in there."

Holding one of the chairs for her at a table with a bright blue umbrella, he waited until she was seated, then sat down across from her. When he realized she was talking about a trip to the ice cream shop, he smiled. "What's your favorite flavor?"

"Mint chocolate chip or maybe mocha fudge or chocolate ripple or…"

"I take it you like chocolate." He'd have to remember that.

Her enthusiastic nod caused her ponytail to bob up and down. "Sometimes I like a couple of different flavored scoops in the same cone. That way I don't have to choose just one. What's your favorite?"

"Vanilla."

She gave him a look that clearly stated she thought he might be a little touched in the head. "You've got to be kidding. Of all the wonderful ice cream flavors, you settle for plain old vanilla? Where's your sense of adventure?"

"I get adventurous once in a while," he remarked, thinking of something a lot more enjoyable than ice cream. Shifting to relieve the sudden tightness in his trousers, he added, "Sometimes, I have a few of those candy things sprinkled over the top."

Completely unaware of the direction of his

thoughts, she asked, "Aren't you afraid that's being just a bit too daring?"

Forcing himself to relax, he grinned. "What can I say, darlin'? I like living on the edge."

A smiling waiter chose that moment to walk over and place menus in front of them, effectively putting an end to their discussion of ice cream flavors. After giving the man their order, Zach noticed Arielle's delighted smile at the sight of a boat slowly motoring its way down the river toward them. Reaching across the table, he covered her delicate hand with his. "On our next trip, we'll take a ride the length of the river."

She paused, then treated him to a smile so sweet he could tell she was beginning to let down her guard. "I'd really like that, Zach. Thank you for bringing me here. Everything is so colorful and full of life. It's absolutely wonderful."

After the waiter brought their food, the rest of the time was spent indulging in some of the best Tex-Mex cuisine in the entire state. Zach watched Arielle polish off the last tortilla chip covered in *queso* from the sampler platter then motioned for their check.

"Why don't we get your ice cream, then walk over to El Mercado before we take a carriage ride," he suggested, handing the waiter his credit card. He needed to get her over to the market as soon as possible.

"I'm absolutely stuffed right now," she remarked, resting her hand on her stomach. "Maybe we'd better get the ice cream after everything else."

Once the waiter returned, Zach added a generous tip to the bill, then signed the receipt, slipped his credit card back into his wallet and stood up to hold Arielle's chair. "Are there any other shops you'd like to visit after we walk over to El Mercado?"

"I can't think of any," she indicated, shaking her head. "Just the ice cream shop will make me happy."

She placed her hand in his and in no time they'd made the short walk to the open-air market where the first part of his plan was about to come together.

"I'd like to buy you something to remember today, Arielle. What about something like this?" he asked, stopping in front of a vendor with an array of silver jewelry. He picked up a finely crafted filigree band with a beautiful solitaire setting. "This ring is nice."

Smiling, she nodded. "I love it. It's gorgeous. But you don't have to—"

He placed his index finger to her perfect lips. "I want to."

"It is made of the finest silver and crystal," the vendor lied right on cue.

Zach checked the attached tag, then gave his old friend, Juan Gomez, owner and master designer of one of the finest jewelry stores in Dallas, a conspiratorial wink. "What size do you wear, Arielle?"

"Five, but—"

"It will have to be resized, but that shouldn't be a problem." Turning to Juan, he retrieved his wallet from the hip pocket of his khaki pants. "We'll take it.

And if you can have it sized by the time we return from our carriage ride, I'll pay double the asking price."

"*Si,* senor," Juan confirmed, nodding happily.

"Zach, you can't do that." Her eyes were wide with disbelief—and he didn't think he'd ever seen her look more desirable.

"I most certainly can and will," he declared, giving his old friend several hundred dollars in order to make the transaction believable. He checked his watch, then placed his hand on the small of Arielle's back to usher her along before she realized what was going on. "We'll be back in about an hour. You'll get the rest of your money when the ring is ready."

His plan had worked like a charm and Arielle didn't suspect a thing. She had no way of knowing that the band was actually white gold and that the solitaire wasn't a crystal, but a white diamond of the finest clarity. Nor did she suspect that when they returned, the "vendor" would be packed up and long gone. Juan would be well on his way back to Dallas to size her one-of-a-kind wedding ring and Zach could check off one more item on his list of things to do before their weekend wedding.

Seven

"I still can't believe that vendor took off with your money and the ring," Arielle complained, shaking her head.

When they'd returned for the ring that afternoon, there had been an empty space in the open-air market where the man and his display of jewelry had once been. And even though several hours had passed since they'd returned to Dallas, changed clothes, had a wonderful dinner at an exclusive restaurant and were now on their way to the first resort Zach had built, she was still fuming.

Considering that Zach was a billionaire, it wasn't as important to him as to someone of lesser means.

And the truth was, the several hundred dollars the man had made off with wouldn't have made a dent in her bank account now—not after Emerald's trust fund to do with as she pleased.

But old habits died hard. From the time she'd graduated college, she'd made her own way on her pre-school teacher's salary and that meant sometimes living paycheck to paycheck. She'd learned to stretch a dollar as far as it would go and until a few months ago, the amount of money Zach had lost to the nefarious man would have represented a month's rent for her.

"Things like that happen," he observed, shrugging as if he wasn't bothered by the incident. "I'm more concerned that it caused you to lose your appetite for the ice cream cone I promised you."

When the driver stopped the car in front of the Forsythe Resort and Golf Course north of Dallas, she waited for Zach to exit the car, then help her out. "I was too angry to worry about eating ice cream," she responded as he closed the car door.

When they started toward the entrance, he stopped in front of the lobby's ornate double doors. Turning to face her, he placed his hands on her shoulders. "I don't want you giving any more thought to the ring, the money or the man who took off with both, darlin'. I didn't lose that much. And if it's the ring you're upset about, I'll buy you another one."

"No, it's not the ring or the amount of money," she said truthfully. "It's the principle."

He leaned down and briefly pressed his lips to hers. "Let's forget about it and go inside. I want to show you around and get your opinion on something."

When he took her hand and placed it in the crook of his arm, Arielle decided to do as he suggested and drop the matter. If he didn't care about being duped, then she probably shouldn't, either.

The doorman held open one of the doors, and Zach escorted her into the opulent lobby. Her breath caught at the beauty of the hotel. From the black marble counter of the reception desk, to the cream-colored Italian marble floor tiles and the expensive paintings decorating the walls, everything was coordinated perfectly. And, although lavish, the lobby still had a comfortable, welcoming feel to it.

"Zach, this is absolutely amazing," she gasped, taking it all in. "I can't believe this was your first resort."

He looked extremely pleased by her compliment. "I really can't take all of the credit. My sister had a big hand in the choice of colors and artwork."

"Well, you both did a wonderful job," Arielle commented, meaning it. "Does your sister help decorate all of your resorts?"

Nodding, he steered her down a wide corridor toward a set of decorative white French doors. "I come up with the theme, layout of the grounds and services we'll be offering at the resort, then Lana goes to work doing her thing with color choices and decorations." When they reached the doors, he stepped forward to open them and ushered her into a small indoor courtyard. "But this is where I need your opinion. What do you think of this room?"

As she took in the bubbling fountain in the center of the glass-enclosed area, the lush green plants and shrubs ringing the marble-tiled floor and impressive stone terrace, she didn't think she'd seen anything more beautiful. "This is breathtaking, Zach."

"Originally, it was my intention to make it a sitting area for guests of the resort." He took her elbow to steady her as they descended the terrace steps and walked over to the fountain. "But it's rare for someone to venture in here and I'm thinking about using it for other purposes."

"I think your golf course adjoining the resort property might have something to do with your guests' lack of interest." She smiled. "I would imagine many of them are bypassing this in favor of getting in a few rounds."

"You're probably right." He glanced around. "One of my employees recently suggested that it could be rented out for small parties and receptions. What do you think? Good idea or not?"

"I think it's an excellent idea," she agreed, nodding. "The white wrought-iron benches and patio tables could be arranged for whatever the occasion dictates." She turned to look back at the terrace with it's ornately carved granite railing. "I could easily see this being used for something like garden club meetings, as well as family anniversary parties and wedding receptions."

"You think so?" He frowned as if giving it serious thought. "I guess it could be used for someone wanting one of those family-and-extremely-close-friends-only affairs."

When he brushed back the sides of his black dinner jacket to stuff his hands in the front pockets of his pants as he looked around the room, he looked more than handsome. He hadn't bothered to put on a tie, instead preferring to wear his white shirt open at the collar. Some fashion magazines might call it the casually chic look, whereas she thought it was just plain sexy.

"I don't suppose it would hurt to give it a try," he acknowledged, walking over to take her into his arms. "Who knows? It just might turn out to be a hit."

"I'm sure it will become quite popular among the Dallas elite for all of their…intimate gatherings," she described, suddenly feeling quite breathless.

His wicked grin sent her blood pressure soaring as he raised her arms to encircle his neck. Wrapping his arms back around her, he pulled her against him. "I've always liked intimate, but it's not a word I've ever associated with more than two people."

"R-really?"

He nodded. "My definition of intimate is you…" His lips brushed hers. "And me…" He kissed her again. "Alone…" Using his index finger, he raised her chin until their gazes met. "Making love, Arielle."

The spark of need in the depths of his dark green eyes and the husky quality to his deep baritone sent desire through her. "Zach?"

His mouth came down on hers with urgency and she returned his kiss with just as much enthusiasm. His tongue mated with hers, demanding that she respond in kind. Meeting him stroke for stroke, the feel of his body against her caused a thrill of feminine power to skip along her nerves.

No matter how often she reminded herself that giving in to temptation again would be foolish, Arielle still wanted him with a ferocity that erased all logic.

When he suddenly lifted his head from hers and stepped back, she realized where they were and why he'd ended the kiss. They were standing in a public area of his resort and anyone could have walked in on them.

Before she gathered her wits, Zach took her hand in his and led her up the terrace to the French doors.

"W-where are we…going?" she finally asked as he hurried her across the lobby of the resort and out to the waiting limousine.

He helped her into the backseat, then gave her a smile that curled her toes inside her sensible one-inch black pumps. "Take us home, Mike," Zach directed to the driver, his gaze never wavering from hers. "To my place."

The short drive to his estate seemed longer than he could imagine and by the time the limousine drove through the gates and up the tree-lined drive, Zach felt as tense as the strings on a finely tuned violin. He'd fully expected Arielle to protest going to his house, but to his relief she hadn't uttered a word of opposition.

Of course, he hadn't given her much of a chance. Back at the resort, he'd recognized the same reflection of desire in her eyes that he was sure showed in his. He hadn't been able to get her out of there fast enough.

As soon as his chauffeur stopped the car in front of the mansion, Zach opened the door and helped her out. When they'd arrived at his resort, he'd noticed several people taking note of who got out of the limo, and that could very well prove to be a detriment. The last thing he wanted was to see a picture of them in the social column with speculation about their relationship. He had a feeling that wouldn't set well with her and could upset his well-laid plans.

Standing beside Arielle, he told his driver, "Take Ray Schaffer, my head of security, drive to the ranch first thing tomorrow morning and bring back my SUV. Then you'll need to meet Arielle's brothers and sister-in-law at the airport on Saturday. I'll be driving myself and Ms. Garnier wherever we need to go for a while."

The usually stoic driver nodded and flashed a rare smile. "Thank you, Mr. Forsythe."

Closing the car door, Zach put his arm around Arielle's waist and walked with her to his front door.

Neither said a word as he punched in the security code to turn off the alarm. By the time they entered the foyer, he wondered if she realized that she was spending the night at his place. Just the thought of having her in his bed had him harder than hell.

But when he turned to face her, his heart sank right along with his hopes of a passion-filled night. Instead of the glow of desire he'd seen on her lovely face earlier at the resort, she looked as if she was ready to drop. And as much as he would like to, he couldn't ignore their day of nonstop activity and that she'd missed her nap.

Wrapping his arms around her, he leaned to kiss her forehead. "I think it's past time we got you into bed, darlin'. You're real close to being asleep on your feet."

"I should have had your driver…take me back to my apartment," she murmured, yawning.

He shook his head, breaking his embrace to place his arm around her shoulders and walk her to the circular staircase. "That would have been a terrible idea. Your apartment is farther away and it would have taken that much longer for you to get to sleep."

"I suppose you're right," she conceded as they climbed the stairs. "I don't know why, but all of a sudden, I can hardly keep my eyes open."

When they entered the master suite, he switched on one of the lamps in the sitting area, then led her over to the bed. "You didn't get a nap this afternoon. The day just caught up with you."

She yawned again and shook her head as she stared at the bed. "I really shouldn't be here. I don't have a nightgown or even my toothbrush."

He chuckled as he reached to pull the comforter and silk top sheet back. "You don't need a nightgown to sleep, darlin'. And don't worry about the toothbrush. I have an extra one." When she looked as if she was going to protest again, he walked over to the dresser and pulled a pajama top from the drawer. "If it will make you feel better, you can wear this," he offered, handing her the silky shirt. Someone had given him the pajamas as a Christmas gift a couple years ago and he'd never worn them. He preferred to sleep without the encumbrance of clothes.

Taking the shirt from him, she entered the bathroom and returned a few minutes later dressed in her panties and his pajama top. She looked so darned sweet, it took everything he had in him not to sweep her up into his arms. But he shouldn't keep her up any longer and touching her would only send him into the bathroom for a cold shower.

After he tucked her into bed, he leaned down to give her a quick kiss. "Sleep well, Arielle."

"Aren't you…coming to bed now?" she asked, sounding increasingly drowsy.

"Nope." He stuffed his hands in his pockets to keep from reaching for her. "I'm going downstairs to the exercise room for a little workout." Turning, he started for the door. "I'll join you in a while."

As Zach walked to the stairs, he blew out a frustrated breath. It would take running several miles on the treadmill and bench-pressing many pounds before he got a wink of sleep.

But he couldn't complain. He'd accomplished another very important detail for their weekend wedding. During the tour of his resort, Arielle had unknowingly given her stamp of approval on their marriage site.

Arielle opened her eyes and looked around the unfamiliar room. It took a moment before she realized where she was. Zach had brought her to his mansion last night. Sometime during the short ride here, her body had reminded her that she'd skipped her nap and fatigue had demanded she get some sleep.

Turning her head, she gazed at the sleeping man stretched out on his stomach beside her. Zach had been so wonderful and understanding when he'd realized that she wasn't up to making love. If she hadn't already been in love with him, she would have fallen for him after last night.

Her heart skittered to a halt as realization sank in. She loved him. Had never *stopped* loving him.

Now she fully understood why her mother had been unable to resist her father the second time he'd shown up. Francesca Garnier had fallen head over heels in love with Owen Larson just as Arielle had fallen in love with Zach. And love defied logic.

"What's the matter, darlin'?" Zach asked, moving to drape his arm over her stomach.

"N-nothing," she lied. "It just took me a minute to realize where I am."

His lazy smile sent a keen longing through her. "You're exactly where you're supposed to be. Here with me."

"What time…did you come to bed?" she inquired, feeling more than a little breathless.

"Sometime after midnight," he replied, rising up to prop a forearm on either side of her. He leaned down to press his lips to hers, but instead of the quick kiss she expected, his mouth molded to hers and he gathered her to him.

Her eyes slowly drifted shut as his warm, firm lips glided over hers, setting off sparkles of light behind her closed lids. When he coaxed her to open for him, she did so on a soft sigh, and the feel of his tongue mating with hers caused the longing she'd felt the night before to come rushing back stronger and more powerful than anything she'd ever felt.

A tingling warmth began to flow through her veins when he slid his hand over her side from knee to waist, and she gripped the sheet with both hands as heat coursed through her body. As Zach caressed and teased her body with his hands and lips, desire began to build inside her. As long as she lived, she would never tire of him touching her.

When he parted her silk pajama top and his palm

skimmed over her stomach to the underside of her breast, Arielle ceased thinking and concentrated on the delicious way Zach was making her feel. She wanted him with a fierceness that stole her breath. She briefly wondered when he had unbuttoned the shirt as he cupped the weight of her, then teased her tightened nipple with the pad of his thumb. But the thought was fleeting when he broke the caress to nibble moist kisses from her collarbone down the slope of her breast to the hardened peak.

A tight coil of need formed deep inside her when he took her into his warm mouth and gently teased with his tongue. As he worried the hardened tip, his hand caressed her down to her hip, then her inner thigh. She quivered from the intense sensations.

"Does that feel good, Arielle?" he prompted. Raising his head, he looked at her as he pulled her panties down her legs, then tossed them to the floor. "I think we have some unfinished business from last night that we need to take care of, don't you?"

Unable to speak, she nodded. When he cupped the curls at her apex and his finger dipped inside to stroke the soft, moist folds, she moaned and arched into his touch.

"Zach, please—"

He entered her with his finger and the coil in her belly grew to the unfulfilled ache of need from his relentless touch. "What is it you want, darlin'?"

"Y-you. Now. Inside…me."

Without another word, his lips captured hers at the same time he abandoned the delicious torture. Using his knee to spread her legs, he moved to lever himself over her. She felt the tip of his strong arousal probe her and as he pushed himself forward, she thought she would die from the ecstasy of becoming one with the man she loved.

Placing his hands flat on either side of her, he held himself off her stomach, bringing his lower body into even closer contact with hers. Never had she felt more filled, more a part of him.

Slowly he pulled his body away from hers, then glided forward to gently thrust into her, his heated gaze never leaving hers. They moved together in a primal dance and each time they met and parted, the blazing need within her grew. All too soon, she felt her feminine muscles tighten around him as she came ever closer to completion.

Zach must have sensed her readiness because he thrust into her a bit faster, a little deeper and suddenly she felt herself spinning out of control, cast into a sweet vortex with no beginning or end. Heat and light flashed behind her tightly closed eyes as wave after wave of sheer pleasure surged through her. Grasping his forearms, she clung to him.

Just as the storm within her began to subside, she felt his body go perfectly still a moment before he threw his head back and groaned. His muscular arms shook from the effort of holding himself off her and his whole body shuddered as the force of his release gripped him.

He moved to her side and collapsed on the bed. His breathing was harsh, but as he gathered her to him, he managed to ask, "Are you all right?"

Snuggling into his strong embrace, she nodded. "I feel wonderful. Thank you."

He leaned back to look at her. "Why are you thanking me? I should be the one thanking you."

She cupped his cheek and pressed a kiss to his firm lips. "Even though I'm pregnant and starting to feel a little awkward, you make me feel sexy."

"That's because you are, darlin'." His smile caused her heart to swell with so much love, she thought it might burst. "All I have to do is look at you and I'm turned on."

Feeling more relaxed and complete than she had in a long time, she couldn't keep her eyes open. "I think…I'll rest a minute or two…before I get up."

"It's still early. Why don't you get a little more sleep?"

When she remained silent, Zach grinned as he pulled the covers over them. He'd been right. Arielle could fall asleep with no effort at all.

As he lay there holding her, he decided that he couldn't afford the luxury of going back to sleep. He had too many plans to make. He had three days left before her brothers and sister-in-law flew into town. He wanted to have Arielle completely convinced that marrying him was best for both of them and have her totally committed to taking a trip down the aisle when her family arrived.

Glancing at the bedside clock, he softly kissed her cheek, then eased his arm from beneath her and got out of bed. He needed a quick shower, a cup of strong, black coffee and a couple of phone calls to some old friends to get the ball rolling. And the very first thing on his To Do list for the day would be to call Juan Gomez to see when he could pick up Arielle's ring.

He whistled a tune as he grabbed some clothes from the walk-in closet, then headed into the master bath and turned on the water in the shower. Everything was coming together nicely and Arielle would be Mrs. Zach Forsythe by the end of the week. Just as he'd promised her she would.

Eight

Arielle found Zach in the master suite's sitting room, reading a newspaper at the small table. Dressed in jeans and a forest-green polo shirt, he looked devastatingly handsome.

"Why didn't you wake me?" she asked.

Looking up, he smiled. "I thought I'd let you sleep in." Folding the paper, he set it aside and, rising to his feet, walked around the table to hold the chair for her. "Do you have any idea how cute you look in my bathrobe?"

A delightful little shiver raced through her at the feel of his warm kisses on the back of her neck. "I—I couldn't find anything else to wear."

He chuckled as he walked back around the table to sit opposite her. "I think it's the first time it's ever been worn."

"You're joking," she said, glancing down at the black silk garment.

"Nope." He shrugged. "What's the use of wearing a robe from the bathroom to the closet? I can wrap a towel around my waist just as easy."

"What happens if you have guests?"

The look he gave her set her pulse racing. "Darlin', the only other person in my bedroom besides me is you and I was under the impression you liked my lack of inhibitions."

Before she could tell him how incorrigible he was, he picked up a wireless device and pressed a button on its side. "You can bring breakfast to us now, Maria."

"*Si,* Senor Zach. I'll bring it right up," a female voice answered.

"Zach, we could have gone downstairs for breakfast," Arielle suggested as he returned the small device to the table.

"Nope." He reached across the table to cover her hand with his. "You need to eat as soon as you get out of bed to avoid getting sick."

"But I'm not used to having people wait on me," she protested.

He nodded. "I understand, darlin'. I like doing things for myself most of the time, too. But I told you that I intend to pamper you and having breakfast brought to you as soon as you wake up is part of that." He grinned. "Besides, you need to conserve your strength."

"Why?"

"Because I have something planned that I think you'll enjoy as much as our trip to San Antonio," he disclosed, rising at the sound of a knock on the door.

When he opened the door, a kind-looking, middle-aged woman with beautiful brown eyes entered carrying a tray to the table. After Zach made the introductions, she smiled. "It's nice to meet you. If there is anything special you would like for breakfast tomorrow, please let me know."

"Thank you, Maria," Arielle replied, instantly liking her. "But I doubt that I—"

"I'll let you know if there is, Maria," Zach interrupted.

The cook nodded. "Enjoy your breakfast."

When the door closed behind the woman, Arielle frowned. "Why would she think that I'll be here tomorrow morning?"

"Probably because I told her you would be here quite a bit from now on," he confessed, lifting the silver covers from their plates. "And before you get upset, I didn't say you would definitely be here. Now, eat. We have another big day ahead of us."

She would have questioned him further, but the food's delicious aroma was far too tempting and she picked up her fork to cut into the omelet. "Oh, Zach," she murmured, closing her eyes as she savored the first bite. "This is wonderful."

"I swear Maria has some kind of magic touch," he agreed, nodding.

They ate in silence and Arielle felt completely full by the time she finished her last crumb of toast. "I don't dare eat here very often," she commented, placing her silverware on the edge of her empty plate. "I'd gain so much weight I'd waddle like a duck."

"You're supposed to gain weight. You're pregnant with twins." His tight tone and the slight frown creasing his forehead surprised her.

"I'm well aware of that and I expect to gain quite a few pounds, especially since I'm eating for three." She scooted her chair back and stood up. "All I meant was that Maria's food is so good, I could easily gain more weight than what the doctor recommends." She started toward the bathroom, hoping she had explained away Zach's concern. "Now, while I get dressed, why don't you carry the tray downstairs, then take me home."

"Why?"

Turning, she searched his face. Why did he suddenly seem on edge?

"You told me that you had made plans for us. Don't you think it would be a good idea if I had something appropriate to wear?"

"Oh, right." He looked a little more at ease as he picked up the tray with their empty plates. "Go ahead and get dressed. I'll be back in a few minutes."

"All right. I'll be ready."

As he watched her walk toward the bathroom, Zach chastised himself for jumping to conclusions. But when Arielle had mentioned gaining too much weight, a flashback of his ex-fiancée and her intention to starve herself into a miscarriage came rushing back.

Descending the stairs, he shook his head at his unfounded suspicions. Arielle was completely different from Gretchen and it was past time he stopped comparing the two women. Arielle was looking forward to the birth of their twins and had expressed nothing but happiness and excitement about the babies.

He took a deep breath as he walked toward the kitchen. He'd feel a lot better about the entire situation once they were married. He'd be in a better position to keep his vow of being there for her and their babies. And if everything worked as he'd planned, he should have that assurance by the end of the day.

After stopping by her apartment where she changed into a sundress and a sensible pair of shoes, Arielle sat in the passenger seat of Zach's SUV, wondering where he was taking her this time. Truthfully, she really didn't care where they went. She was enjoying the few days he'd asked her to spend with him and looked forward to whatever he had planned.

She knew it was absolute insanity to be getting in way over her head so quickly. But where Zach was concerned, she didn't have a choice in the matter. She loved him, had never stopped loving him and understood why her mother hadn't been able to resist her father. And just like her mother, there was a chance she would end up getting hurt again.

But as Zach steered the truck into a parking lot, she abandoned all speculation when she realized he was taking her to the Dallas Arboretum. "I love gardens. How did you know?"

His deep chuckle caused her insides to quiver. "Darlin', I wish I could tell you that I had some kind of insight into that. But I didn't. I just figured most women like flowers and it was a safe bet you would, too."

"Good call," she responded, smiling.

When he got out of the SUV and came to help her from the passenger side, he grabbed a medium-size insulated backpack from the backseat that she hadn't noticed before. "What's that?"

"There's a really nice picnic spot in the Pecan Grove area of the arboretum and I had Maria prepare lunch for us." He slung the carrier over one shoulder, then, taking her hand in his, started through the main entrance.

"What a nice idea," she remarked. "I haven't been on a picnic in years. At least not one without several dozen preschoolers to keep track of."

"Score one more for Zach," he declared, grinning.

"Oh, so now you're trying to make points with me?" she teased, laughing.

He leaned down to give her a quick kiss. "Darlin', I've been trying ever since walking into your office last Friday morning to plead Derek's case."

She could have told him that he was succeeding, but as they walked along the tree-lined paths, Arielle's attention was claimed by the acres of perfectly kept lawns and immaculate beds of brightly colored flowers. Shades of bright pink, purple and red were everywhere and mingled with lush green shrubbery and various nonflowering plants, the gardens were absolutely breathtaking. Enjoying the fresh spring air and gorgeous scenery with Zach was wonderful and before she knew it, they were walking toward a beautiful picnic area among a grove of pecan trees.

"A dollar for your thoughts," Zach offered as he placed the backpack on a shaded picnic table and began unzipping the front flap.

"A dollar?" Seating herself on one side of the table, she smiled. "I thought that used to be a penny."

"Inflation has set in, darlin'," he explained, laughing as he removed a navy and tan checkered cloth from the side of the pack. "I think Maria said we have turkey and Swiss on wheat bread, some kind of cold, chopped vegetable medley and sparkling grape juice. I hope that's okay."

"I'm starved and it all sounds yummy," she stated, helping him spread out the small tablecloth. "But these days, I'm always hungry."

"Very true," he agreed, handing her two plates, two sets of cutlery and two wineglasses. "But very understandable considering you're having twins."

"My mother mentioned one time that she ate so much when she was pregnant with Jake and Luke that she gained fifty pounds." She arranged the plates and cutlery, then waited for Zach to pour the grape juice into the goblets. "It's odd how I can remember something like that, but not the sound of her voice."

"Didn't you tell me you were ten when she was killed in a car accident?" he reminded, his voice gentle. "That was a long time ago and you were only a child, darlin'. Time has a way of making things like that fade away."

"I suppose you're right."

Staring at the empty plate in front of her, she thought about their time in Aspen and the details she'd shared about her life. But Zach hadn't revealed anything about himself when they'd first met, and beyond his name, his career and the fact that he had a sister and nephew, she knew nothing about him now.

"What about your parents?" she asked, looking up to find him watching her. "Are they still living?"

He shook his head as he placed wrapped sandwiches on the plates, then opened the container of vegetables. "My mom died when I was six. There were complications from having Lana that she just couldn't overcome."

"Oh, Zach, I'm so sorry."

"It's been almost thirty years and about the only things I remember clearly about her is that she loved baking cookies and reading stories to get me to sleep at night." He sat down at the table across from her. "After she was gone, my dad hired Mattie to take care of me and Lana while he worked the ranch. Then he passed away from a heart attack when I was in my junior year at college."

Her heart went out to him and she reached across the table to place her hand on his. "I know that had to have been devastating for you and your sister."

"Lana was only an infant when Mom died, so she doesn't have any memories of her. But we were both close to Dad and it was pretty rough for a while," he admitted, staring off into the distance. When he turned his attention back to her, he asked, "What about your dad? Is he still alive? I don't remember you mentioning anything about him."

Spooning some of the crisp vegetables onto her plate, she shook her head. "There's really nothing to tell. I never got to meet him and never will." When Zach raised a questioning eyebrow, she added, "My brothers and I recently found out that he was killed in a boating accident a couple years ago."

Zach looked surprised. "I'm sorry to hear that, Arielle."

"Don't be." She took a sip of her grape juice. "You don't miss what you've never had."

When their gazes locked, she nibbled on her lower

lip as she decided how much to tell him. Not knowing anything about her father and having never met the man, she'd glossed over his nonexistent role in her life when they'd been in Aspen.

But maybe it was time to tell Zach what she'd recently learned about the man. Maybe then he'd understand why she'd been so hurt by his actions in Aspen. And why she'd been afraid that the same thing that happened to her mother had happened to her—that although the man she loved was fond of her, he couldn't love her.

She sighed as she continued to stare at him. They had to start somewhere or they'd never build the trust between them needed to raise their twins together.

"The relationship between my mother and father was anything but conventional." She took a deep breath. "They were together twice, ten years apart and only for a few months each time. But both affairs resulted in unplanned pregnancies."

He remained silent, mulling over what she'd said. "It's a shame that things couldn't have worked out between them." He took a bite of his sandwich, then after chewing thoughtfully, asked, "Your mother never found anyone else?"

Arielle shook her head. "Whether he was worth it or not, my father was her one true love and she wouldn't settle for anything less." She poked at her vegetables with her fork. "But the story doesn't end there."

He raised his brows. "There's more?"

This was the part she had trouble believing herself. "A couple of months ago, my brothers and I were contacted by a representative for our paternal grandmother. That's when we learned our father's real identity."

As she watched, Zach slowly lowered his sandwich to his plate. "He lied about who he was?"

She could tell by his expression that the uncanny parallel to their own situation wasn't lost on him. "Our father used an assumed name and Mama never knew that the man she fell in love with wasn't who he said he was. Nor did she ever learn that during the ten years between their affairs, he fathered three more sons by three different women. None of whom he bothered to marry."

"Did he know about his offspring?"

"Every one of them," she confirmed, nodding.

The frown on his handsome face left no doubt that Zach didn't approve of what her father had done. Not in the least. "Did he offer to help these women raise his children?"

"No."

"What the hell was he thinking?" Zach shook his head disgustedly. "How can a man just walk away from his kids and never be there for them or at the very least, see that their basic needs are met?"

"I don't know." She took a bite of her vegetables. "Apparently, being an irresponsible liar who preyed on women unfortunate enough to fall in love with him was one of my father's biggest character flaws."

Rising from his seat, Zach came around the table to her side, then, straddling the bench, took her into his arms. "I give you my word that I'll always be there for you and our children."

"You're going to be a great dad," she observed.

He nodded. "Or die trying." His warm smile caused her to tingle all over. "And I know you're going to be the best mom any kid could ever have."

"I'm going to do my best," she vowed, returning his smile.

A sudden gust of wind threatened to sweep their lunch off the table and, looking up, Arielle realized it was going to start raining soon. "I'm pretty sure we're about to get wet."

"We'd better pack up the picnic and head back to the truck," he responded, getting to his feet.

"Good idea." She hurried to help him gather up everything and put it back into the insulated back-pack. "I may start waddling like a duck soon, but I just don't seem to have the same fondness for getting wet."

Laughing, Zach caught her hand in his and hurried her toward the parking lot. "Besides not wanting you to get wet, we need to get back to the house, anyway."

"Why?"

"I have a couple of things I need to take care of for this evening and you need a nap."

When he helped her into the passenger seat, his grin sent shivers of anticipation through her and she knew he was up to something. She waited until he rounded the front of the SUV, then slid into the driver's seat before asking, "What do you have up your sleeve this time?"

There was enough wattage in his wide smile to light the entire city of Dallas. "You'll have to wait and see. But trust me, darlin'. You're going to love it."

"Oh, Zach, I absolutely love this," Arielle said as she closed her eyes and savored the last cold bite of mint chocolate chip ice cream.

Seated across from her in the restaurant at his Dallas resort, she could hear the smile in his voice. "I thought you might. That's why I had it flown up here from the ice cream shop on the River Walk in San Antonio."

Opening her eyes, she sputtered. "I can't believe you did that. I wouldn't have known the difference if you'd had the kitchen staff open a carton from the local grocery store."

"But *I* would. Besides, I promised I'd get that ice cream for you." The tender look in his dark green gaze stole her breath as he reached across the table and covered her hand with his. "And unless there's a damned good reason, I always keep my promises, darlin'."

"Always?" she asked, knowing he was referring to something far more important than ice cream.

Nodding, he continued to hold her hand as he rose to his feet. "Come with me, Arielle."

"Where are we going?" she asked as they walked out of the restaurant and into the hotel lobby.

"Somewhere a little more private," he explained, whispering close to her ear. When they reached the doors of the indoor courtyard, he smiled. "Close your eyes."

"You're certainly being mysterious about this."

He leaned down to brush his lips over hers. "Just another little surprise. Now, close your eyes."

When she did as he requested, he opened the French doors to the courtyard and guided her inside. Even with her eyes closed, she could tell they were standing in complete darkness. "Zach?"

She heard what might be the sound of a switch being flipped on. "You can look now, darlin'."

Opening her eyes, Arielle's breath caught at the sight of tiny white lights tastefully threaded throughout the foliage surrounding the room. Even the fountain had been adorned with special lighting that made the bubbling water appear to be a cascade of sparkling diamonds.

"Zach, it's beautiful," she declared, walking to the edge of the terrace. "How did you get this done so quickly?"

"Darlin', you can accomplish just about anything if you're willing to pay the price."

He took hold of her elbow and they descended the stone steps. He escorted her to one of the patio tables covered with a pristine linen cloth. "I thought you might like to see what this will look like for those intimate gatherings we talked about last night."

"It's perfect," she mused, sitting down in the seat he held for her. "It looks like something Cinderella might have seen when she arrived for Prince Charming's ball."

"I'm glad you like it," he noted, lowering himself into the chair next to her.

As she took in the elegance of the little courtyard, intuition told her they were there for more than her approval on the room's transformation. Turning to face him, she caught him watching her closely.

"Zach, what's going on?"

His smile sent a warm rush flowing through her veins. "Do you love me, Arielle?"

"Zach, I thought we agreed—"

"Just answer the question, darlin'."

Her heart skipped several beats and time stilled as she stared back at him. She could tell him no, but they both knew it would be a lie.

"Yes," she finally answered, surprised at how steady her voice sounded, considering her body had started to quiver uncontrollably.

His smile caused her heart to pound hard against her ribs. He removed a small black velvet box from his suit jacket. Placing it on the table, he removed the ring she'd thought the vendor in the marketplace had stolen. "Arielle Garnier, will you do me the honor of becoming my wife?" he asked, taking her left hand in his.

"You agreed not to insist on our getting married," she stalled.

He shook his head. "I'm not insisting that we get married, darlin'. I'm asking you to marry me."

Everything within her wanted to tell him yes, that she would love nothing more than to be his wife and build a wonderful life with him and their children. But although Zach had asked her if she loved him, he hadn't admitted how he felt about her.

"Do you love me?" she asked, finally getting her vocal cords to work.

His gaze held hers for what seemed like forever before he replied. "You have to know that I care deeply for you, Arielle."

Her heart felt as if it dropped to her feet. "That's not what I asked you, Zach. I want to know if you love me."

"We're good together," he responded, placing the ring on the table. He cupped her face with his hands. "We can have a good life."

"Really?" Tears filled her eyes as an ache like she'd never known filled her heart. But she blinked the moisture away. "You think so?"

"I know so, darlin'." He gave her an encouraging smile. "I like doing things for you and getting things I know you'll like."

"I-Is that what you think...I want?" she prodded, her chest tightening with so much emotional pain, she wasn't sure she could draw her next breath. "Material things?"

His expression became guarded. "I promise you'll never want for anything, Arielle."

"Y-You're wrong, Zach." She shook her head. "There's only one thing I want from you. And you can't or won't give that to me."

"What's that?" he asked. They both knew what she wanted and they both knew she wasn't going to get it from him.

"All that I've ever wanted," she professed, standing up. "Your love."

Rising to his feet, he stammered, "You have to understand that—"

"P-Please...don't," she begged, backing away from him. She couldn't bear to hear him tell her that he could never love her.

"Everything will work out, Arielle. And I give you my word that I'll never do anything that would hurt you or isn't in your and our twins' best interest."

"It's too late for that, Zach," she concluded as her heart shattered into a million pieces. "You just did."

Nine

"What's going on, Zach?" Lana asked Friday morning as she slowly walked into his den. "And don't tell me nothing because I know better."

"Hey, sis." Seated in one of the chairs in front of the fireplace, Zach motioned for her to join him. "You look like physical therapy is working wonders. You're walking a lot better than you were last week."

"Don't do that," she insisted, shaking her head as she eased down in the chair beside him. "You're not going to distract me after I skipped therapy to drive over here. I want to know why you haven't been in the office all week and why you look like you've lost your last friend." She frowned. "How long has it been since you shaved?"

"A couple of days." He reached up to scratch the growth of stubble covering his cheeks as he stared at the empty coffee cup in his hand. "I just felt like taking a few days off from everything, that's all."

Lana gave an unladylike snort. "I wasn't born yesterday, so don't feed me that line of hooey. You haven't missed a day shaving since you scraped three or four hairs off your chin when you were thirteen. And you never take time off unless you're visiting one of the resorts, which we both know are working vacations. So what's wrong?"

He'd known he wouldn't be able to avoid telling his sister the truth. Even before their father had died, he and Lana had been close. She knew him better than anyone else and was just as protective of him as he was of her. There was no way she was going to leave without answers.

"In about five and a half months, I'm going to be the father of twins," he said without preamble.

His sister's silence proved his news was not expected. "Are you serious?" she finally asked, her voice reflecting her stunned shock.

He nodded. "You know I wouldn't joke about something like that."

"Dear God, Zach, I know I was out of the loop there for a while, but how did I miss this?" Lana gave him a pointed look. "I lived here with you for several months after my release from the hospital and you weren't seeing anyone."

Explaining the events in Aspen and his recent reunion with Arielle, Zach finished by telling her what happened when he proposed. "After I took her to her apartment, I came here. End of story."

"Not by a long shot, brother." Lana slowly shook her head back and forth. "I don't blame her for telling you to hit the bricks. I would have, too. If you want her back, you have some serious groveling to do."

"I don't grovel," he retorted, suddenly irritated with his sister. They usually agreed on just about everything and it irked him no end that she wasn't taking his side.

"Well, I'd say if you want a future with this woman and your twins, you'd better start." Lana placed her hand on his arm and her voice took on a gentle quality. "I know what happened five years ago has a lot to do with the way you handled this, Zach. But Arielle isn't Gretchen. From everything you've told me, she loves you and is thrilled to be having these babies. And unlike Gretchen, she obviously adores children or she wouldn't have made pre-schoolers her career."

"I'm well aware of that."

"Then stop holding Arielle accountable for something she hasn't done and wouldn't think of doing."

He shook his head. "I'm not."

"Aren't you?" Lana gave him a meaningful look.

"I know you blame yourself for not seeing what Gretchen was doing, but that's in the past and you need to let it go. And if you'll admit it, your pride took the biggest hit back then."

"How do you figure that?" he demanded, more irritated with each passing second.

"You thought Gretchen loved you and wanted the same things you did. But that wasn't the case and you can't accept that you were wrong about her." Lana sighed. "Don't you see, Zach? It's just a matter of semantics. You say you care deeply for Arielle, but you can't bring yourself to use the word *love* because you might be wrong about her, too. And that scares you to death."

His sister's insight was hitting a little closer to home than he was comfortable with. But he wasn't about to concede. "You don't know what the hell you're talking about, Lana."

"Don't I?" Her tone and knowing expression were filled with confidence as she used her cane to stand up. Then, leaning down, she kissed his cheek. "Don't let your stubborn pride get in the way of the happiness you could have with Arielle. Admit to yourself how you feel about her and take another chance, Zach. From everything you've told me about her, Arielle is more than worth the risk."

It took several minutes after Lana closed the door behind her for Zach to think rationally. At first, his sister's observations had him so angry he could have bit nails in two. But the more he thought about what she had said, the more he wondered if she might be right.

Had he been holding Arielle accountable for the sins of another woman? Was he reluctant to take another chance on love simply because he wanted to protect his ego?

As he sat there contemplating the possibilities, he couldn't stop thinking about the way the crushed look on Arielle's beautiful face and the tears filling her eyes had made him feel. Just knowing that he'd caused her so much emotional pain created a tightness in his chest that threatened to suffocate him. And every minute of every day he was away from her, those feelings intensified.

He took a deep breath, then another. The way he saw it, he had two choices. He could play it safe, continue to deny how he felt about her and be the most miserable bastard west of the Mississippi. Or he could swallow his selfish pride, tell her how much he loved her and risk finding the happiness and completion that he knew in his heart only she could bring him.

With everything suddenly crystal clear, Zach stood, walked out of the study and climbed the stairs. He needed a shower, a shave and a pair of pants with reinforced knees. If he had to, he'd spend the rest of his life on his knees, begging Arielle's forgiveness for being such a fool and asking her to give him one more chance to make things right between them.

* * *

Arielle sat down on the couch, trying to gather the courage to call her brothers and tell them not to come to Dallas for the weekend. She wasn't looking forward to telling Jake and Luke not to visit, even though she would love to see them and could really use their emotional support. But the last thing she needed was to have two brothers in full "overly protective big brother" mode telling her what they thought she should do, while she was trying to deal with a badly broken heart.

Fortunately for her, she'd already handled the situation, broken off all contact with Zach, at least for the past few days, and was deciding to merge the preschool back into the Emerald, Inc. umbrella of companies and move to San Francisco.

When the doorbell began ringing insistently, her heart skipped several beats. She only knew one person in Dallas besides her coworkers at the preschool, who at this time of day were all at work.

As she walked the few feet to the door, she considered telling him, through the door, to please leave her alone to get on with her life. But knowing Zach, he wouldn't listen.

"Arielle, we need to talk," he declared as soon as she opened the door.

She shook her head as much to deny his request as an attempt to stem the fresh wave of tears that seeing him caused. "I think we've said all there is to say, Zach."

"No, we haven't." Before she could stop him, he placed his hands on her shoulders, backed her away from the door and into the foyer, then kicked it shut behind them. "First off, are you all right?"

No, she wasn't all right and might never be again. But she wasn't going to let him know that.

"I'm doing okay," she said cautiously.

"Good."

When he continued to stand there staring at her, she took a step away from his disturbing touch. "Why are you here, Zach? What do you want from me?"

"I told you, darlin'." He stuffed his hands in the front pockets of his jeans and rocked back on his heels. "We have some things to discuss."

"No, we don't." She pointed toward the door. "Now, please, just go."

"Not until you hear me out. Then, if you still want me to leave, I will."

Knowing how futile it was to argue with him, she motioned toward the couch. "Would you like to sit down for this?"

"That might not be a bad idea," he agreed, nodding. "This could take a while."

Arielle sighed as she walked over and lowered herself onto the couch. "Let's get this over with."

He gave her a short nod, then to her surprise, sat down on the coffee table directly in front of her. She immediately leaned back against the cushions to put a bit of distance between them. If she didn't, she wasn't entirely sure she wouldn't throw her arms around him and hang on for dear life.

"About five years ago, I was an arrogant jerk who thought he had it all," he began, propping his forearms on his knees and staring down at his loosely clasped hands.

"And how is that different from the way you are now?" she asked before she could stop herself.

Glancing up, he gave her a self-deprecating smile. "I guess I deserve that, don't I?"

His concession surprised her, but it wasn't in her nature to be cruel. "I'm sorry. I shouldn't have said that."

"You had every right to say it and a lot more."

Why did he have to look so darned good to her? And why couldn't he sit somewhere else? Didn't he realize how hard it was for her to love him the way she did, knowing that nothing was ever going to come of it?

"As I was saying, five years ago I thought I was on top of the world and completely invincible. I was barely thirty years old and had just made my first billion, was engaged to a woman I thought loved me and had a baby on the way."

In all of her wildest imaginings, she'd have never dreamed that what he thought he had to tell her included a fiancée and a baby.

"Why are you telling me this, Zach?" She didn't want to hear that he'd been able to love one woman, but couldn't love her.

"Because I want you to understand why I've had a hard time letting myself love again," he said, his dark green gaze unwavering when it met hers. "Why I've been such a coward."

His frank assessment of himself shocked her. But before she could comment, he rose to his feet and began pacing the room.

"We hadn't been engaged long when we found out about the pregnancy," he continued, his tone reflective. "And I thought everything was going great. I was thrilled about the baby and she assured me that she was, too."

"I take it that wasn't the case?" Arielle guessed.

Zach's harsh laughter caused her to cringe. "Not even close. As soon as she heard the word *pregnant,* she started doing everything she could think of to lose the baby."

She sensed what he was about to tell her next and instinctively placed a protective hand over her stomach.

"After a few weeks of starving herself and refusing to get the rest she needed, she was successful."

"I'm so sorry, Zach," Arielle sympathized. As excited as he'd been about their babies, he must have been devastated by the woman's intentional miscarriage.

Nodding, he reached up to run his hand through his thick dark brown hair. "I'd been busy opening the Aspen resort and wasn't paying enough attention to realize what was going on." He shook his head.

"Maybe if I had, I could have convinced her to have the baby for me to raise."

It suddenly became clear why he'd been so determined to see that she ate right and when she mentioned anything about gaining weight, he'd become irritable. It also explained why he made sure she took a nap every day. He didn't trust her when she told him how excited she was about having a child and was making sure nothing happened to jeopardize the pregnancy.

"I'm not her, Zach."

"I know, darlin'. And I'm sorry for holding you accountable. I'm the one at fault for not seeing it sooner." He shook his head. "The same as I am for not recognizing what she was doing."

"You can't blame yourself for what happened, Zach. It sounds to me that no matter how attentive you were, your fiancée would have found a way to end the pregnancy."

"You're probably right," he agreed. "But at the time, all I could see were my dreams of having a family fall apart."

With sudden insight, she realized that just like her, his lack of a conventional family while growing up was what made having one of his own so important to him. "I'm sure that was extremely hard for you."

"I survived." He gave her a hesitant look. "But not without losing a good chunk of my pride."

"I'm afraid I don't understand," she commented, wondering what his pride had to do with it.

He walked back over to sit down in front of her on the edge of the coffee table. "I've always had this thing about being right. And when I think I am, come hell or high water, I won't back down."

"Mattie mentioned that when you're convinced of something, you can be extremely stubborn," Arielle relayed, recalling how insistent he'd been about her having the flu.

"That's right, darlin'. And when I discovered I'd been wrong about my fiancée, it sent me into a tailspin." She watched his chest rise and fall as he drew in a deep breath. "It was hard for me to admit that I'd been wrong about her and her feelings for me. But it was that much harder when I realized I was wrong about the way I felt for her."

"No one likes having to accept they've made a mistake and especially about something like that, Zach." She knew firsthand how difficult it had been for her to concede that she'd been wrong about him never being able to love her.

He nodded. "But then I made an even bigger mistake when I made the conscious choice not to put myself in that position again and risk taking another hit to my pride."

"In other words, you decided not to love anyone or trust that they would love you," she recapped, realizing as never before that the situation between them had been hopeless from the beginning.

"But I was wrong." He stared down at his hands a moment before he lifted his gaze to hers. "Only I didn't realize it until you came along."

Her heart squeezed painfully and she had to force herself to breathe. She couldn't bear to hear him make a false confession of love, simply to get her to marry him.

"Please don't, Zach."

"What? Don't tell you that I fell in love with you the minute I saw you out on that ski slope?" He took her hands in his as he shook his head. "I can't do that, darlin'."

Tears filled her eyes and she forced herself to pull away from his touch. She wouldn't, couldn't, allow herself to believe him. If she did and it turned out that he was lying, she'd never survive.

"I think…you'd better…go."

When he moved to sit beside her on the couch and took her into his arms, her body began to tremble uncontrollably. "I can't do this…Zach."

"I know you don't believe me and you think I'm just telling you what you want to hear," he observed gently. "But I swear with everything that's in me that I do love you, Arielle. And I'm sorry for all the heartache I've caused both of us."

"I wish…I could believe—"

Suddenly turning her to face him, he cupped her

cheeks and forced her to look at him. "Darlin', don't you think that if I was going to lie to you about how I feel, I'd have told you what I knew you wanted to hear the other night at the resort?"

What he said was true. He could have easily told her he loved her then. But he hadn't. He'd been painfully honest about his feelings for her.

"But why…now?" she mumbled, sniffing back a fresh wave of tears. "What caused you…to change your mind?"

He smiled tenderly. "I didn't change my mind. I just came to the realization that all the pride in the world isn't worth having without your love. Without you, darlin', my life means less than nothing."

The sincerity in his eyes convinced her that he meant every word he said. "Oh, Zach, I love you so much, but—"

"I know you're afraid, Arielle." He brushed his lips over hers. "But if you'll give me a second chance, I'll spend every day for the rest of my life making sure you never doubt how much I love you."

"Third."

"What?" he asked, frowning.

"You asked for a second chance. But you've already had that. This will be your third chance." She gave him a watery smile. "And I think it's only fair to warn you that it's your last. You'd better get it right this time, Mr. Forsythe, because there won't be another."

He crushed her to him then and gave her a kiss that left both of them gasping for breath. "I love you, Arielle Garnier. Will you marry me?"

She laughed. "You don't waste time do you?"

"There's been enough time wasted already," he confirmed, smiling. "But you didn't answer my question, darlin'."

Knowing she had no other choice in the matter, she nodded. "I haven't been able to resist you from the moment we met and that hasn't changed. Yes, Zach, I'll marry you."

The tears she'd been holding back spilled down her cheeks. She watched as he reached into the front pocket of his jeans and pulled out a black velvet box. He opened it, took her left hand in his, then slipped the ring on her third finger.

"How about tomorrow?"

"What about it?" she asked, loving the feel of his ring on her finger.

He chuckled. "If you'll remember I told you that I'd like to get married on the weekend."

"But I can't possibly get everything arranged in such a short amount of time," she explained, wishing with all of her heart that she could.

"Actually, there's not much to be arranged," he countered, giving her a sheepish grin.

"What have you done?" she inquired, loving him more with each passing second.

"You mean besides getting Juan Gomez to meet

us in San Antonio to have your ring sized, decorating the courtyard and fountain, arranging for the resort to cater the reception and asking my old friend Judge Morrison to sign a waiver allowing us to get married without the required waiting period and to perform the ceremony?" He chuckled. "Other than that, I haven't done a thing, darlin'."

She marveled at how thorough he'd been. "When you showed me the courtyard, you were actually getting my approval for our wedding."

"Yes. I was in denial at the time, but I realize now that everything I did, every plan I made, was because I love you and wanted to make that day as special for you as I could."

"I love you so much, Zach. And I really appreciate everything you've done, but you weren't supposed to press the issue of marriage," she reminded, putting her arms around his neck.

"I love you, too. But technically, I didn't press you about getting married," he argued, kissing the tip of her nose. "I promised I wouldn't talk to you about it. But I never promised I wouldn't *do* something about it."

As they sat on the couch holding each other, Arielle nibbled at her lower lip. If they were going to be husband and wife, there shouldn't be any secrets between them. And she still had a big, rather bizarre secret she hadn't shared with him yet.

"Zach, do you believe in fairy tales?"

"If you mean the happily-ever-after kind, I didn't until today," he confessed, resting his cheek against her head.

She smiled. "Let me tell you about my fairy god-mother."

Epilogue

The following evening, Zach stood by the fountain in the courtyard of his first resort with Arielle's brothers—all five of them—and marveled at how much they looked alike. Except for the twins, Jake and Luke, the other three all had different mothers. But there was no doubt they were related. All five men were well over six feet tall, had muscular athletic builds and bore a strong facial resemblance. Each accepted Zach into the family, in his own way.

"You do know that our little sister is always going to be right and you're always going to be wrong, don't you?" Luke asked, grinning.

Zach grinned right back. "Yep."

"And all she'll have to do is say the word and one of us will show up to kick your sorry ass," Jake proclaimed, laughing.

Nodding, Zach's grin widened. "I wouldn't expect anything less."

Caleb Walker spoke up. "I think he's going to work out just fine for our little sister, boys."

"Looks like it," Nick Daniels agreed.

"Welcome to the family, Forsythe," Hunter O'Banyon added.

When Arielle told Zach about the discovery of her three half brothers, he hadn't realized they'd all formed a bond in such a short time. But considering the mutually unique relationship they shared with Emerald Larson, they did have quite a bit in common.

His gaze drifted over to the white-haired woman sitting at one of the tables with her personal assistant, Luther Freemont. It was no wonder Arielle thought of the old gal as a real-life fairy godmother. She'd not only made Arielle's dream come true of owning her own preschool, but Emerald had brought them together again. And that alone was enough to convince Zach that she could work magic.

Checking his watch, he glanced at the French doors. Where were Arielle, her brothers' wives and Lana? As soon as the women had first congregated at his estate, they'd whisked Arielle off to find a dress to wear for the ceremony and he hadn't seen her since.

"Getting a little antsy there, Zach?" Jake noted as the other men discussed the homes Luke's construction company was building for them. "There's still time to run like hell."

"Nope. I've waited all my life to find your sister. I'm not about to lose her now," Zach declared solemnly.

"Oh man, you've got it bad," Jake observed, shaking his head. "And I thought Luke was lost when he figured out he loved Haley."

"Your time will come." Zach laughed. "And when it does, you'll go down like a ton of bricks."

Jake snorted. "Not me. Not when there's a smorgasbord of women to choose from."

"Never say 'never,'" Zach advised as the French doors to the resort's courtyard opened.

At the first sight of Arielle, dressed in a white knee-length gown, her dark auburn hair swept up into a cascade of curls, his heart stalled. He had to be the luckiest man alive and he intended to spend every moment of his life letting her know just how much he loved her.

Walking over to the terrace steps, he offered her his hand. "I missed you today, darlin'."

"And I've missed you."

"Do you have any idea how beautiful you are and how much I want you right now?" he whispered close to her ear.

Her pretty smile damned near knocked him to his knees. "Probably as much as I want you."

"Then what do you say we get this little gathering started so that we can go upstairs to the bridal suite and get started on the intimate part?" he teased.

"Excellent idea, Mr. Forsythe," she agreed as they walked over to the fountain where the Judge waited to make them husband and wife.

"Luther, isn't she the most beautiful bride you've ever seen?" Emerald proclaimed proudly, dabbing at her eyes with her lace-edged linen handkerchief.

"Miss Garnier does make a striking bride," her personal assistant concluded in his usually stoic manner.

Emerald surveyed the gathering. Nearly everyone in the room was a member of her family—a family she'd taken great lengths and spared no expense in finding. And one that she was extremely proud of.

As her gaze settled on Jake, she frowned. He seemed to be more like his father than any of her other grandsons and was, without question, the one she worried about the most.

But unlike her irresponsible son, Jake was complex and felt more than he wanted people to believe. And unless she missed her guess, he had been more deeply hurt than any of the others by their father's abandonment.

She sighed. Only time would tell if his devil-may-care attitude was nothing more than a smoke screen to hide his true, caring nature. And once he moved to Kentucky, taking charge of the enterprise given him as part of his legacy, the clock would start ticking.

"I now pronounce you husband and wife," the judge declared, drawing Emerald's attention back to her now-married granddaughter and her handsome new husband.

"Well, Luther, we've been successful in setting things right once more," she asserted, smiling.

"Yes, madam, it's worked out just as you planned," he agreed.

"Is everything in place for Jake's move to Louisville?" she asked, rising from her seat.

Luther gave her a stiff nod. "The documents have been signed for him to take immediate possession of the Hickory Hills Horse Farm the first of next month."

"Excellent."

Emerald smiled contentedly as she and her assistant walked over to congratulate the lovely couple. She and Luther made a good team and had successfully helped five of her six grandchildren find true happiness.

Kissing the bride and groom and wishing them a long and happy life, Emerald placed her hand in

Luther's folded arm as they walked toward the buffet table on the far side of the room. "Well, Luther, that's another one down. And only one more to go."

* * * * *

Don't miss Kathie DeNosky's next novel,
The Billionaire's Unexpected Heir,
available September 2010.

VALENTE'S BABY

BY
MAXINE SULLIVAN

Dear Reader,

This is the last book in my Valente series.

Matthew Valente may be the youngest of the three brothers, but he is no less compelling and commanding. And while he may be the last of the Valente men to get married, he unknowingly was the first to father a child.

Can you imagine finding out that you're the father of a little girl? Wouldn't the thought of having never found out upset you greatly? Your daughter could have grown up never knowing her father and you never knowing her. It's a heartbreaking thought.

Yet Lana Jensen has her reasons. And she's upset too. She knows she's in trouble when Matt discovers her secret. And did I mention that Matt is drop-dead handsome?

I'm sad to say goodbye to my Valente men, but giving them all a happy ending with the women they love has been such a thrill for me. There's nothing better than being a writer.

Happy reading!

Maxine

Maxine Sullivan credits her mother for her lifelong love of romance novels, so it was a natural extension for Maxine to want to write her own romances. She thinks there's nothing better than being a writer and is thrilled to be one of the few Australians to write for the Desire™ line.

Maxine lives in Melbourne, Australia, but over the years has travelled to New Zealand, the UK and the USA. In her own backyard, her husband's job ensured they saw the diversity of the countryside, from the tropics to the Outback, country towns to the cities. She is married to Geoff, who has proven his hero status many times over the years. They have two handsome sons and an assortment of much loved, previously abandoned animals.

Maxine would love to hear from you and can be contacted through her website at www.maxinesullivan.com.

To the three men in my life –
my husband, Geoff, and sons, Anthony and Kevin.
You are my heart.

One

"You're a father."

Matt Valente broke into a grin as he sat down on the hotel bed. "I didn't know I was pregnant."

"Don't be smart, Matthew," Cesare Valente snapped down the telephone line. The founder of the House of Valente perfume dynasty was clearly not amused. "Remember Lana Jensen?"

The smile dropped from Matt's lips. "She was my top accountant a while back, so yeah, I should remember her." That perfect body…that beautiful face…those Nordic blue eyes hinting at a Scandinavian heritage that seemed as clear as crystal but were in fact deep and hiding lies.

"She had your baby."

A baby?

No way.

The only thing she'd *had* was him.

They'd both been a little tipsy at the office Christmas party and she'd taken advantage of his inebriated state to seduce him. They'd made love on the sofa in his office.

Not that he'd been any less to blame for succumbing to her charms, despite her giving him the come-on for months, her blue gaze skittering away every so often, teasing him with a sensual game of cat and mouse.

Afterward he'd regretted not keeping to his golden rule of no personal involvement with office staff. As chief financial officer for the family business, he didn't need any complications in the workplace.

"I don't believe it. She's lying."

"I saw the child with my own eyes, Matt. I was in my Mercedes waiting for the light to change when Lana crossed in front of me pushing a small child in a stroller. I checked out the birth certificate. Your name's on it."

Matt's hand tightened around the phone. "Dad, that's a breach of privacy."

His.

Hell, if *his* name was on that birth certificate he needed to sort it out.

"Matt, I did what needed to be done. And that included a background check on Lana."

Matt's lips twisted. "Why am I not surprised?"

"It was necessary. She's the mother of my grandchild."

"And she'd suitable?" he asked with a touch of sarcasm.

"As far as I'm concerned, yes. Her parents are dead, and she has an uncle who lives in France and is a respected businessman. Do you want to know more? There's some other information on her family. I can send you the report."

"No, thanks." He knew all he needed to know about Lana Jensen. More than enough.

And he needed to make his father see sense.

"Dad, look, you can put any name on a birth certificate. I didn't think you'd fall for that old trick."

"She's a Valente, *figlio mio*." *Son of mine.* "She looked just like you. There's no doubt in my mind."

Something odd bounced around in Matt's chest. "It's a girl? Er…I mean, she's a girl?"

"Yes. And I'm delighted. It's about time we had another little girl in the family."

Matt grimaced. Girl or boy, it didn't matter to him. "Well, I'm not."

"You will be once you see her."

"Who said I was going to see her?"

"She's my granddaughter, Matt. If you don't go to her, then I'll bring her to you."

Matt's jaw clenched. "This is to trick me into getting married, isn't it? You may have forced Alex and Nick to marry, but I'm not falling for it, Dad."

A year ago they'd been about to branch into the North American market with their top-selling perfume, Valente's Woman, when Cesare had threatened to sell the business out from under Alex's feet if he didn't marry. Then a couple of months ago, Cesare had promised to give the Valente estate to anyone but his second son, Nick. Both his brothers had been given no choice but to do what their father wanted or lose what they loved most. As youngest son, Matt had decided there was nothing his father could do to him to make him marry.

"Matt, I admit I had no compunction in forcing your two brothers to marry, and I would have found a way to force you to marry, too. Only now I don't have to, do I? You've brought a daughter into this world and you will give that daughter your name. She will be known as a true Valente."

"Don't dictate to me, Dad. If this child is mine, and I'm in no way convinced of it, then I'll give her my name. You can count on it."

"That's all I wanted to know. The family jet is at Brisbane Airport waiting for you. Nick and Sasha are already there and will attend the conference dinner in your place."

His father was like a damn bulldozer at times. Not even the heart attack had stopped his interfering in his sons' lives.

"I've got a date for the dinner tonight."

"You *had* a date. I suggest you break it and get back to Sydney tonight and go see the mother of your child as soon as possible. I like Lana and I'm sure she'll be reasonable."

At the mention of Lana, his gut clenched, but there was no way he wanted his father to know that. Cesare would somehow use that knowledge in future if he could. He could imagine the older man's reaction if he ever told him Lana was a thief and that *he'd* covered up for her without telling anyone. And he couldn't wholly blame his decision not to report their theft on Cesare's heart attack at the time either.

"What woman is ever reasonable, Dad?" he mocked.

Cesare laughed and said goodbye, and Matt hung up the phone and went to stand at the window in his hotel suite. He looked out over the sweeping coastline of Queensland's Gold Coast as the rolling surf of the Pacific Ocean tumbled onto the golden beaches of Australia's tourist capital.

Tonight he'd planned a romantic dinner and a night of lovemaking with a lady friend of his.

Now he could only think of one woman.

Lana Jensen.

She'd been the only woman he'd made love to without a condom. He'd been so hot for her, and the alcohol he'd consumed had lowered his guard.

But if that child was his—if Lana had lied to him about being protected from a pregnancy—then she'd done more than stolen that fifty thousand dollars from the House of Valente.

She'd just stolen his freedom.

* * *

"Oh my God!" Lana gasped a split second after opening her apartment door and seeing the man on the other side. Panic raced through her at the speed of light. It couldn't be him. It just couldn't be.

"Yes, you'd better start praying," Matt Valente declared.

Recovering hastily, she played for time even as she edged the door shut a fraction. "Matt, what are you doing here?"

"You know the answer to that."

"I do?"

"Invite me in, Lana."

Not for all the tea in China.

"Sorry, no. I'm going out shortly." She started shutting the door with more haste. "Perhaps if you have something to say you can telephone me tomorrow and—"

He pushed past her into the apartment, despite his haste, gently moving her out of the way. "I've got plenty to say and I intend on saying it *now*."

She tried to hold back her agitation. "Look, you just can't come in here and—"

"Where is she, Lana?"

Lana froze. "Where is who?"

"My daughter."

Dear Lord, until that moment she'd been hoping this wasn't what his visit was about.

"So you know?" she whispered.

"It's true, then."

She bit her lip. "No. I mean...er...sure, I had a baby but—"

"Give it up, Lana. She's my daughter. My father saw you with her on the street and he checked out her birth certificate."

She gaped at him. "But...but that's an invasion of my privacy."

"Do you think he cares?"

Just then a child's babble issued from the living room and Matt shot her a dark look.

Lana stepped in front of him. "Matt, please. Just leave. Don't do this."

"No chance in hell," he growled, and stepped around her, taking a few paces to the doorway. He went stone still as he saw the little toddler standing up against the playpen railings.

Lana tried not to think about how he must be feeling right now. She told herself not to feel sorry for him. Matt Valente was a playboy who wasn't ready to settle down or have children. If he was here, it was only because his father had made him come.

"What's her name?"

Surprise kicked in. "You don't know?"

He didn't move a muscle. "What's her name?" he said rawly.

"Megan."

A moment slid by, then, "Megan Valente."

Apprehension slithered down Lana's spine. "Actually, it's Megan Jensen."

"Soon it will be Valente," he said with the full superiority of a Valente male.

Her mind reeled. "What do you mean?"

He ignored the question as he walked over to Megan, crouched down in front of the eleven-month-old and looked at her through the bars.

Lana could see his reflection in the decorative wall mirror. There was awesome wonder on his handsome face as he took in each and every feature of the beautiful little girl.

Her heart tilted. For Megan's sake she wanted Matt to love his daughter. For her own sake she wanted him to deny parentage, leave and never come back.

"Hello, Megan," Matt said softly, not touching, not moving, not doing anything except capturing her attention.

Megan stared back entranced, her brown eyes so like her father's. She looked so cute, a little dark-haired doll with chubby cheeks and bow-shaped lips that had recently learned to blow a sloppy kiss for her mother.

Oh God.

Suddenly Megan transferred her gaze to Lana and within the space of a second her face began to screw up and she let out a wail.

Lana rushed forward and lifted her out of the playpen. "It's her bedtime," she said, soothing her daughter with a "shh" and patting her back until the little girl hiccupped and quieted.

Matt got to his feet, his expression unreadable. "Put her to bed, then we'll talk."

She hesitated.

"Put her to bed, Lana."

"If you insist." She hitched Megan higher on her hip. "Take a seat. I'll be back in a minute."

"No. I'm coming with you."

She swallowed. That sounded ominous. "Why?"

"I'm interested in everything my daughter does."

"*Our* daughter."

"At least you're admitting it now."

Trying not to show how upset she was with all this, she hurried past him and down the hallway to the smaller bedroom. She had stenciled Megan's room with a variety of farm animals, adding a musical mobile that played a lullaby above the crib, and giving her daughter plenty of soft toys to cuddle. The room looked lovely.

Megan had fully settled down by now as Lana changed her diaper. She lay there quietly, her eyes on Matt in the doorway as if she was fascinated by him despite herself.

Don't let him get to you, sweetheart, Lana wanted to say. *Ignore him and he'll go away.*

She hoped.

Then she kissed Megan on the cheek. "Good night, pumpkin," she murmured, then put her in her crib.

She was grateful when Matt stepped back to allow her to leave the now-darkened room without having to squeeze past him. "Coffee?" she said, heading for the kitchen, needing something to do.

"Don't you have something stronger?"

She shot him a look over her shoulder. "Sorry. I don't usually drink."

"Yeah, I remember."

His sarcasm had her spinning to face him. "That was different. It was Christmas and—"

"You thought I'd be a good lay."

The breath caught in her throat. "It wasn't like that."

"It wasn't? Then perhaps you thought I'd be a good sperm donor and future moneymaker?"

"No! I—"

She'd been so attracted to Matt back then, and working for him the two years previously had made her crazy with want. Yet in spite of them both having a few drinks too many, it hadn't been cheap.

Not for her anyway.

It had been intense and overwhelming, and she hadn't been able to help herself when she'd literally run into him coming out of the elevator as she went to collect her purse from her desk after the party. He'd held her to stop her from falling and that had been all it needed. She'd lifted her mouth up toward his and he'd groaned and backed her into his office.

"Yes?" he prompted now, a sudden sensual look in his eyes telling her he remembered.

Everything.

"Let's just forget it," she muttered. "We both acted out of character that night."

"Oh, I'd say you acted right *in* character. You knew exactly what you were doing."

She swiveled away before he could see the hurt in her eyes. If he knew her he'd realize she'd never seduce a man just to father a child. Forcing a man to be a father never worked.

With shaking hands she put the coffeepot on, then took a ragged breath and turned to face the one person who could unravel her perfectly constructed life once again.

He stood with his lower back against the sink, his arms crossed against a well-muscled chest. "So, Lana, you lied to me, didn't you? You told me afterward that you were on contraceptives. You told me there was nothing to worry about." His eyes seared her. "But there was, wasn't there?"

She hesitated, then, "Yes."

"Did you think I would tell you to get rid of it?"

She hesitated again, but only briefly. "The thought did cross my mind."

"No bloody way!"

An odd feeling turned inside her chest at his emphatic reply. She'd thought about that scenario of course, but had come to the conclusion Matt would want his child. Playboy or not, he had strong family ethics, and if he'd known he was about to be a father, nothing would have stopped him from being involved in the baby's life.

And now he knew.

God help her.

"You should have told me as soon as you realized you were pregnant."

Her throat turned dry. "I couldn't, Matt."

"Why?"

She hadn't wanted to risk him taking her child away from her. If he'd thought his son or daughter was better off with the Valentes, he would have had no hesitation in instigating a custody battle.

And he'd have won, too.

She'd seen it time and again at the boarding school her uncle Dan had paid for her to attend. Some of the rich thought they were above reproach. That money and privilege gave them the right to do what they liked. Usually, they got their way.

He could still win.

She swallowed hard. She couldn't tell him the truth. If he knew her fears…if he knew she'd do anything to keep her daughter…he'd take advantage of her biggest vulnerability.

Her love for her child.

"I realized you wouldn't want to be a father." That was true. "You're far too busy being a playboy. The two things don't mix."

"I'm a father now, and you don't see me running."

"We both know you feel obligated and nothing more."

"Don't presume to know what I'm feeling." A pulse

beat in his cheekbone. "Why put my name on the birth certificate if you didn't want the truth known?"

That had been her one weakness.

"I had to," she admitted. "In case anything ever happened to me. I needed her to know."

He gave her a look sharper than a knife. "Were you ever going to tell me, Lana? And what about our daughter? When were you going to tell her?"

She inclined her head. "When she was older. It would have been up to her to decide whether she wanted to make contact with you."

"And in the meantime you would have poisoned her against me. And I would have missed out on her growing up." His eyes stabbed her with his disgust. "So you're a cheat and a liar as well as a thief?"

"No, I…" She shook her head to clear it. "*What* did you say?"

Then she got it.

"Matt, I know you may think my keeping Megan from you is stealing but—"

"I meant the money you stole from the House of Valente."

Her fine brows drew together. "Money?"

"Don't play dumb, lady. Remember that little sum of fifty thousand dollars? I found the paper-work after you left. You covered your tracks well, but not well enough to fool me."

She rocked back in shock. "I didn't steal any money."

"You're lying again."

She shook her head. "No, I'm not."

"Don't play games. You're caught out. There's nothing you can say to convince me otherwise."

A threat of hysteria rose in her throat. "I didn't steal any money. I wouldn't. I'm an accountant, for heaven's sake. I'd lose my job and my livelihood."

"Which is part of why I didn't report the theft. For some reason I felt I owed you that. Lord knows why," he said with total self-possession. "If my father hadn't had his heart attack, I might have changed my mind."

"You should have reported it. At least then I could have proven you wrong."

"That's not possible."

"Look, if you think I stole money, what did I do with it, then?"

He glanced around the kitchen, with its shiny new appliances. "The deposit for this apartment must have been expensive."

She blinked in surprise. He didn't know that her uncle Dan had bought this apartment for her? How could he not know? She was sure he would have checked out her background and found out all sorts of things about her family.

Or perhaps that was still in the works.

If it was, then no doubt Matt would discover how wrong he was about this stolen money.

If it wasn't, no way would she tell him anything. Her uncle Dan had been very kind to her and she loved him dearly, and she wouldn't repay him by having the Valentes delve into his private life. She knew that her uncle was bisexual, with him married to Aimee but having a gay lover, Julien. It wasn't common knowledge, and she'd only found out about Julien on their last visit to Australia—the same time Dan had discovered she was pregnant.

She couldn't—wouldn't—open Dan's personal life up for gossip. Not even to prove to Matt that she wasn't the person he thought she was.

"What? No answer?" he mocked.

She lifted her chin. "You're wrong about me."

"I don't think so." His eyes hardened further. "Now it's payback time."

"Payback?" The fine hairs on her arms rose in warning.

"We're getting married. For a year, so that my daughter will be known as a Valente."

Her mind stumbled in shock. She'd never expected him to offer marriage. She didn't come from a moneyed background, nor was she of good stock. Marriage to Matt Valente just hadn't been an option.

And she wouldn't have pushed for that option even if it *had* been. She'd sworn never to marry for the sake of a child. She wouldn't make the same mistake her mother had made, she'd promised herself years ago. Megan would not grow up in a hostile household like Lana had. There was nothing as bad as a husband who felt trapped. It brought out the worst in a man.

She shuddered. Her own mother had been preg-

nant with *her* when she'd married Lana's father.
Valerie Jensen had loved her husband and she'd
prayed he would come to love her in return, only he
hadn't. He'd used that love against her every day of
their married live.

Would Matt do the same?

Somehow Lana managed a strangled, "This is ludicrous. You can acknowledge Megan as your
daughter without marrying *me*."

"No. I want this official. I already have the license
for this Friday at three o'clock." She gasped but he
ignored it. "Believe me, Lana, if you try to run I'll find
you and I'll make sure the judge at the custody hearing
learns all about how you stole money, about how you
always put yourself first, how you were unwilling to
give your daughter the best in life, and how you put
Megan's life at risk by running. I'll get full custody of
my daughter. And that's not a threat, that's a promise."

"You wouldn't," she muttered. It was her worst
nightmare.

The line of his mouth flattened. "Try me."

"She's my daughter, Matt. I carried her and I
gave birth to her while you were out sleeping around
with other women. You have very little right to her."

A nerve pulsed near his temple. "I'm her father.
But don't worry. I don't plan on sleeping with you.
We'll have separate bedrooms."

"For all your comings and goings?" She shook
her head. "I won't have you parading your girl-
friends in front of Megan."

"I'll take no lovers for the next year. And that's out of respect for my child, not you."

Defeat weighed heavily on her shoulders, but she was determined not to let him see it. She tried to think and could only come up with one thing that might help her.

"Okay, but I'll only marry you if I can come back to work for you. I want to find the real thief." She would prove her innocence without bringing Dan into it.

"Do you really think that's going to happen?" he scoffed.

"I mean it, Matt," she said, remaining firm but knowing she didn't have a leg to stand on if he refused her request.

He shrugged. "As you wish. But just don't plan on stealing any more money from us."

His comment offended her. "If I wanted to do that I'd steal it from my current job, wouldn't I?"

He looked surprised. "You work?"

The question would have amused her at any other time. "I have to earn a living somehow."

"Not anymore," he dismissed arrogantly. "I'll support you and Megan. There's no need for you to work at all."

He was unbelievable!

"I *like* working. It's part of who I am." She saw his eyes narrow and realized she was giving away too much about herself. She didn't want that.

Nor did she want to be supported by him, she

decided, getting back to the point. It would only be for Megan's sake if she accepted a little help from him.

And come to think of it, this would actually work out well. The one thing she regretted as a single mum was not having as much time to spend with her daughter as she'd like.

"I'll work a couple days with you and the other days I plan on staying home with Megan. Agreed?"

He paused, then, "Agreed."

"But after the year's up, I get my divorce, right?" She couldn't imagine being connected to this Valente for longer than that. "Promise me, Matt."

"I can guarantee it."

Two

"If any person can show just cause why these two people may not be joined together, let him speak now or forever hold their peace."

Lana's heart fluttered with anxiety in the ensuing silence, wishing that someone…anyone…would put a stop to this lunacy. If only Megan would cry, she might have the confidence to say no to this marriage.

The registrar continued with the ceremony.

And suddenly it was too late.

"You may now kiss each other."

Oh Lord.

As if Matt knew that she couldn't look at him to save her life right now, he put his hand on her arm and turned her toward him, a solemn look in his eyes.

He lowered his head and she repressed a shiver; in the mere few days since he'd come back into her life she could not ignore his compelling presence.

And then his lips touched hers in a precise kiss that said he was cool and in control and in no way did he want a response from her.

She was glad to oblige.

It would be her secret that his touch still made her tingle. She'd take that secret to the grave, she knew, as he moved back, his eyes dark and inscrutable.

The registrar smiled at the small gathering. "I present to you Mr. and Mrs. Matthew Valente."

Her heart dipped, but Matt's family—their only guests—started congratulating them, giving Lana time to compose herself. She'd told them she had no family to invite, except an aunt and uncle who were off on a jaunt to South Africa. Of course, it was the truth, but she played it low-key. And she hadn't wanted to invite the few single friends she'd drifted away from since having Megan.

The Valentes were it.

Yet she couldn't complain about their treatment of her. They were just so delighted to have a new addition in Megan, and they even seemed genuinely pleased *she* was joining them. She'd thought they might think she'd tried to trap Matt, but Cesare and Isabel had been kindness itself.

She could even set aside her resentment with Cesare for his breach of privacy over the birth certificate, after he'd handed her a gorgeous posy of flowers on arrival today, the bright colors a perfect foil against the soft femininity of her cream suit.

And Isabel had put one of the flowers from the posy in Megan's dark hair. Both gestures had been a little "family" touch that had overwhelmed Lana and she'd had to blink rapidly to hold back the tears.

"We need a photograph of the bride and groom, and then one of the whole family," Isabel said, pulling Lana from her thoughts.

"Smile," Matt murmured, smiling at her. "I want my family to at least think we can be pleasant to each other."

"That'll be a stretch."

He blinked at her words, and gave a low chuckle, and she found herself smiling back genuinely for the first time.

At that moment the camera clicked.

"Hey, that'll be a great picture," Nick said, looking at the screen on the digital camera. "Yes, it is. Now let's try a few more, and then we'll get someone to take a picture of us all together."

Lana continued to smile, but she was grateful the camera hadn't clicked a moment ago, or it might have caught her expression reeling from the effects of Matt's devastating smile.

Matt Valente could only be described as terminally handsome, with his sophisticated good looks and attitude of self-command making a woman hard-pressed to turn her eyes away.

And he was now her husband.

And Megan's father, she reminded herself, not allowing herself to forget the reason she was here today.

After the photographs, everyone headed out of the building to go to Cesare and Isabel's apartment, where a late lunch with the family was to be held in their honor.

Lana had just climbed into the limousine when there was a flash as someone raced up and snapped a picture of them. Thankfully she'd been blocking a view of Megan at the time.

Matt swore and quickly shut the door behind them. "Bloody journalists," he growled. "I don't like them taking pictures of Megan."

Lana's brow rose in surprise. She felt the same but, "Isn't the point of our marriage to get her known as a Valente?"

"Not with pictures. I was raised in front of the press, but it's a different world now and I'll be damned if I'll let them use her. That's not what our marriage is about."

His words warmed her and she quickly buried her face in her daughter's dark curls. For the first time she didn't feel as though Megan would be alone in the world if anything happened to *her*. Dan would do his best from France of course, but it wasn't the same as being cared for by a father who loved her.

She'd marry a thousand men like Matt to do this for her daughter, she admitted, then realized how ridiculous that thought was. There *was* no other man like Matt Valente.

Alex and Nick Valente were men in their own right.

And so was Matt.

He was one of a kind.

And he knew it.

Lana couldn't help but feel a little reserved once they arrived at his parents' apartment. Matt stayed by her side for a while, then left her to walk around with Megan in his arms.

As she watched him she wished she could believe that their daughter was some sort of trophy to him, but she knew that wasn't true. He was a proud father, that's all.

Occasionally he'd look her way and he'd smile at her for the benefit of the others, but Lana was sure they weren't fooling any of them. She only had to look at his two brothers to see the truth in their eyes. They knew Megan was the reason Matt had married her.

As did their wives, Olivia and Sasha. Olivia was the daughter of a famous movie star, which had to be hard at times. And poor Sasha's father had been charged with fraud and was due to be sentenced soon.

Yet both women were just so nice and unaffected by the trappings of wealth. They even mentioned getting together for lunch, but Lana held them off.

And she planned on holding them off for as long as she could. It was no use her getting too close to these women. She'd be gone before they knew it, she told herself, sipping at her champagne and watching Alex and Olivia's eight-year-old son, Scott, and their newly adopted six-year-old daughter, Renee, playing together.

Just then Matt moved into her line of vision to talk to Alex. Megan was still in his arms and her poor darling was cautiously looking up at her father as if she wasn't sure whether to cry or not.

And Matt wasn't letting go.

And didn't she know how *that* felt? Matt was paying no notice to Megan's nervousness, just as he paid no notice to *hers*.

Suddenly Matt looked at Megan and kissed her cheek and without warning Megan gave her toothless little grin. Lana's heart tripped over when she saw that.

Megan and Matt would be okay together.

"You've done the right thing for her," Isabel said gently, coming up beside Lana.

Lana started, then gave a small smile. "I know, Isabel."

"Matt will be good for her."

"Yes, he will." She would never have married him if he wasn't.

"And you'll be good for my son."

Lana wrinkled her nose. "I'm not so sure about that."

"*I* am. He needs someone like you."

Lana shook her head. "No, you're wrong. I'm nothing special." Matt needed someone who liked to go out and party. And probably someone from a high-profile family would be even better.

The older woman considered her. "Don't put yourself down, Lana. You're a lovely person, and any woman who puts her child first like you're doing by marrying my son is someone we're proud to have in our family."

Lana swallowed hard and blinked rapidly, touched by the words. "Most mothers would do what I'm doing."

"No, sweetie, they wouldn't," Isabel said, turning to gaze at her three sons.

Lana remembered then that Isabel was actually Alex and Nick's stepmother, not their real mother as she was Matt's. From what she knew of the Valentes, Alex's mother had died when he was little and Cesare had then married Nick's mother, who'd walked out when Nick was a baby. Cesare had then found long-term happiness with his third wife, Isabel, who'd been a proper mother to the three boys.

Lana inclined her head. "You're right, Isabel. Not all mothers are the same."

A short time later, Cesare tapped his champagne glass with a spoon to get everyone's attention.

"First of all, I'd like to congratulate my youngest son and his new wife on their marriage." He held up his glass. "To Lana and Matt. May your marriage be strong and happy."

"To Lana and Matt," the others toasted, and Lana

felt her cheeks warm. Was she the only one to see that cynical look in Matt's eyes?

"And now," Cesare said, "Izzie and I have a special gift for all our beautiful daughters-in-law. To each of you, we give the very first of our new Valente's Woman Limited Edition perfume."

Isabel handed out the gorgeous bottles of scent and Lana was grateful Olivia and Sasha's excitement made her own more sedate response fade into the background. She felt like such a fraud. She didn't deserve to be a part of this. She only had to look at Matt to know he was thinking the same thing.

Thankfully, the party finally ended two hours later. Megan was tired and had begun to cry and Matt declared they were leaving, for which Lana was relieved. It had been a long afternoon and Megan had been a little angel through it all, but now she needed her bed.

And that bed should now be at Matt's place. In the days leading up to the wedding she hadn't thought to ask where that was, but he'd told her he'd have all Megan's things and anything Lana wanted transferred to his apartment while they were busy with the ceremony.

Twenty minutes later Matt turned the car into the gated driveway of a large house that had a picturesque garden and lawn. Then she saw the high fence had a board with a Sold sign across it.

She twisted toward Matt in disbelief. "Tell me you didn't buy this house for us?"

His satisfied look completely disappeared. "Yes, I did."

"When?"

"Yesterday."

Her eyes widened. "But we're only going to be married for a year."

"So? It'll be a good investment. Anyway, my apartment wasn't suitable for a child."

"I can just imagine," she muttered.

His eyes turned cold. "There were only two bedrooms."

"I could have shared with Megan."

She certainly wouldn't have shared with *him*.

"Megan needs her own space." He paused. "And you need your sleep if you insist on working."

Okay, so she couldn't fault that.

Her irritation subsided a little; then she thought of something else. "You could have just left us at my apartment, you know. And you could've stayed at yours."

"No."

Her lips pressed together, even though she hadn't much hope he'd agree. "I've lived there for almost a year now. There's nothing wrong with it."

"That doesn't mean it's suitable for Megan."

That stung.

"I see." Obviously *she* could live in a dump for all he cared, but Megan needed to live somewhere befitting the Valente name.

Then she felt bad.

It sounded as though she was jealous of her daughter, and she wasn't. *She* had the Valente name herself now anyway, even if she wasn't going to use it, having decided to stick to Jensen. After hearing herself referred to as Mrs. Matthew Valente at the Registry Office today, she needed this to keep a sense of independence.

No, it was Matt's dominating way that really irked her. He thought he knew what was best for her and Megan. He should have asked her opinion.

Clearly having had enough, Matt pushed open his car door. "Come on. Let's go inside." He got out of the car and opened the back door, ducking back in to release Megan from her car seat. "Leave her things. I'll get them later."

Lana alighted and then went to take Megan out of his arms. "Here. Give her to me."

"No, she's heavy. I'll carry her." He walked away and up the front steps, leaving Lana to grit her teeth and follow them.

Matt produced a key and opened the door wide and they stepped into an entry foyer. A glimpse at the formal living room on the right confirmed the place was stunning.

"Did you even take the time to look around before you bought this place? You didn't, did you?"

His aristocratic brow rose. "Why? It's not good enough?"

She waved a dismissive hand, parroting his offhandedness. "Don't be crazy. It's lovely. I just wondered, that's all."

"I always think before I act, Lana."

Not always, was her immediate thought as their eyes met and she saw that same thought in him. She flushed. The one time he *hadn't* thought things through was the reason they were here now.

"We have a housekeeper starting tomorrow," he said, somewhat in a clipped tone. "She has her own apartment at the back of the house."

She nodded and glanced down the hallway as if she was looking around, but it was more about not looking at *him*.

"I'll give you a tour later. For now I'll show you the bedrooms." He started down the hallway and she tensed as once again she followed him until he turned left into a wing. He opened the first door. "This is your room. You've got your own en suite."

At least they didn't have to share a bathroom. Nor that beautiful, king-size bed, which she pretended she didn't even notice. "Very nice."

"There's a connecting door to Megan's room." He walked to the next room. "This is hers." He pointed to the door farther along. "My room's next to this one."

Lana's heart missed a beat as the impact of their circumstances started to roll over her. She was going to be sharing a house with the man who had the monopoly on high-powered virility.

God help her.

All of a sudden Megan saw her crib and squirmed to get to it. "She wants to go to bed."

Matt nodded. "Everything's here, so I'll leave you to it while I go get the rest of her things from the car."

"Okay. Just put her down on the carpet while I get organized."

Once he'd left, Lana stood looking around. Megan's furniture appeared miniscule in this room that was painted in pale yellow with nursery rhyme characters stenciled around the walls. Her daughter was going to love looking at them from her crib.

But for now…

"Right, madam. Let me get out of this jacket first," Lana said, slipping off her cream jacket and placing it on a chair, leaving her cream camisole top above her short skirt. "That's better."

She gathered a few items. "Now it's your turn."

Lifting Megan up, she laid her on the change table while she gave her a top-and-tail with a wash-cloth and then put on a clean diaper.

She chatted as she went. "You were such a good little girl today. Mummy is very proud of you. I think you…"

Five minutes later Matt stood in the doorway, letting Lana's voice flow over him as he watched her preparing Megan for bed. It was an odd feeling watching these two new women in his life.

His daughter he loved already.

And the other he….wanted.

His gaze traveled over Lana's profile. Her short blond hair was always stylish, but she'd done something special to it today and it looked fantastic.

Her cream suit fit her perfectly, but now she'd taken off her jacket and was standing there in a lacy top with spaghetti straps curved over her shoulders, leaving her smooth skin free.

And that short skirt and silk stockings showcased her long legs, one of which she'd kicked out behind her as she leaned over their daughter on the change table.

His groan kicked into gear in reply. This woman had to be the sexiest mother he'd ever seen.

And dammit, he still desired her.

As if sensing his presence, she looked over at him and he quickly blanked out his expression. It was going to be tough enough being in the same house, without her knowing that he wanted to strip those clothes from her body.

"You'll have to teach me how to do that," he said, determined not to let her know his thoughts.

Her elegant eyebrows rose a fraction. "*You'll* change her diaper?"

"I think I should know how to do these things. I want to be a hands-on father."

She relaxed with a wry smile. "Oh, changing diapers will certainly give you that experience," she said, picking Megan up in her arms and turning toward the crib, but not before Lana's smile swept into him.

"Wait," he managed to say as he approached them. "I want to give her a good-night kiss." He leaned forward to kiss his daughter's chubby cheek. "Sweet dreams, Megan Valente." She smelled of baby powder.

But as he eased back he caught a tantalizing hint of "Valente's Woman," the special perfume that was taking the world by storm. All the Valente women wore it—and now Lana was truly entitled to wear it, too.

It suited her.

Only for a year, he reminded himself, growing angry with disappointment at the woman she was. Damn her for stealing that money. He didn't want a thief for a wife, or for the mother of his child.

A year, that's all.

And then she could damn well wear whatever perfume she pleased.

"There's some food and coffee in the kitchen," he snapped, as he walked to the door.

"Thank you, but I'll be fine."

He stopped to look at her. "Neither of us had much to eat today."

"You'll join me?" she said with clear surprise.

"Is that a problem?"

She sent him a cautious glance. "No, I guess not."

"The kitchen's down the hallway on the right," he said, leaving them alone.

He hated that her attraction got to him. She was

fiery and icy at the same time, and watching her just now only served to remind him what he could have if he chose to bed her.

He cursed under his breath. This wasn't the way it was supposed to be. And definitely not from their first day together.

Five minutes later she entered the kitchen. She'd slipped her jacket back on, but if she thought it would provide some sort of protective shield she was very much mistaken. The fine material might have veiled the bare shoulders and firm breasts beneath her camisole top, but the clingy fabric couldn't fully conceal the outline of that willowy figure beneath her short skirt.

She caught him looking at her and her blue eyes flared before darting away to nervously glance around the room.

Look at me again, he wanted to say, then immediately severed the thought.

Don't look.

Don't touch.

"This is a magnificent kitchen, Matt," she began to chatter, still looking everywhere but at him. "Your housekeeper is sure to love it."

"She's your housekeeper, too," he pointed out.

Her gaze flew to him. "But I've never had a housekeeper before."

"You're a Valente now. You'll have to get used to it."

Anger flashed in her eyes; then her chin angled.

"Actually, I'm keeping my own name. Megan's the Valente now, not me."

The comment shouldn't have surprised him, but it did. Most women he knew would jump at any chance to be Mrs. Valente.

He frowned. Or was her show of independence merely for his benefit? She might not have wanted this marriage, but she certainly knew how to take advantage of an opportunity.

"So you're a liberated woman?" he drawled, not bothering to make an issue of it. He had her measure.

"I don't see any point in taking on a name I have no intention of keeping."

He gave a careless shrug. "Fair enough."

She stared for a moment. "You're not going to argue about it?"

"No. I agree. It makes sense."

"Oh." She seemed to be at a loss. "Good." Then she swung away and viewed the selection of food on the marble countertop. "This all looks very appetizing."

The muscles at the back of his neck were taut. The only thing that looked appetizing was *her*. "My mother thought we might be hungry."

"That's sweet of her."

Funny, his mother had called Lana sweet. It worried him. He didn't want his family drawn in or upset by her. His parents would be shocked if they knew what she was really like. It would be a hard pill to swallow knowing that the mother of their grandchild was so untrustworthy.

He gestured for her to sit on one of the tall stools. "Help yourself to the food," he said tightly, moving around the other side of the countertop, not wanting to be too close to her right now.

She slid onto the stool and picked up one of the delicious-looking sandwiches, appearing to be at ease, but he knew she was anything but.

He took one of the sandwiches for himself. "Speaking of my mother, you were having a good chat with her this evening," he said casually, remembering how he'd watched them and felt the urgent need to part the two women.

A wary look crossed her face, then vanished. "Were we?"

"You both looked deep in conversation."

"Then we probably were," she said, and took a nibble of her sandwich.

His brows drew together. It appeared as though she was hiding behind that sandwich, not eating it. That made him suspicious.

"I hope you're not planning on worming your way into her good books."

Her eyes widened and the sandwich lowered from her mouth. "Why would I do that?"

"My mother is predisposed to liking you. That makes her vulnerable to being hurt."

She frowned. "I don't plan on hurting her. Or anyone else for that matter."

"Don't you?"

She slowly put the sandwich down on the plate

and shot him a glare. "You know, you really are a bastard."

All at once everything within him rose like bile. "No, my daughter was the bastard."

She drew in a sharp breath. "I can't believe you just said that."

"You don't like to hear the truth?" The air held tight with tension. "I'm suddenly married to a treacherous beauty who not only stole money from my family, but who stole almost a year of my daughter's life from me. I think I have fifty thousand and one reasons to be pretty damn angry right now, don't you?"

Her chin angled. "You may think that, and that's your choice, but you've also got one very good reason for at least showing me some respect as your wife. And *she's* in that bedroom back there."

Megan.

Reluctant admiration fought his animosity, and lost. "Admit you stole the money. That'll make me respect you more."

"I can't confess to something I didn't do."

Frustration clawed through him. "Stop lying, Lana. Just…stop the lying."

She jumped off the stool. "I hope you choke on your food, Matthew Valente," she muttered, and raced out of the room.

Matt watched her leave, his appetite deserting him. He felt bad, but dammit, he'd done the right thing.

He had to remember—and keep on remembering—that his new wife might look like an angel, but beneath that sweet facade she was as devious as they come.

Three

After the way Matt had verbally attacked her last night, Lana hadn't expected to sleep soundly, but when she awoke the next morning she felt much more able to cope with being married.

And cope with Matt's attitude toward her, she decided, determinedly propelling herself out of bed. She had to get on with what life had dished out.

Megan was still asleep when Lana opened the connecting door. Lana's heart softened as she looked down at her child. Matt could think bad of her all he liked, and he could give her a hard time for the next year, but as long as Megan was safe, healthy and happy, she could withstand anything.

Even a charismatic womanizer like Matt Valente.

Pleased to have the time to shower without getting Megan sorted first, Lana returned ten minutes later dressed in tan slacks and a dark brown knit top, and found her daughter sitting up in her crib making noises and playing with her toys.

"There's Mummy's little darling." Giving her little girl a big kiss, she changed her diaper, then carried her to the kitchen to prepare her breakfast. She wasn't sure what was on the agenda today, if anything.

"You must be Mrs. Valente," a middle-aged woman said, coming forward to shake her hand as soon as they stepped into the large, airy kitchen.

Lana blinked at the name, then smiled. "Please call me Lana."

"Lana, then. I'm Ruth, your new housekeeper." She looked at Megan. "And this must be Megan. My, isn't she like her father?"

"I hope that's a good thing, Ruth," Matt said, coming into the kitchen and turning on the charm. He promptly leaned over and kissed Megan on the head.

Lana almost gasped. For a moment she thought he was going to kiss *her*. There was a knowing look in Matt's eyes as he moved away.

"Of course it is, Mr. Valente," Ruth said, pulling Lana back to the moment. "Now, breakfast will be served in the sunroom. What would the little one like?"

Lana told her, then watched in surprise as Matt took Megan from her arms and headed for the sunroom. She followed them, annoyed at his sheer arrogance.

"Excuse me," she hissed. "But do you have to do that?"

His brow rose. "What?"

"Take Megan off me like that. She's not a parcel, you know."

He slipped Megan into her high chair. "I thought I was helping. She's heavy."

"Yes, and I've managed to carry her around longer than you," she said pointedly.

His eyes hardened. "And whose fault is that?" he snapped, turning back to do up the strap. He fiddled with it, then muttered something under his breath. "How do you do this thing up?"

She shot him a look that said she was pleased he didn't know everything. "Like this. See."

He watched her show him. "You make it look so easy."

"That's because it's childproof."

One corner of his mouth twisted upward. "Are you trying to tell me something? No, don't answer that," he mocked, sitting down and reaching for the coffeepot. "So, what do you think of Ruth?"

She frowned while he poured her a coffee without asking. "She seems very pleasant and efficient."

"She comes highly recommended. She also has a degree in first aid and child care and has agreed to look after Megan while you're at work."

Lana stiffened. "You mean she'd be her *nanny*?"

He poured himself a coffee. "Yes."

"But Megan goes to day care already." She'd informed them it would only be for three days a week now instead of five, and Lana planned on spending those two other days with her daughter.

"I'm afraid that's not suitable anymore."

This set Lana's teeth on edge. "So I just move her because you snap your fingers?"

He put the coffeepot back, his mouth tightening. "This isn't about me. It's about our daughter."

She counted to five and then expelled a slow breath. "Look, don't you think with everything else new in her life it might be a good idea to keep some things the same?"

"Things can't stay the same, I'm afraid. Megan's a Valente now. Remember the press trying to take a picture of her after our wedding? Do you really want her at risk like that at the day care center? Or worse?"

Lana's heart jumped with fright. "Don't."

"This is only temporary. Once things settle down we'll try and find a day care center close by where we know she'll be safe, okay?"

She nodded, not sure she wanted to let her baby out of her sight ever again. She was just overreacting, of course, but she wanted Megan to have a normal life. Now that her daughter was recognized as a Valente, that would be impossible.

Just them, Ruth came into the room with a bowl of baby cereal. Lana thanked her then concentrated on feeding Megan, aware of Matt watching her.

"By the way," he said as she placed a spoonful of mush in Megan's mouth. "My mother has offered to look after Megan at any time, especially if we need to go out for an evening."

"That's good of her but I can't see it being necessary."

"There may be some events we can't avoid."

The spoon stopped midair. "Our marriage was to give your name to Megan. That's it." He'd made that more than clear, and she was more than happy with that.

"I don't like it either, but there are particular obligations that go along with being a Valente. Would you prefer I take another woman as my partner?"

The thought of him with other women had always made her feel sick to the stomach, but only because she'd wanted him so much herself. She'd hated being one of many.

And yet surprisingly she'd let him make love to her without a condom. She may have been slightly drunk, but somehow deep down she'd trusted him. It was crazy that she *still* trusted him in that respect.

She managed to school her features. "For Megan's sake, I wouldn't want you out and about with another woman, but that's your choice."

He swore softly. "Of course I'm not going to take another woman, but I wanted you to see how ridiculous the situation is. If I need someone to accompany me anywhere, then you're it, Lana. For Megan's sake," he reminded her.

The little girl in question started to babble and reach for the spoon in Lana's hand. "Sorry, pumpkin," she said, continuing to feed her.

When she turned back to look at Matt, he was pouring some muesli into a bowl and adding milk. She let his comment pass. Fine, so there were some things she would have to do as Matt's wife.

A few minutes later he pushed his empty bowl to the side. "There's a park around the corner. We should take Megan."

"A park? Today?" It was Saturday, but it was the last thing she expected he'd suggest the day after their wedding.

"Why not? The weather's supposed to be nice and the fresh air will do her good."

So he'd checked out the park as well as bought a new house? He'd been busy. If only he wasn't so involved…no, that was an idiotic thought.

"She would enjoy that," she said, and received a mocking look from him that *she* wouldn't.

Half an hour later, Lana gave Matt a quick lesson in changing diapers and dressing Megan in a playsuit, then she placed Megan in her stroller.

"I'll push it," Matt said, coming up behind her.

She was used to doing it herself. "No, that's okay."

"I don't mind."

She could see he wanted to do it, so she relented.

It was a funny feeling walking to the park with him. Never in a million years would she imagine her and Matt Valente together like this.

Married.

Parents.

Not lovers.

Once there, Matt looked like any proud father, pushing Megan on the swing, taking her down the slide, taking her on the small merry-go-round where he insisted Lana join them. A couple of times, she had to give herself a mental shake to stop believing this was real.

It was only real for him and Megan.

It wasn't real for them as a family.

A few yards along the small lake a man started tossing pieces of bread at the swans, who quickly began snapping it up. Suddenly Megan started to giggle.

Matt darted an amused glance at Lana. The man threw more bread and the swans ate it and Megan giggled louder. Her laughter was infectious and love rose in Lana's throat, not only for her little girl, but that she could share this moment with Matt.

It was a moment to treasure.

Suddenly Matt looked down at his daughter in his arms. "Oh God, she's gorgeous!" he said in awe, sending an odd tenderness through Lana.

"Yes, she is."

Their gazes touched for a brief moment before Megan began squirming in his arms and Matt turned away. "Come on," he said. "It's time to go."

Their morning was over.

Once back inside the house, Matt lifted Megan

out of the stroller and handed her to Lana without looking at her. "I'm going into the office. I have some work to catch up on. You and Megan will be fine here."

He left them to it and that smarted.

Clearly he had no idea she had her own workload to consider. She'd put in her resignation and now she had one week to tie up as many loose ends as she could. There was a ton of work to be done this weekend. Work she'd planned on doing whenever she got a spare moment.

Unlike Matt, who could just walk out the door and forget his obligations for a time.

She looked at Megan. "Well, pumpkin. It's just you and me again. Would you like the house tour?"

Megan stared at her.

"Right. The house tour it is," Lana said, refusing to let her irritation with Matt spoil the rest of her and Megan's day.

The one-level house was spacious and exuded elegance and style, encompassing every possible luxury. There were four bedrooms, one of which was Matt's, tempting her to peek inside but she decided not to.

There was a formal dining room she probably wouldn't use in their short married life, certain Matt would be careful about inviting anyone for dinner.

And she really loved the informal living room that allowed her to look out a wall of windows over a swimming pool and feature garden. She was especially pleased to see the pool was surrounded by the legally required child resistant fence.

It was a beautiful house, far different from the one she'd been raised in. Her parents' house had been moderate, but those four walls had shaken with yelling and abuse more often than not.

Shuddering, Lana put that to the side. This house was one she would be proud to own if her marriage had been a true one. As it was, she'd try to enjoy being here without letting herself get too attached to it.

Just as she wouldn't let herself get too attached to the Valentes.

For lunch, Ruth suggested Lana take Megan out on the patio in the sunshine. Megan played happily in the playpen they had set up beside the table, while Lana took the opportunity to unwind away from Matt's presence.

Half an hour later, Megan started getting cranky and Lana put her to bed. Thankfully she went straight to sleep.

Now it was work time for herself.

Quietly closing the connecting door between them, she kicked off her shoes and spread the paperwork out around her on the bed. No doubt Matt would want to use the study, and while she could, too, she'd be able to concentrate better in her own space.

Sunlight streamed through the window, making her sleepy. She continued to work until the warmth made her too tired to think. Perhaps she could take a quick power nap….

She shook herself awake. No, she needed to get this monthly report done. She couldn't let herself fall asleep. She needed this time while Megan was asleep or she'd have to stay up half the night working.

But that sunlight was so warm…so…

Something touched her shoulder and her eyes flew open to see Matt standing beside the bed. The sunlight had waned and shadows now darkened the room.

"Lana, it's almost dinnertime."

She sat up in a rush. "What? How?"

"Don't ask me questions I can't answer," he drawled.

She ignored that.

Good grief, had she really slept the afternoon away? "Where's Megan?"

"Ruth and I have been looking after her for the last couple of hours."

She ran her fingers through her hair. "Hours? I can't believe I didn't hear her crying."

"She was fine. I came home and she was playing happily in her crib. We've been in the living room getting to know each other. Then Ruth helped me bathe her and give her dinner. She'll be ready for bed soon."

Lana had the feeling that she was rapidly becoming "surplus to requirements" where her daughter was concerned.

"You've been working?" Matt asked abruptly, his gaze on the various papers and files.

She swung her legs over the edge of the bed and grimaced, more at herself than not. "I was *supposed* to be working, but I fell asleep before I got much of anything done."

His dark brows knitted together. "Why are you working on a weekend in the first place?"

Her lips tightened. Was it okay for him to work on a weekend and not her?

"I put my resignation in, remember? I've got a load of work to do before I leave."

"Surely they could get someone else to take over?"

"Eventually, but I don't like leaving them in the lurch." She pushed to her feet and smoothed her knit top down over her slacks. "At least after that sleep I'll be able to work late tonight."

"No."

She'd been about to step into her shoes, but the comment snapped her head up. "What did you say?"

"I said no. You've had a busy week. I don't want you working through the night."

Her growing anger cooled a little at his concern.

"And Megan needs a mother who's fit and healthy, not exhausted," he added, undoing the momentary good feeling she'd had toward him.

So this was about Megan again, not her. She didn't mind him being right about Megan needing a fit mother; he just wasn't right about *her*.

"You seem to have forgotten that *you* went into work today and *you're* Megan's father. Should I be questioning *your* fitness?"

His eyes reflected a glimmer of surprise; then he frowned. "How much work have you got?"

She glanced at the files on the bed. "A lot."

He remained quiet for a lengthy pause. "Okay, here's the deal. I'll look after Megan tomorrow if you take it easy tonight."

Her eyes widened. "*You'll* look after her?"

"I'll take her to my parents' place for a few hours, and then Ruth can help me when I get back. Deal?"

She thought about Matt sharing the responsibility for Megan's well-being. She'd been so used to doing everything herself that it took a second to rethink it.

All at once it hit her how much change this marriage would make to her life. When it had been just her and Megan, she'd been fully occupied with being responsible for every aspect of her daughter's life and juggling it with her own. Now she had no cooking, no cleaning, no food shopping, and nothing much to do each night at all. She certainly wouldn't have to sit down and work out the bills. In fact, she'd have plenty of time to spare.

And she'd have to learn to share her daughter. Coming to terms with that would take some time.

She looked up at Matt. "I'd appreciate all that, but I'll still need to work tonight to catch up." Their conversation at the breakfast table came to mind. "Unless you have other plans for us tonight?" As soon as the words left her mouth she felt herself blush. "I mean, we're not expected to go out or anything, are we?"

Derision entered his eyes. "No, we're not expected anywhere. I'll be going out myself after dinner anyway."

"Oh." Not wanting him to read her expression, she concentrated on putting on her shoes. "Then there should be no problem with me working tonight once she's down."

There was a moment's silence.

"Not one," he muttered, and left the room without waiting for her.

For a moment she sat back down on the bed, her heart constricting. Was he going to see another woman tonight? He'd said he wouldn't have any affairs for Megan's sake, but would he stick to that promise?

Could he?

Four

"Peekaboo!" Cesare said to the little girl sitting on his lap, and Megan giggled.

Matt watched his father in amusement. "You're such a pushover for a pretty face, Dad."

"How can I not be a pushover? She is so beautiful."

Matt felt himself swell with pride. He'd never been conscious of wanting his father's approval before, but it was a nice feeling knowing he had it now.

"He's a softie when it comes to his family, Matt," Isabel said, coming into the room with a small teddy bear in her hands.

"He's not the only, Mum," Matt said pointedly.

She smiled. "I'm allowed to spoil my grand-daughter."

Matt held up his hands. "Hey, don't let me stop you."

Isabel sat next to Cesare and waved the teddy bear in front of Megan's face. Megan immediately forgot the peekaboo game and reached for the stuffed animal. Matt laughed at the affronted look on his father's face.

Then Cesare turned to him, a sharpness in his eyes that had been there all along. "So the marriage is going well?"

Matt kept the smile on his face. "I've only been married two days, Dad."

Isabel tutted at her husband. "Give them time, Cesare."

Matt didn't set her straight. He hadn't told any of his family that the marriage was temporary, not even his parents. But they had to know he wasn't in love with Lana.

Thankfully Megan started to get a bit irritable just then, and Matt looked at his watch. "Speaking of time, Megan's due for her morning nap." He pushed to his feet, relieved to have something to do. "Here. Give her to me, Dad," he said, and scooped up his daughter.

Isabel stood, too. "Come on. I'll show you the spare room. We've put a crib in there for her."

Matt grinned wryly. "You haven't turned the room into a nursery, have you?"

His mother's lips twitched. "Not yet."

After that, Megan didn't wake up for a couple of hours, so it was mid-afternoon before he arrived back home.

Lana rushed out of the study when he opened the front door, taking Megan in her arms and fussing over her as if she'd been gone a week instead of a couple of hours.

"I've brought her back in original condition," he mocked, and wondered what it would be like if Lana fussed over *him*.

Don't go there.

"Is everything okay? No problems?" she asked, still frowning.

"Sorry to disappoint you. Not a one."

"Good." She suddenly had a smug look about her that set his antenna on high. "Because Ruth's gone to visit her sister in the hospital this afternoon and may not be back until late."

"So?" She obviously thought he couldn't handle his own daughter.

"Do you think you'll be able to look after Megan for the rest of the day?"

"Of course. We'll be fine."

"Oh." Her bubble burst. "Well, just call me if you need me."

Not on your Nellie, he mused, then noted the tired lines under her eyes. "How's the work going?"

"Moving along."

"You'd better get back to it, then."

"I'm here if you need me."

"We won't," he said, more snappish than he'd intended.

She handed Megan back, then headed for the study, but not before he saw her flinch. His jaw clenched. Why the hell was he feeling sorry for snapping at her? When all was said and done she'd had Megan to herself the last eleven months.

It was his turn now.

All at once the thought of her keeping Megan from him…of him possibly never knowing he had a daughter…never hearing his little girl giggle as he'd done with the swans yesterday…made his heart harden even more.

One thing was for sure. He wasn't going to rent out his old apartment now, after it had proven the perfect escape last night. He could always go out on the town, he supposed, but suddenly he didn't feel like it.

The rest of the afternoon was spent playing games with Megan on the living room floor, then letting her play with her toys while he sat down for a much-needed rest and a flick through the television channels with the remote to see what was showing.

The next minute her cry had him jumping to his feet. Quickly he scooped her up and checked her over, but she didn't appear to be hurt.

Maybe she was hungry? Yep, he could open a jar of baby food for her.

Only, it didn't soothe her.

Nothing did.

Lana appeared in the kitchen doorway. "Is everything okay in here?"

He looked up with a touch of relief. "I don't know. She won't stop crying and nothing I do will help."

Lana's brows drew together as she came forward, her gaze going over the little girl. "She's had a couple of big days. I think she's just overtired." She took the spoon out of his hand. "Come on, pumpkin. Let's eat this nice dinner, and then you can go to bed."

It sounded simple.

And it *was* simple when Lana did it, Matt mused, watching her in slight awe when half an hour later she finally put Megan down in her crib and the little girl shut her eyes and went to sleep.

"You've got a way with her," he murmured, stepping back to allow her to leave the bedroom.

She pulled the door closed, then tipped her face up to him. "Not always."

Their eyes met.

Neither of them blinked.

They were standing very close and the scent of Valente's Woman stirred his nostrils—and his groin. If it had been any other woman he'd pull her up against him and make passionate love to her.

But not this woman.

This woman and passion mixed only too well.

His pulse thudding with thick desire, he pivoted before he could do something he regretted. "I think I'll go take a shower."

A long, cold shower.

Lana's heart raced as she watched Matt stride toward his bedroom and close the door behind him. For a minute there she thought he'd been about to kiss her. It had almost been the office Christmas party all over again.

Except neither of them had been drinking.

They'd been standing too close.

And she'd been feeling grateful for him taking care of Megan today.

And both of them were probably drained from the events of the past week, that's all.

Yes, that's all it was.

It couldn't be anything else. Matt blamed her for keeping his daughter from him. He thought she'd stolen money from him. He'd hate himself in the morning if he made love to her.

And she'd hate herself, too.

She'd have to make sure they didn't get too close in the future, she decided, making her way to the kitchen, where she put the casserole Ruth had left for them in the oven. She'd do another hour of work before dinner.

She'd just sat down at the desk when her cell phone rang. It was her boss, Mr. Wainwright.

A couple of minutes later she flung the study door open with steam coming out of her ears.

She couldn't believe it.

She *didn't* believe it.

How could a man who took such pride in his own work not expect she'd take pride in her work too?

Giving one quick knock, she stormed into Matt's bedroom. "How dare you!" she hissed, keeping her voice low so as not to wake Megan next door.

He frowned at her. "How dare I what?"

"You rang Mr. Wainwright! He says I don't have to finish up my week. He's releasing me from my contract early."

"And you've come to tell me you're grateful?" he joked.

"I can't believe you did this." Her lip curled. "On second thought, I can. The high-handed Valentes do what they like, when they like, and damn everyone else."

His jaw set. "As far as I'm concerned, if you want something you go and get it."

She flashed him a look of disdain. "What did you offer him? A bit of business thrown his way? You scratch my back and I'll scratch yours? Is that the way it is, Matt?"

A muscle pulsated in his cheek. "That's business."

She glared at him.

Glared for all she was worth until…

Something powerful drew her gaze downward.

And her eyes hit the hard contours of his chest.

His broad, *bare* chest.

All at once she realized he'd been in the middle of getting dressed and that his hand was still at the opening of his trousers. Her eyes flew back up to his face.

Zip.

He finished the job, sending the sound rushing through her veins, the blood rushing to her cheeks, but it was his knowing look that helped pull her together. He knew his half-dressed state had taken her off-guard. Knew he had made her knees go soft.

The arrogant devil!

She angrily gathered her thoughts. "My career is *none* of your business. And I mean that quite literally."

"I want you home with Megan."

She gasped, then bristled with indignation, forgetting all about his bare chest and the back scratching and the sexy sound of a zipper sliding up.

"You're not one of those men who don't want their wife to work at all, are you? Please tell me you don't want me pregnant and barefoot in the kitchen?"

His eyelids flickered and darkened. "Of course not. I meant this week, that's all. You said yourself she would find everything new and strange. I was just trying to make sure you spend some time with Megan until she gets used to it."

He was being caring of Megan? She believed that. But did he have to tread all over *her* to do it?

She set her chin in a stubborn line. "You could have asked me that yourself. But I suppose that's not worth your time. I'm still working three days a week with you. So don't try and renege on the deal, Matt."

"I don't renege on deals."

She stared at him. He seemed to have no idea he'd done anything wrong. Or more than likely he just couldn't acknowledge any wrongdoing.

"Don't interfere in my career again." She turned to leave the room.

"Lana?"

She stopped but didn't look back.

"Don't forget I'm your boss now. Your career both now and in the future is in my hands."

Lana swallowed. His tone was steel covered in velvet.

This time she did turn around. "Don't *you* forget something, Matt. I'm a Valente now. I can play dirty, too."

Then she turned on her heel and went back to the study, her mind spinning from the sheer arrogance of her new husband. If he thought he'd browbeat her, then he had another thing coming. She might no longer have a job to go to at Wainwright's, but she had a free day tomorrow before starting at Valente's. She would work her fingers to the bone to finish up as much as possible. It was a matter of pride, not to mention a small victory over Matt's attempt at controlling her.

Five minutes later she heard the front door close and Matt's car drive away. Evidently she'd be eating dinner alone tonight.

She told herself she was glad about that. She didn't want to break bread with a man who demanded she do what he wanted. A man who rode roughshod over everyone, and too bad for them if they didn't like it.

Yet she felt a chill. Memories of her father leaving the house for a night out on the town colored her thoughts. Where was Matt going? Who was he meeting? Would he come home smelling of alcohol? Of another woman? Dear Lord, she didn't think she could do this for a whole year.

At eleven she heard him return, heard his footsteps stop outside the study door, then she let out a slow breath as they continued on their way. That was exactly how she wanted it to stay, she told herself. She wanted to be just a small pause in his life until it was time for him to move on.

Five

Matt's face was shuttered when he walked into the sunroom the next morning, but Lana knew she flushed. She didn't want to think about her comment last night in his room on scratching backs, or the sound of a zipper going up or running her palms over his muscular chest, yet she couldn't seem to help herself.

She knew he saw it, too, and something reciprocal flashed in his brown eyes before he turned to focus on Megan.

He swung his gaze back to Lana.

"What do you plan for today?" he asked, surprising her with the question.

"Just a quiet day at home with Megan." No need

to tell him she planned on working until she'd finished her commitments to Wainwright's.

He stared for a moment. "Have a good day."

"I will."

He left not long after, and Lana roped in Ruth's help this one time to keep an eye on Megan, so by mid-afternoon she was able to take the paperwork over to Mr. Wainwright.

She felt such a sense of accomplishment as she handed over the files, but that soon disappeared on the way out when one of the female staff made a smart comment about her being lucky enough to marry Matt Valente.

Lana held her head high and ignored her. She wasn't feeling terribly lucky right now.

Far from it.

Arriving back at the house, she was disconcerted to see Matt's car in the driveway. She'd meant to ask Ruth not to say anything about today, but had forgotten in her rush to get out of the house.

Not that it really mattered if Matt knew what she'd been doing all day. Serve him right if he got a guilt attack from it. She pulled a face. Who was she kidding? Matt Valente didn't know the meaning of guilt.

She found him sitting on the leather sofa bouncing Megan on his lap, the pair of them laughing together. Her heart ached a little to join in the fun.

She stepped into the room. "You're home early."

His head turned to face her, the animation dying on his face. "I wanted to see Megan."

She felt as though she was intruding in something special.

As she was.

"Of course," she murmured, ready to leave them to it.

"Ruth said you'd gone to Wainwright's."

His words spun her back to face him. She shot him a defiant look. "Yes, I did. And I finished it all, despite your attempts to make me do otherwise."

"So I believe." A light of admiration entered his eyes. "Good for you."

His reply stunned her.

Then she quickly turned away, murmuring that she'd go change. She was confused and heartened in the same instant. Just when she wanted to hate him, he did or said something to make her change her mind.

Not that the feeling lasted long, she decided after dinner when he mentioned he was going out again, sluicing any softening toward him right down the drain.

Nonetheless, the next morning she was secretly glad of his company when they stepped out on the eighth floor of the House of Valente together. She wasn't actually nervous about it all, more uneasy. The real thief could still be here and could be watching her.

His middle-aged personal assistant greeted her warmly. "Lana, it's so nice to have you back."

"Thank you, Irene," she said, feeling cheered by the reception. She'd always enjoyed working here. Until her awareness of Matt had grown out of control.

Her eyes fell on Matt's office, and out of nowhere memories of the Christmas party came flooding back. She felt her cheeks begin to heat up, but thankfully the others didn't appear to notice.

Irene handed Matt a pile of messages. "You're late for your first appointment," she scolded in motherly fashion.

"I know, Irene, but we have a child who comes first now. Everyone else can wait." He turned to Lana, his eyes distant. "Irene will show you to your office." He turned and walked into his office and shut the door, leaving behind an awkward moment.

Typical.

Irene smiled at Lana. "New fathers are always cranky," she mused.

Lana forced a smile but said nothing. What could she say anyway? The press might have put a spin on their marriage being a love match, but it wouldn't take long before word got around the office once they saw her and Matt together. Loving they were *not*. Hopefully everyone would think they were just being private.

"Which office has he put me in, Irene?"

"The end one."

Lana got a sinking feeling in her stomach. "That's a single office, isn't it?"

"Yes, that's right. I'll show you. Then I'll take you around to meet the staff. There are some new faces."

Lana went with her, embarrassment and anger warring beneath the surface. Matt was certainly making sure she started off on the wrong foot with her co-workers.

Of course that wasn't hard to do with Evan Rogers, one of the other accountants, whom she'd worked with before. He was so swarmy that if she suspected anyone of stealing money, it was him.

"Lana, how lovely to see you back," he gushed at her in front of the others. "And you've got the end office now, too. How…fortunate."

Lana kept the smile on her face and ignored his dig. She actually hoped it *was* Evan who'd stolen the money. No one else deserved to go to jail like he did, she mused, determining that Evan's accounts would be a great place to start investigating. He might not have been stupid enough to take money that led straight back to him, but perhaps he'd made a minor mistake somewhere…anywhere….

After that she managed to focus as she got reacquainted with the financial aspects that concerned her job, and by late morning she felt right at home. The work was so familiar she could do it with her eyes shut, though she knew that therein lay the danger. She had to keep her eyes open for any sign of fraud. Not just by Evan but by anyone else. She would bide her time; it might look strange if she started looking up old accounts straightaway. She would do that once she felt able to without suspicion.

She didn't see Matt until he came to get her to go home.

"How was your first day back with us?" he said, leaning against the doorjamb.

He looked gorgeous and noticing it made her angry with herself. And damn, but she was still angry with him anyway.

Her mouth tightened. "You shouldn't have given me this office."

His eyes narrowed. "Why?"

"I didn't have one by myself before. I shared with three others."

"You weren't my wife before."

"Exactly. You shouldn't show me any favoritism." She only just refrained from saying that perhaps he should share that particular point with the others instead of ignoring her as he had all day, but then it sounded as though she actually *wanted* him to spend time with her.

"Maybe I should put you in my office with me," he quipped, his lips curving sensually.

Her heart jumped in her throat. "I hope you're kidding."

All at once his smile disappeared and his face shuttered up. "Obviously," he muttered, straightening. "Are you ready to leave?"

"Give me a moment to finalize something and I'll be with you."

"I'll go talk to Irene until you're ready."

She nodded, glad for him to take his presence out of her sight. If only he could take the memories of being in his office with him. Maybe coming back here wasn't a good idea after all.

No, she had to prove to Matt that the mother of his child wasn't a thief. It was important to her.

She said nothing more in the car, but she was glad when they arrived home and she got to kiss and cuddle Megan. She missed her little girl when she went to work, though she knew she'd miss her work if she stayed home all day, too. She had the best of both worlds right now. It was one of the positive things about this situation.

Matt insisted on feeding Megan again that night, and with Ruth around the atmosphere was quite jovial.

Then he went to take a phone call and Lana put Megan in the bath, laughing at her little girl splashing the water with her toy duck.

Megan thought her mother laughing was funny and she splashed the water with her duck again, only this time the water splashed on Lana's knit top.

"Megan! Look what you've done to Mummy," Lana said, chuckling, not minding in the least getting wet.

Splash.

"Ooh, you little devil," she said, and gently splashed the water so that it slapped against her daughter's belly.

Megan giggled, then splashed the water again. Lana returned the favor.

"You two look like you're having fun."

Lana's head swung to the doorway. The smile froze on her lips. "Er...she likes her bath time."

"You look like you do, too." His eyes dropped to her wet top, his pupils dilating before he lifted his gaze back to her face. "Keep playing. I like watching."

Lana's breath hitched. She dared not look down, but she was sure her nipples were beaded and easily seen, and after that glance of his she almost expected to see steam come off her clothes.

She swallowed. "No, she's finished her bath. It's time for bed."

Lana took the toy duck out of Megan's hands and went to pick her up, but before she could the little girl made an outraged sound and hit the water with her fist, then stuck her bottom lip out in an angry pout.

Something in her expression looked so much like Matt at that moment, Lana could only exclaim, "Lord, she's the image of *you*."

He looked startled. "Actually I was just thinking how much she was like you."

It was her turn to be surprised. She didn't think her daughter had any of her features and she was pleased.

But a pout?

"I don't pout," she said with a rueful grin.

The corners of his mouth quirked upward. "Well, I certainly don't."

They stared at each other, and Lana felt her smile slip. He turned and left the room.

Swiftly she turned back to Megan and concentrated on getting her ready for bed. And when she sat down to dinner, it was alone. Matt had already gone out.

At work the next day Lana was placing some reports on Irene's desk when Cesare called to her from inside Matt's office. She frowned as she stepped up to the doorway.

"Come in, Lana." He got to his feet and came to give her a kiss on the cheek, making her feel like one of the family. "Welcome back, *cara.*"

She wasn't used to such affection. Her parents had been too full of hatred for each other to have anything left over for friendliness.

"Thank you, Cesare." She didn't look at Matt, nor did she let her thoughts show on her face.

Cesare led her to one of the chairs. "Sit down here." He waited until she did, then went back to his own seat. "I was just telling Matt that his mother and I have ballet tickets at the Opera House for Friday night."

Lana eased into a smile. Now, *this* was a nice safe subject. "How lovely."

"Do you like the ballet, Lana?"

"Love it," she said with enthusiasm. She'd only ever been once, but she—

"Then you and Matt can go in our place."

She darted a look at Matt, then back at her

father-in-law. "I…we couldn't possibly take your tickets, Cesare."

"You would be doing us a favor, Lana. Both Izzie and I have a full day on Friday and we'll be just too tired to go out that night, as well. And the friends who gave us the tickets would be insulted if we didn't use them."

"But—"

"Thanks, Dad." Matt cut across her. "We'll be happy to take them off your hands."

Lana's eyes snapped back to Matt, but her glare bounced off him.

"Good. Your mother and I will look after Megan."

Lana tensed as she turned to Cesare. "Won't she be too much for you both after such a long day?"

"She's our granddaughter. She'll never be too much."

Her heart did a roll. "That's sweet of you, Cesare, but—"

"No problem, Dad." Matt cut across her again. "That'll work out just fine. We'll be able to enjoy ourselves knowing Megan is being looked after so well."

Cesare nodded with satisfaction. "Good. Your mother said to say that you should leave Megan with us for the night. That way you won't have to worry about waking her up and taking her home again. It would only unsettle her." With that bombshell, the older man stood up. "I must get back home now. I just dropped by to see how things were going here."

"Business is booming, as you well know," Matt teased.

Cesare kissed her cheek, and Lana barely waited for him to close the door behind him to get her words out. "Damn you, Matt. You shouldn't have accepted."

"I didn't have much of a choice. I don't want him to overdo things by going to too many events. And he will accept the invitation himself if we don't go."

"Wouldn't Nick or Alex like the tickets? I'm sure Sasha or Olivia would jump at the chance of going to the ballet."

"They've already made plans they can't break."

Her lip curled. "Do you know that for a fact, or are you just guessing?"

He nodded at the telephone. "Call them and see. My brothers are attending a charity dinner on Friday. I'd already gotten out of that one, but I didn't expect this."

Okay, so she could accept that. "He's matchmaking, you know."

"You may not have noticed but we're already married," he mocked.

"He's still matchmaking."

All at once his eyes closed in on her. "*Now* I see where this is coming from. You're worried about being alone in the house with me all night." He paused. "You have nothing to worry about, Lana."

"That's obvious," she said before she could stop herself.

He pinned her with a stare. "What does that mean?"

She realized she had to tread carefully. She didn't want him thinking she cared. "Just that you've been spending a lot of time out each night."

His look sharpened. "Do you have a problem with that?"

She raised one slim shoulder. "Not at all. It was just an observation."

Seconds crawled by.

"Do you think I'm with another woman?"

"Are you?" she challenged, despite not being sure she was ready to hear this.

A pulse beat in his lean cheek. "Perhaps I might just be trying to stick to the deal we made about separate lives. It doesn't necessarily mean I'm out with other women."

Silly relief raced through her veins but she quickly held it at bay. Was he just telling her what he wanted her to know? "I'm glad to hear it. For Megan's sake, of course."

"Of course." His eyes held hers, then flicked over her tailored business suit. "Do you have anything to wear Friday night? If not, get yourself something and charge it to me. As a matter of fact, you'll need a new wardrobe anyway."

Her back went rigid. "I don't need any clothes and I definitely don't need your money. I can afford to buy myself something if I need it."

"I don't want my wife walking around in department store clothes."

Her pride felt bruised. Not all her clothes were

off the rack. This suit certainly wasn't. She liked nice clothes as much as the next woman and sometimes she found real bargains.

She angled her chin at him. "There's nothing wrong with department store clothes."

"I didn't say there was. I just don't want my wife walking around in them." She went to speak and he held up his hand. "Do you really want to be the only one wearing cotton instead of silk?"

"Do you really think I care?"

He scrutinized her response, brows drawn together. "No, I don't think you do."

Her stomach fluttered.

"You're lucky, Lana. You've got style. You could wear cotton and make it look like silk anyway."

She gave the softest of gasps, then held her breath, knowing she had to keep this on a professional level.

"Then it won't matter if I wear department store clothes, will it?" Not waiting for an answer, she quickly stood up.

There was a moment's pause before he muttered throatily, "Wear what you want."

"I will." Suppressing a shiver of trepidation, she walked to the door and didn't stop until she reached her office, putting some distance between them.

Had she misheard that low pitch to Matt's voice back there?

Or had it been wishful thinking on her part?

She prayed *not*.

For either thing.

* * *

"Anything good on television tonight?" Matt asked, p'.opping down on the living room sofa later that day.

Lana had been watching the end of a current affairs program and now she looked up in shock. "You're staying in?"

"You would prefer me to go out?" he drawled.

"No." She looked back at the television. "No, it will be nice to have some company," she admitted, not realizing until this moment how lonely she'd felt each evening.

And that didn't make sense. She'd always enjoyed her own company, so why was she feeling lonely when nothing really had changed?

"What's on tonight?" Matt asked, interrupting her thoughts.

"Um...I was going to watch a movie after this."

"A chick flick?" he said with something like disgust.

She had to smile. "No, not a chick flick. It's a spy film."

His gaze rested on her lips a moment; then he turned to the television. "Death and mayhem. That's more like it."

Lana swallowed hard, her mind racing. That low pitch had been in his voice again, the way it had today in his office. Oh, she didn't think he was planning any type of seduction. She had no doubt he was as determined to keep their marriage as platonic as she was.

So why was her trepidation increasing? More importantly, why was her heart thudding with growing excitement? Hadn't she learned her lesson at all?

The tension in her shoulders relaxed. Her comment about him going out every night must have found its mark.

Yes, that's all it was.

A few minutes later the movie began and for a little while she even managed to forget about Matt's presence, until there was a break and he started talking about a review he'd read some time ago.

Trying to appear nonchalant, Lana responded but she wasn't actually listening. Another part of her was watching his velvet brown eyes, down to those firm lips, over the shadow of his jaw darkened by the end of day, to the bob of his Adam's apple cushioned by that strong throat.

All of him.

Her gaze traveled back up to his eyes, and she swallowed hard at the awareness in them.

He knew.

Thankfully the movie came back on and she dragged her gaze away until the next break when she decided she couldn't sit still any longer.

"Would you like some coffee?" she asked, jumping to her feet. "And some cake. Ruth did some baking today."

"That sounds good." He unfurled from his chair and stood up, too. "I'll go check on Megan while you do that."

They went their separate ways and in the kitchen Lana came up for air. Heavens, she felt like such a novice. Her face was giving away her thoughts as if she were handing them to Matt on a platter.

Oh, look, Matt. I'm hot for you tonight. I need you to make love to me. Come and take me.

She smiled grimly. Maybe someone would come and take her—away. And they should lock her up until she had her head examined for wanting a man who would never commit to any woman.

Ten minutes later they were eating cake and drinking coffee, and she was feeling very proud of herself for focusing back on the movie instead of on Matt.

"You've dropped some cream on you," he muttered.

The spoon stopped halfway to her mouth. "I did? Where?"

"There."

She looked down to her cleavage, where a blob of cream had fallen. She could feel her cheeks redden. Quickly she scooped it up and licked it off her finger.

"You've left some." He leaned forward with his napkin. "Here. Use this."

She waved it aside. "That's okay. I've got a napkin around here somewhere."

"Use this," he all but growled, and she looked up and saw a hot flash in his eyes that said he'd lick the cream off himself if she didn't hurry up and do it.

Her pulse skittered as if it were on an icy road.

Hastily she found her napkin. "Look, I've found it," she exclaimed, holding it up. She wiped the spot, then gave an awkward smile. "This cake is so nice, isn't it?"

A nerve pulsed near his temple. "Very nice."

Flushing, she turned back to the television. The air throbbed with painful sensuality between them, but somehow she got through to the end of the movie.

As soon as it ended, a starter pistol went off in her mind, but she pretended to yawn oh so casually. "I guess I'd better go to bed," she said, slowly pushing to her feet when all she wanted to do was run to the door.

"Me, too." He flicked the remote and turned off the television. "I'll just make sure everything's locked up first."

Her gaze slid to him. "Well, good night. See you in the morning."

There. That was a warning.

Do not disturb.

A moment crept by, then, "See you tomorrow."

There was a clipped sound to his voice and she breathed a sigh of relief as she hurried to her room to take a shower. Not that she expected Matt would come after her. The danger had been back there in the living room.

Half an hour later she lay in bed wide-awake. She couldn't settle. Her room felt claustrophobic and her pulse was still jumpy from being in Matt's company all evening. She needed to get up and move around, do anything but lie here and think of things best left alone.

She didn't bother putting her bathrobe on over her short, satiny chemise; she figured Matt would have gone to bed.

All was quiet as she opened her door and padded along the plush carpet to the living room, moonlight guiding the way. She could see the lights from the swimming pool casting shadows ahead and—

"What are you doing?"

She gasped and whirled around. Matt had come up behind her in the doorway. "Oh, you frightened me!"

There was a tiny pause. "You're supposed to be in bed," he said, making it sound as if she'd gone back on her word.

"Er…I couldn't sleep." She noticed he was still in the same clothes. "You're supposed to be in bed, too," she said, almost accusingly.

"I'm on my way there now."

It sounded like an invitation.

She moistened her mouth. "Well, I must go." She went to hurry past him. She'd been unwise to come out here in her night wear.

He caught her by the arm. "Next time put on a robe," he rasped, holding her still, his touch sending little zings of full awareness through her bare skin.

He let her go.

She hurried to her room and leaned back against

the door, her heart thudding beneath her breast. Oh Lord. The danger wasn't so much back there in the living room.

The danger was in herself.

Six

The next day Lana decided it was time to do some investigating. Now that she was part of the furniture, she could blend in more easily and be a bit more adventurous in her search for the truth.

But she waited until Matt came into her office to take her home before saying anything. "I'm going to stay back here for a couple of hours tonight."

He sent her an exasperated look. "It's a waste of time if you ask me."

"I'm not asking you, Matt." She was getting nowhere with clearing her name. She had to do something. "If you could put Megan to bed, I'd appreciate it." This once she would have to miss seeing her daughter. Heck, the main reasons she was doing this was for Megan.

He scowled. "What time will you be home?"

"I don't know. Eight, perhaps. I'll catch a taxi."

"I don't like it."

"Really."

"I'll come back and get you at seven. Ruth can look after Megan."

"But—"

"No buts. I'll be here at seven."

She took one look at his hard features and knew he wasn't going to budge. "Okay, but not before seven. I want a chance to actually get some work done." She didn't mention anything else out loud, in case the walls had ears.

Matt turned and left, and Lana took a deep breath. Right. Now she could concentrate without his skepticism in her face.

An hour later the whole floor was quiet, and after doing a check that everyone had gone, she was focusing intensely on the reports on her computer screen when Evan popped his head around the door.

"What are you doing here so late?" he asked, making her jump.

"Oh, Evan! You frightened me." She caught her breath. "Anyway, I could ask you the same question."

"I had to go see someone on the next floor." He stepped into the office. "Can I help you with any-thing?"

Inside she was panicking, but outside she

casually clicked on her screen saver, then leaned back on her chair. "Not, not really. I'm just catching up."

He frowned. "You were always on top of things before."

"These days I'm a married woman with a child."

He looked at her strangely, then he smiled a false smile. "Let me know if you need any help."

"I will."

Like hell.

"I'm going home now. Good night, Lana."

"Good night."

He left, but she didn't move for long moments. It wasn't until she heard the whisper of the elevator door closing that she let herself relax. Then she unlocked her computer screen and started searching the reports again.

At seven, Matt returned. "Find anything?" he said from the doorway.

"No." She hated to admit it.

"I told you."

She couldn't let herself be beaten. "I'm close to finding something. I can feel it."

He eyes said he didn't believe it. "Grab your things and I'll take you home."

His attitude shouldn't have disappointed her, but it did. She tidied her desk and picked up her handbag. "By the way," she said on the way to the elevator. "I've decided to work tomorrow. Ruth won't mind looking after Megan for the day, too."

He raised a brow, his eyes hardening. "Don't you think this is going too far?"

"No."

He shrugged. "Your choice."

"Yes, it is."

"Can you send this out by courier please, Irene?" Lana said, holding out some paperwork.

Irene picked up her ringing telephone, but nodded at one of the trays on her desk. "Just put it in that pile so Matt can check it first."

Lana frowned as the other woman turned away to deal with the person on the other end of the line. Her heart sank. Was this procedure something new? Or was this just for *her*?

She waited for Irene to finish her call.

"Does Matt check everyone's work now?" she asked as casually as she could.

Irene bit her lip. "Oh dear. Lana, he's just looking out for you. I told him he was being overprotective, but I guess it comes with being married now."

How she managed to keep a straight face right then, Lana didn't know. Here she was, working hard to clear her name, and all he cared about was keeping an eye on her in case she stole his precious money. Oh, how she wished she could come clean about Dan buying the apartment. She'd love to see the shock on Matt's face.

She grimaced inwardly. Unfortunately, then he'd be asking her where the fifty thousand dollars went.

And when she couldn't tell him—she was innocent, after all—he'd start investigating her background more than he'd evidently done already. And then Dan's private life would be at risk of being leaked to the newspapers.

No, she couldn't let that happen.

"You may be right, Irene," she said, and went back to her office, running into Evan along the way. The man had a knowing look in his eyes that set her blood boiling again. For Irene to know that Matt was checking her work was totally humiliating. But for Evan to know, and possibly the others—it made her want to sink right through the floor.

Unable to sit still a moment more, she strode back down the corridor. Irene was nowhere to be seen, but she wouldn't have cared anyway. This was between her and her husband.

Through the open door, she could see the man in question sitting at his desk. Without pause she stepped inside his office and shut the door behind her.

He looked up as she approached the desk.

"Damn you, Matt."

He put down his pen and leaned back in his leather chair, looking very much the employer. "I'm sure you're going to tell me what the problem is."

She hated his complacency. "This is the second time this week you've gone over my head."

"And this is the second time you've stormed into a room uninvited."

A picture of her storming into his bedroom came to mind, but she shook it off. He was just trying to knock her off balance because he knew he was in the wrong here.

"You've been checking all my work. You've embarrassed me greatly, Matt."

"As opposed to being embarrassed if one of the others found you stealing money?" he derided.

She drew a sharp breath. "I *didn't* steal anything."

"Prove it."

"I will when I get a chance, but you're undermining me. If the real thief thinks you're checking my work, then he might suspect we know the money is missing. He might realize that you're blaming me. And then he'd have to know I'm trying to prove my innocence."

Matt got to his feet and came around the desk. "How do you know it's a he?"

She was taken aback. Was he actually beginning to believe her?

She lifted her shoulders. "I *don't* know. It may not be a man. I was just assuming it might be."

He stopped right in front of her. "Don't assume anything, Lana. It could get you into trouble."

She frowned. "What's that supposed to mean?"

"Assuming can be dangerous." A purposeful gleam appeared in his eyes, his tone silky. "Like last night for instance. When I saw you in that short nightgown I could have assumed you wanted me to make love to you."

She caught her breath. "I wasn't…I didn't…"

"Didn't you?"

"No! I can't believe you thought—"

He fastened his mouth on hers and for a stunned second everything held still. Then his firm lips began to move. Her heart kick-started again just as his tongue slipped inside and took command.

Her legs buckled at the intimacy. She wanted to pull away, not to let him have such control over her, but the incomparable richness of his tongue on hers was a lure she couldn't resist.

He wrenched his mouth away.

And suddenly it was over.

He let her go.

"Next time you storm into my office," he growled, "*this* is what you'll get."

She was at a loss for words.

Lost for want of him.

His eyes burned into her. "And heaven help you if you ever storm into my bedroom again like you did Sunday night."

Panic stirred in her chest, but she somehow subdued it.

She pulled her shoulders back. "For the record I did not go out in my nightgown to seduce you," she said icily. "And for the record I did not steal any money."

She spun on her heel and left him to it, vaguely aware of her brother-in-law Nick coming out of the elevator and saying hello, as she muttered a reply and swept past him to her office. Right now she wasn't feeling too kindly to any Valente.

Her hands were shaking by the time she got back to her desk. Oh God. That kiss had shot down all her hard-earned defenses. And now, somehow, she had to scramble to put them up again.

"Now, that's one pretty pissed off lady," Nick drawled, entering Matt's office.

Matt schooled his features and returned to his chair, silently cursing himself. "Mind your own business, Nick."

"Hmm. Touchy, are we?"

"No." He watched Nick park himself on the chair opposite. Damn him. Brothers could be such a pain at times, and *his* brothers in particular. They always thought they were right.

Nick's mouth quirked. "You know, Matt. I haven't told you this before but I find something really funny."

Okay, he'd bite.

"What?"

"I find it hilarious that after Alex and I warned you about Dad's plan to make you marry, you ended up doing it to yourself."

"Shut up, big brother."

It took a moment for the amusement to leave Nick's face. His eyes sharpened as he seemed to realize this was more than serious. "What's the problem?"

Matt winced. Okay, so his brothers liked to tease,

but they were always concerned for his welfare. "Sorry. It's not a good time to be discussing my personal life right now."

"So things really aren't going well between you and Lana?"

"Let's say they could be better."

Nick considered that. "Sasha and I had some rough patches, too. Not in the bedroom, mind you. We always seem to be communicable on that level." He looked at Matt speculatively. "Oh, hell. You two haven't slept together, have you?"

Matt's mouth twisted. "We did once. It's how Megan came to be here."

Nick waved a dismissive hand. "I mean since you've been married."

"No."

"Then there's your problem."

He shook his head. "We've got more problems than sex, Nick."

"Such as? You've got a beautiful wife and daughter. A great house, a good job, terrific brothers— well, at least one," he joked.

Matt ignored the last bit.

He looked sourly at his brother. "Don't you have an office of your own to go to?"

Nick gave a quiet chuckle. "No wonder Lana can't put up with you. You're a grouch."

"And you've outstayed your welcome," Matt pointed out, grateful for his concern but equally grateful he was letting the subject drop.

"Okay, I'll leave. I only came to give you some good news. Valente's Woman is a finalist in the Fragrance of the Year Award."

Matt felt a rush of pleasure. "That's terrific. Dad will be so proud."

"You bet. Alex asked Dad to come down to the office. We'll open a bottle of bubbly." Nick pushed to his feet and headed for the door. "See you in about fifteen minutes?"

"Fine."

Nick stopped briefly. "By the way, Matt. That's a nice shade of lipstick you're wearing."

Matt smiled grimly at the parting shot even as thoughts of Lana returned.

Hell.

If he wasn't careful he'd be making love to her again and then they'd be right back where they started. And if that happened, for all her talk to the contrary, she might even want to make this marriage permanent.

Not a chance.

He might want her physically more than he'd ever wanted any woman, but that didn't mean he was ready to be tied down. This marriage was only temporary, and if she tried to make it permanent, then she was in for a shock.

No way.

Getting up from his chair he went into the bathroom. Sure enough, he had a smear of Lana's peach-tinted lipstick on his top lip.

And the soft honeyed taste of her in his mouth.

* * *

Lana was relieved when Matt went out that evening after dinner. There'd been a hint of danger in his eyes ever since this afternoon. That kiss had shaken her, and it seemed it had shaken him, too. They were both in deep trouble.

Together they were an explosive combination. If she wasn't careful there'd be nothing left but to pick up the pieces. She'd done that once before. She wasn't sure she could do it again.

So she wasn't sure why she went out the next day and bought herself a new dress for the ballet that evening. It wasn't just to cheer herself up. Nor was it because her money worries were nonexistent right now and she could afford silk instead of cotton.

Could it be that she *wanted* Matt to be proud of being seen with her? Okay, it was a very feminine reaction. She could admit that.

And so was defiance, she thought, somewhat smugly as she stepped into the living room that evening and saw Matt standing at the windows with Megan in his arms, looking out at the swimming pool.

He turned around when he heard her.

And that dangerous gleam stirred.

"Is that a new dress?"

She smoothed the front of the peacock-blue material over her stomach in a nervous gesture. "Yes."

"Did you charge it to me?"

That brought her chin up. "No."

His eyes swept over her, trickling down her form

like a soft powder. "You look lovely," he said, his voice a touch husky.

Her throat went dry. She wasn't used to such compliments from Matt. She feared she could get used to it.

"Thank you." She moistened her mouth, wanting to say how nice he looked himself, but that would have been an understatement. In his dark suit and white shirt, he was sex appeal personified, his sophistication imprinted on him like a birthmark.

The Valente birthmark.

Thankfully Megan babbled something, and not for the first time Lana was grateful for her daughter's presence.

They drove to Cesare and Isabel's apartment and dropped Megan off for the night, the older couple delighted to have their grandchild and neither looking the least bit exhausted.

"Your father seems to have weathered his day well," Lana said pointedly, once they were in the car and heading toward the city center.

"Don't let him fool you. He's good at hiding things."

Cesare wasn't the only one, Lana pondered, stealing a look at Matt's profile, then turning away when he caught her gaze. He looked so handsome he quite took her breath away.

In what seemed like moments, they were parking the car in the Opera House car park. He cupped her elbow as they walked to the elevator that would take them up to the concourse area, but she broke contact with him when they stepped around a crowd of people chatting.

"We might run into some people I know," he said in a clipped tone, cupping her elbow again. "So do you think you could look like you actually want to be with me?"

She tried to ignore the tingle of his touch. "You don't have to put on a show tonight, Matt. Everyone must have figured out by now why you married me."

"I don't give a damn what everyone thinks they know, but I do have some pride. You're a beautiful woman and they would expect that we're having a physical relationship."

"Then they'd be wrong," she said, but her mind was on his comment.

He thought her beautiful.

Just as quickly another thought replaced it.

He also thought her a thief.

They went straight to their seats. As the dance started, she got caught up in the stirring power of the ballet. The superb music accompanying the emotional tale wowed her until she forgot all about her problems and Matt beside her.

Until intermission arrived. The curtain lowered and she felt his eyes upon her.

"You're enjoying yourself?"

It was silly to feel a bit self-conscious. "Yes, very much."

"Good. My father will be happy."

She was glad she could make *someone* happy.

She stood up. "I think I'll go find the ladies' room."

He got to his feet, too. "I'll meet you in the bar."

They parted ways not long after and once she'd finished in the ladies room, she was walking along the corridor to the bar when she saw a wallet on the floor.

Automatically she picked it up and gasped when she saw the wad of hundred-dollar bills inside. The name "Arthur Taran" was on the driver's license. She was about to go hand it into management when she caught sight of one of the staff. She gave it to her instead and the woman promised she'd find the owner.

Lana soon forgot about it on reaching the bar and finding Matt talking with a debonair young couple around his own age. He handed her a drink of wine and introduced them as Justin and Sara.

"So you're Lana," Sara said warmly. "I saw your wedding picture in the paper and thought you looked beautiful, but it didn't do you nearly enough justice."

Lana immediately liked the other woman. "And I was having a bad day, too," she said with a wry smile.

They all laughed, including Matt, whose smile made her heart skip a beat, even with that slight hardness in the back of those eyes.

Sara turned to Matt. "Matt, she's not only beautiful but has a sense of humor. And I bet she's a really nice person."

"Would I have married anyone who wasn't?" Matt drawled.

"If she was beautiful, yes!" Justin joked, then winked at Lana. "I went to school with him."

Lana smiled. "You clearly know him well."

Sara laughed, then, "Oh, I'm so glad we ran into each other."

A short time later it was time to return to their seats.

"Let's come back here and have a drink afterward," Sara suggested. "We don't have to rush back home tonight. Justin's parents are looking after our little boy."

"Sounds good," Matt said, drawing a glance from Lana, but his face gave nothing away.

On the way back to their seats he didn't clarify whether she wanted to have a drink afterward with his friends. Not that she minded spending time with them. It was preferable to going home and knowing it was only her and Matt alone in the house.

Just the two of them.

She winced inwardly. There was nothing to worry about. She and Matt would have that drink, then go home and go to their separate rooms, just as they did every night.

And just because Matt kissed her in the office yesterday, and just because now there was an increasing awareness between them, didn't mean a thing. She would concentrate on enjoying the ballet. And then she'd enjoy his friends.

And that would be that.

The curtain lifted and the performance continued, and Lana became absorbed in the movement once again.

After the ballet had finished to much-deserved applause, they met up with Sara and Justin in the bar, where the other couple had found a secluded table near a window that gave an amazing night view of Sydney Harbour.

"Do you enjoy the ballet, Lana?" Sara asked, once everyone was seated. "It's ages since I've been."

"I haven't been to the ballet since I was twelve," Lana admitted. "My mother brought me as a treat for my birthday." She sighed. "She's gone now."

Sara reached out and squeezed her arm. "I'm sure it's a memory you treasure."

Lana warmed to her even more.

"Here she is, Mr. Taran. This is the lady who found your wallet."

Lana looked up to see the staff member to whom she'd given the lost wallet, and an older gentleman standing by their table.

He pumped Lana's hand. "My dear, thank you so much for returning my wallet."

Lana smiled. "It was my pleasure, Mr. Taran."

"I'd like to give you a reward."

She waved that aside. "No, but thank you for offering."

"No, thank *you*." His smile encompassed the others then he walked away.

"See, I told you she was nice," Sara said, but

Lana was aware of Matt watching her with an odd look in his eyes.

She ignored him and actually began to relax and enjoy herself as she talked about kids with Sara, watched Justin joke with Matt about being a new father, and generally had a good time over two glasses of wine.

An hour later she felt warm and even pleasant toward Matt and he even seemed to be more relaxed around her.

He really was a heartbreaker, she mused, peeking beneath her lashes at him, caught out with a knowing look that glinted on the verge of hot. Yet suddenly she didn't seem to care. The wine was making her feel good.

"I think it's time we let these two lovebirds go home to bed, Justin," Sara said, then yawned delicately. "Besides, I need my beauty sleep."

The words made Lana wince. Was she really looking like a lovesick idiot? Or was Sara seeing more than there was?

Definitely.

She wasn't in love with Matt. She wanted him, certainly. He made her ache for him physically, but that had nothing to do with affection.

Everyone agreed to meet up soon, then Matt put his hand on her elbow as he walked her back to their car.

Thankfully the night air kept her head clear.

"You handed in that wallet," he said, once they were in the car, his eyes inscrutable.

"It was the right thing to do."

"You weren't tempted to keep it?"

She met his eyes without flinching. "No."

She hadn't handed in the wallet to get his approval, but it would have been nice for him to acknowledge her honesty.

"No one would have known," he pointed out.

"*I* would have known."

He studied her and an odd expression flickered across his face before he turned away to start the engine. "My friends really like you."

"And that surprises you?"

"Not at all. You're very charming."

So was he.

Except with *her*.

"I gather you're happy with my performance tonight, then?" she said with an underlying note of sarcasm.

"Performance?"

"They think we're happily married."

He glanced at her only briefly. "It'll do."

She sighed with frustration and left him to concentrate on the driving. It didn't matter what she did, his opinion of her wasn't going to change. He wanted to think bad of her and he would continue on that path.

So why on earth had she been worried about spending the night alone in the house with him? He'd kissed her in his office to punish her, not because he'd had an overpowering need to feel her lips beneath his.

Not the way she did his.

All at once he cast her a sideways glance, and his gaze dropped to her mouth and darkened. "Don't," he growled, before returning to the road.

Startled, she felt her thoughts fumbling to catch up to him. Then she realized. Until that moment she hadn't been aware of touching her mouth with her fingertips, remembering him there.

The mouth that he had kissed.

Heavens.

Had she given herself away?

The tension was palpable for the rest of the journey, but Lana didn't know how to disperse it. The two of them seemed to create a sexual energy together that was multiplied by the confines of the car.

It made her skittish and eager to get home so she could hide in her room.

Yes, hide.

Somewhere that she wouldn't be tempted to make love to him. She was a coward and she could admit it.

They arrived home shortly after, but he surprised her by parking the car near the front door and not in the garage. Was he going out again?

To another woman?

She felt a moment's squeezing pain. Wasn't it unrealistic of her to believe he could remain celibate? It wasn't as if they had a love match. He was a virile man.

She avoided his eyes until they were inside.

"Lana?"

The intensity in his voice trapped her where she stood.

"Look at me, Lana."

Her heart bumped her ribs into action. She swung toward the kitchen. "Coffee. Do you want—"

"*You.*" He caught her by the waist and smoothly put her up against the wall. "That's what I want."

She swallowed hard. "Matt, in the car, if you think I was—"

"Oh, you were." His eyes zeroed down to her mouth. "You were thinking of our kiss."

She shook her head, unable to speak, unable to deny it with words.

"Yes, you were," he murmured huskily.

She could feel the heat of his hands, attacking her defenses, trying to climb the barrier she'd fought hard to maintain.

She had to find her voice. "It wasn't a come-on."

"No, it was a turn-on." He began to nuzzle her neck.

Oh Lord.

She gave a shaky breath. "We're more than this, Matt."

He stopped nuzzling and leaned back, the look in his eyes pure passion. "Are we?"

It was honesty at its most basic.

He wanted her and she wanted him and that's what this was all about. It was what they'd been about the first time they'd made love, and nothing had changed between them on that front.

Did she really want to deny either of them the pleasure?

Worse, if she did, would he go find another warm body?

Would he walk out that door and leave her alone tonight? And then she would go to her bed and sleep alone and there would be no Matt to take her over the edge into fulfillment. No Matt to ease this profound hunger inside her. She didn't think her body could handle that right now. She was ripe for making love, no matter how much she wanted to refute that.

Her small purse slipped from her hand and fell to the carpet with a soft clink. "Oh God, I want you, Matt," she whispered, wrapping her arms around his neck.

His eyes flared with a triumph that normally would have her retracting her statement, yet this time it did nothing but thrill her.

She wanted him so badly.

He took her mouth in a fierce, hungry kiss and she parted her lips in full capitulation and kissed him back, rejoicing in his tongue slipping inside to devour her softness.

She moaned and he replied with a sound of satisfaction deep in his throat, his hands tightening on her waist as he pressed her up against the wall, leaving her with no illusion that he was fully aroused.

But his touch merely fueled the ache deep inside her, and she moaned again.

A deep, heartfelt moan.

She soon matched him stroke for stroke as a hypnotic blend of sensuality and seduction tantalized her senses.

His taste was heady.

He smelled…intoxicating.

He began showering kisses on her eyelids, down her cheek, along her chin, returning to her mouth time and time again, demanding a response she freely gave.

His hand closed possessively over her breast and a whimper escaped her throat as he explored the sensitive flesh through the material, teasing her, rubbing his thumb over her nipple. Could he feel the hammering of her heart? she wondered as a river of anticipation raced through her veins.

Soon it wasn't enough.

For either of them.

He swung her up in his arms and started down the hallway with her, twice stopping to kiss her boneless, turning her into a melting puddle of need by the time they reached his bedroom.

She registered a fleeting glimpse of the room decorated in olive and black before he was back to kissing her, carrying her over toward the bed, but not laying her down on it.

He stood her on her feet and in the catch of a breath, he unzipped her dress and pushed it down to the floor, along with her panties and silk stockings. Her shoes were somehow missing, so she must have already kicked them off along the way. He straightened and undid her lacy bra and tossed it aside.

Time came to an instant standstill.

She was naked.

Fully naked.

She realized he'd never seen her like this before.

His eyes drank her up and he made a guttural sound as he reached for her.

And time started ticking again.

They had to have each other.

Soon she tingled under his fingertips, making her ache in secret places that craved the heat of his arousal. Adrenaline pumped through her veins, her need shocking her.

Suddenly she couldn't wait a moment more to have Matt inside her. Giddily she pushed aside the flaps of his jacket and started to unbutton his shirt. Where his tie had gone she didn't know.

She must have been too slow because he groaned and stepped back, not to strip off his clothes as she thought, but to undo his trousers and free himself.

She gasped; then need kicked in and with her response matching his own urgency, she reached out to explore the hard lines of him.

"Stop," he growled as he reached down to the bedside drawer where he took out a condom.

She was about to say that she was on contraceptives to help with her monthly cycle, but she was suddenly…consciously…mesmerized by him rolling the condom on himself.

The words escaped her.

Then he was leaning her up against the bedroom

wall and maneuvering her body. She felt his erection at the tip of her entrance, felt him ease her onto him.

He slowly thrust upward and slid fully inside.

"Matt!" she cried out, gripping his shoulders, her eyes widening as her body adjusted to him.

A dark flush spread across his cheeks. "You feel so good."

"You, too," she gasped.

He lifted her and with a groan drove himself into her again, this time more firmly.

Their bodies locked and her senses spun.

She pressed a kiss against the hard cords in his neck. "Take me, Matt. Take me please."

"Where?" he muttered.

"Anywhere. As long as it's with you."

He began to thrust in and out, causing a pure and explosive pleasure within her. Before too long her body started to vibrate in ripples, radiating outward and pulling everything in its path back within her, including this man inside.

The center of her being became a whirlpool of sensation, flooding her with desire. She came with a rush as it sucked her into its incredible and mind-blowing depths.

A minisecond later, Matt followed her into the sensual vortex.

Seven

Matt shuddered to an awesome climax as Lana's body clenched around him, holding him tight, not letting go until she'd taken everything from him.

Finally he caught his breath and his head cleared—and he shuddered for a very different reason. This woman had her grip on him in more ways than one.

He gave her a hard kiss, withdrew from her to lay her down on the bed.

What the hell had he done? he asked himself as he strode from the room to the bathroom. He stood at the bathroom mirror. Making love to her just now had been so good. So bloody good he'd wanted her again almost immediately.

Dammit, he'd been caught in a snare of his own device.

And all because of that kiss in his office the other day.

And because of that wallet tonight.

And because in the car she'd caressed her mouth with her fingertips. Seeing her do that had sent him over the edge.

It hadn't helped that he hadn't been with a woman for weeks now. Nor had he ever had a more sensual relationship with a woman without actually having sex with her.

He wouldn't be caught out again.

She could hand in as many wallets as she liked and it still wouldn't matter. She could walk around in that sexy nightgown and he still wouldn't let her tempt him.

She could even parade naked in front of him.

He grimaced. Well, maybe not naked. He *was* a man, after all. He had his limits.

And he'd reached his limit tonight.

He would have to stop this right here.

He went back into the bedroom and stopped at the sight of her. Her short blond hair was tousled around her beautiful face, and she'd thrown her dress on but hadn't done up the zipper, the material falling away and leaving a smooth shoulder. In one hand she held her lacy bra and as she straightened with her panties in the other hand, he caught a glimpse of bare cheek.

Desire licked at his insides.

He swallowed hard. "I'm sorry, Lana, but this was a mistake."

She colored a little. "A…mistake?"

His lips formed a hard line. "I don't want you getting the wrong idea about this. It happened, but it's not going to happen again. It'll just get too complicated otherwise."

Something shifted in her expression. "Fine."

Her comment brought him up short.

He scowled. "It is?"

Her lips twisted. "Matt, you can forgive yourself for wanting someone you despise."

He felt a punch to his gut. "I don't despise you."

"Don't you? Funny, I thought you did."

"Lana, look—"

"Matt, really, I understand. We'd both had a few drinks tonight and—"

"One. That's all I had."

She blinked. "One?"

"I don't drink over the limit and drive."

She crinkled her nose. "Okay, so *I* had a couple of drinks and let down my guard. Seems to be my modus operandi. But at least we don't have to worry about a pregnancy this time."

The words jarred him. "That's something, I suppose."

Her chin angled with pride. "Now, if you'll excuse me, I'd like to go to my room and get some sleep. I need to get up early and go pick up Megan."

She was taking it so well.

Too well?

"*We'll* pick up Megan," he insisted as she passed him by.

She inclined her head and he let her go, one part of him amazed that for the first time he was letting a woman walk away from his bed while he still wanted more of her.

That's the way it had to be.

With Lana it was a necessity.

There was always a price to pay for happiness, Lana reminded herself as she sat on her bed and pressed her fingers to her temples.

And she'd just paid it.

Heavens, had she really made love with Matt again? Really melted at his touch? Had she really reached out and touched him like that?

Oh yeah.

It hadn't been quite as fast as the last time they'd made love in the office. Back then there had been no time for more than quick touches and furtive glances. No time for savoring each other. He'd thrust inside her before she'd known it and she'd welcomed him, joining him in a long, simultaneous climax. It had been the most incredible feeling she'd ever experienced.

Tonight had been just as incredible.

More so.

A mistake, he'd called it.

She winced. Yes, it had been a mistake. She'd reached that conclusion herself the moment he'd left her alone and sanity had returned. Oh, there'd been no doubt he'd wanted her and she'd wanted him and it had been enough at the time.

But now she had to wonder about the true reason behind it all. Had it merely been masculine pride? His friends had liked her and he'd said others would expect they'd have a physical relationship.

Or perhaps she'd been a convenience more than anything? She'd been unwittingly available when he'd wanted a woman.

Any woman.

Maybe her handing in the wallet had convinced him for a short time that she wasn't capable of stealing? And afterward reality had hit him with a thud and he was back to believing the worst of her again.

And now his guard was truly up.

Except the reality was that she hadn't expected anything more.

And he had no need to be on guard.

They'd merely been a man and woman in the wrong place at the right time. That's how she'd look at it. No need to get worked up about it all, right? She'd simply be grateful Matt wasn't feeling guilty and wanting to rectify the situation by insisting their marriage become permanent.

Thank God he hadn't.

Flinging aside her thoughts, she put on her nightgown, slid beneath the covers and turned off the light. And she'd try not to go over their lovemaking in minute detail. From now on she'd try and forget it ever happened.

Tomorrow they'd both move forward like mature adults.

Thankfully Lana was kept busy over the weekend. They both slept late in their separate beds, so that by the time they went to pick up Megan it was almost noon and Isabel insisted they stay for lunch.

Lana felt uncomfortable with Isabel's and Cesare's eyes on them, even guilty. If she and Matt had been on friendlier terms, she'd jokingly confess she felt like a teenager who'd had sex with her boyfriend and was trying not to let her parents know it.

As it was, they acted civil to each other until it was time to go home. She fully expected him to go out that evening, but to her surprise he went to the study. It was as if he was showing her he could be around her without making love to her again.

Or perhaps he was trying to show himself.

And that made her wonder, especially when she caught him watching her at odd times, his eyes darkening before he'd blank them out, as if a dial were turning on without his permission and he had to turn it off deliberately.

Unfortunately for her, she couldn't stop her thoughts from turning to their lovemaking. If only she could turn that part of her mind off, perhaps she could get some peace. If only Matt didn't affect her, she might have a chance at it. Truth to tell, she was dismayed at the way her body continued to want him again. It was as if there were still lively little sparks of desire floating in the air between them, in spite of her best efforts to put them out.

Her only consolation was that both of them were fighting this thing. She knew for sure that Matt wouldn't attempt to make love to her again.

And she wouldn't let him.

Thank heavens by midweek they were almost back to normal. Normal for them, that is.

Subsequently, when Matt walked into her office before lunch on Thursday she pretended she could ignore him.

"What are you doing?"

She glanced at him, then back to the computer screen. "Guess."

He expelled a breath. "Lana, I've checked those old accounts and there's nothing else there. If there was, I would have found it."

"No, there's something more. I can feel it. I—" She fell back in her chair as a thought made her heart skip a beat. "Are you saying you believe I didn't do it?"

His eyebrow slanted. "Let's say I'm giving you the slight benefit of the doubt."

"How kind," she drawled, pretending that even his halfhearted support didn't thrill her. It did. Perhaps he was getting to know the real her. He had to know she wasn't a person who would steal from others. Hadn't returning the wallet made him see that?

She mentally slumped. She shouldn't give too much credence to what he said. If he could make love to her while believing her a thief, then he could as easily change his mind about this.

"Come on. We're going out to lunch," he muttered.

Her mind whirled in surprise, then withdrew. "I'd rather stay here and look through these."

"I want to go shopping."

She sat up straight. "I told you I don't want any clothes."

"It's not for you. I'm going to buy some things for Megan's room."

"Things?"

"Furniture."

She lifted her chin. "I spent a lot of money on her furniture." She saw his eyes flicker. "Not stolen money," she said, feeling as if they were back where they started.

He inclined his head. "And you did well," he conceded, "but I want her to have the very best. Now that she's used to her new room, it's time for new furniture."

His words reminded her of a discussion at the ballet. "Didn't I hear your friend Justin talking about buying baby furniture for his son's room?"

He scowled. "Yeah, so?"

She tilted her head. "You don't have to one-up him, you know."

"I won't even bother to reply to that," he snapped, then looked at his watch. "I've made a booking and we're going to be late."

"Since when does that worry you?"

"It doesn't."

Sighing, she grabbed her purse and stood up. "I've already had a piece of cake for morning tea."

"Your figure can handle lunch."

The compliment sent the blood rushing to her head, but she concentrated on getting out of the room. He took her elbow as she passed him by, bringing her close but not too close as he walked her from the room and down the corridor. She wasn't sure if his hold was to remind everyone she was his wife, or to let *her* know who was boss.

Probably both, she mused, knowing in either case it was a proprietary gesture and nothing more.

Ten minutes later they were seated at a restaurant with a glorious view of the Royal Botanic Gardens. The weather was perfect for a lunchtime walk or a jog, and many people were doing exactly that along the pathways. Others were sitting on the grass and taking in the harbor view.

Lana wished she was sitting out there in the sunshine, rather than sitting in here with Matt. Out there she could escape being close to him. In here there was no escape.

"We need to talk," Matt said, once they'd ordered a light lunch. "About Megan."

Her heart seemed to squeeze tight. Did he want

a divorce already? No, then he wouldn't want to furnish Megan's room.

A wave of apprehension swept through her as her old fear rose. Perhaps he wanted Megan, but wanted to get rid of *her?* Perhaps he'd found a way to push her out of her daughter's life?

He leaned back in his chair. "I've located a new day care center for her."

Lana's shoulders slumped. "Is that all?"

He scowled. "What did you think I wanted to talk about?"

"I thought you were going to finally offer to buy Megan off me."

His eyes narrowed. "Would you sell her?"

She looked him straight in the eye. "I'd rather die first."

Silence; then he said with a twitch of his lips, "Defeats the purpose, don't you think?"

"You know what I mean."

His humor disappeared. "I wouldn't ask that of you, Lana. I can see you love Megan more than life itself."

A warm feeling bounced inside her chest. "Thank you."

Their gazes linked, and all at once Lana felt they connected on a level beyond the bedroom. For a moment they both saw a true part of each other, not the facade they sought to present.

Then the waiter provided a diversion by returning with their drinks, and she broke eye contact and took a sip of her mineral water to give herself something to do.

"Now, back to the day care center," Matt said brusquely once they were alone. "I've found a suitable one not too far away."

Suddenly Lana felt apprehensive. "You have?"

His eyes narrowed. "What's the matter? I thought you'd be happy."

"I am. I mean, I am, but I'm not."

"That makes sense," he drawled.

She grimaced. "I'm frightened for her safety, Matt. I didn't have to worry about that before, but now it's a real threat."

He considered that. "I'll make sure she's safe, Lana."

She let out a slow breath of relief. "I know you will."

He held her gaze, a pleased look in his eyes. "Have you considered that she may not need to go to day care at all? She's only little. It might be best for her to continue staying at home with Ruth on the days that you're working. What do you think?"

That thought had occurred to her, too, but she shook her head. "No. She needs to get used to it again. Next year there'll be just me and her and…"

"You don't have to worry about any of that," he said, his face closed now.

She paused a moment. Then said, "You know, Matt, I don't say no just to be difficult. I do whatever's good for Megan, despite what's good for us."

He held himself stiffly. "I appreciate that."

Suddenly she felt sorry for him. His whole life had changed. "But I have to admit it's been a new experience for me, sharing responsibility for her like this," she conceded. "It takes time to get used to it."

A friendlier look entered her eyes. "She's *our* responsibility, Lana. Don't forget that."

His words sent a quiver of delight through her veins. He wasn't being possessive of Megan, or arrogant toward *her*. He was merely acknowledging their mutual love for the most important person in their lives.

As it should be.

Lunch arrived, and Lana fought back disappointment at the interruption. She and Matt had bonded a moment ago and she liked the feeling.

If only…

What?

If only Matt could really believe she wasn't the bad person he thought she was?

If only he didn't need proof she hadn't stolen the money?

If only they could end up friends for Megan's sake?

She sighed, knowing that wasn't possible. There was too much between them now for them ever to be friends.

They finished eating in silence, then had coffee. She drank hers down quickly, wanting to get this over and done with and get back to work. The less time spent in Matt's company the better. She was getting too soft where he was concerned.

Matt took a last mouthful of coffee. "Right. Let's go shopping."

He drove them to a baby boutique that she remembered Justin mentioning. She shot him a wry look as they got out of the car.

"He recommended it, that's all," he defended, but she saw the humorous gleam in those dark eyes, and a soft glow filled her.

The manager came out to greet them the minute they stepped inside the store. "Mr. and Mrs. Valente," he welcomed, and Lana shot Matt another knowing look, which he ignored this time.

The store manager knew a good sale coming and he was extremely helpful. As for Matt, he was businesslike on the outside, but she could see he was enjoying himself. He ordered a new crib, then saw something better that would turn into a bed for Megan's future use, and ordered that one instead. He did the same with a toy box and a stroller. And he wanted to buy the biggest playpen there.

Lana saw the playpen and laughed.

"What's so funny?" he asked as the store manager went off to see about delivery.

"You. You're like a kid in a toy store."

He shrugged. "Hey, it's not every day a man gets to buy things for his daughter. Besides, we *are* in a toy store."

"Enjoy it while you can. I doubt she'll let you when she gets older."

They shared a smile that could have deepened to something more, only her cell phone rang. It was Ruth saying Megan had a high temperature and wasn't well.

"We'll be right there," she said, seeing Matt pull his shoulders back as if expecting a blow.

"Megan?" he muttered after she'd ended her call.

Lana nodded, worry already eating at her. "She's got a temperature."

Matt put his arm under her elbow, speaking to the store manager as he guided her to the front door. "Our daughter's sick. I'll get my PA to call you and arrange payment."

"Very good, sir. I hope your daughter is okay."

"So do I," Matt said, his voice as rough as gravel.

Lana's heart was in her mouth as they drove home. "She might be teething, Matt. That's probably all it is."

"Teething doesn't make them sick."

She glanced sideways at him. "How do you know that?"

"I've read some books about it."

That surprised her. "A lot of doctors say that teething doesn't make them sick, but I've heard it lowers a child's resistance to picking up germs."

"Germs?" he asked, as if she'd said a dirty word.

"Cold germs, that's all." She could see the grimness on Matt's face and she felt sorry for him. The playboy was truly gone right now, and in its place was a very worried father.

"Do you have a family doctor?" he asked.

"Not really."

His mouth tightened as he used his cell phone to call his mother, telling her the situation and shooting out instructions.

He hung up. "Mum will get our family doctor to pay a visit."

"Good," Lana murmured.

She usually visited the local medical center if she or Megan needed a doctor, though she wasn't sure Matt could understand that. He had wealth and connections, and for the first time ever, she thanked God he did. She wanted the best for her daughter.

As soon as Ruth opened the door, Megan cried out to Lana, who hurried forward and took her daughter in her arms. Lana's heart lurched at Megan's rosy red cheeks, stained by tears. She wore only a diaper and felt hot to the touch.

Then Megan saw Matt, gave a loud cry and threw her arms out toward him, wanting to be held by her father. Lana looked at Matt and her legs almost gave out at the sheer love for his daughter on his face. She willingly handed Megan over to him.

"I've given her some medicine," Ruth said calmly as they moved inside. "And I've been cooling her down in the bath."

"Thank you, Ruth," Lana said, looking at her daughter with a worried frown. "Let's take her into the living room, Matt."

"I'll just go wet this washcloth again for her," Ruth said.

Once in the living room, Megan whimpered and Matt looked helpless all of a sudden. "Shouldn't we take her to the hospital?"

Lana tried not to show her worry. "Let's give the medication a chance to work until the doctor gets here."

Megan started crying again and he tried to soothe her. "Dammit, where is that bloody doctor?"

Lana wiped her daughter's nose with a tissue. "Try not to worry, Matt. Kids can look so sick one minute and the next they're up and running around." She gave a sympathetic smile. "Believe me, there were some nights I walked the floor with her when she had a cold or colic and I would have sworn she had pneumonia or something worse."

Matt stiffened. "I would have been there if I'd known."

She groaned inwardly. "It wasn't a criticism of you."

Megan continued crying and he shot Lana a dark look. "Really? It sounded like it to me."

She knew he was panicking deep inside, so she allowed him his snide remark. "Matt, I was only trying to say she'll be back to normal in no time. Just take it easy."

"Like you're doing?" he snapped, as Megan continued crying. "You seem to be taking this real easy. But you're an old hand at this, aren't you?"

She angled her chin. "That's enough, Matt."

"No, it's—"

"Mr. Valente," Ruth warned, coming back into the room with the washcloth. "This is not the time or place to be arguing. Your daughter is sick. She needs you to remain calm." She sounded like a schoolteacher reprimanding one of her students, and Matt's face blanched.

A moment crept by.

He let out a slow breath. "You're right, Ruth." He looked at Lana. "I'm sorry, Lana. I didn't mean to snap at you."

"I know, Matt."

After that the doctor came and said it was probably only a virus but to keep an eye on her. The medication had worked by then, so the little girl soon fell asleep.

They continued to anxiously check on her throughout the evening, unable to sit still for long. By midnight she woke and was cool to the touch, and they each breathed a sigh of relief. It appeared the worst was over. After a drink of water, she fell asleep again.

"Lana, I'm really sorry about snapping at you today," Matt murmured, standing by the crib.

She realized she had finally given himself permission to relax now that Megan was on the mend. "Matt, I understand. You were scared something serious was the matter with her."

His mouth flattened into a grim line. "It doesn't excuse me taking it out on you. Hell, I can only imagine how it must feel to be alone and carrying the full weight of it all."

"Don't beat yourself up about it."

He stood still for a moment longer, looking down at his sleeping daughter. Then he looked up. "Why don't you go to bed," he suggested quietly. "You should get some sleep."

"But you're the one with work tomorrow." She at least had a day off.

"I don't have to go in if she's not better." Then he heaved a sigh. "I suppose we should both go to bed," he said, nothing remotely suggestive in his words.

Lana nodded. "It's been a long day."

He went to move away, then stopped. "Call me if I don't hear her."

"I will."

He left the room and exhaustion swooped over Lana. The thought of bed and sleep sounded like heaven.

Only, once she'd had her shower she felt incredibly thirsty and decided to get a cool glass of milk or she wouldn't sleep until she did.

And this time she remembered to slip on her satiny bathrobe over her chemise nightgown.

Just in case.

It was as well she did. At the kitchen door she got a jolt to find Matt standing there in his pajama bottoms, looking out the window over the back garden, the moon giving enough light for her to see his knuckles gripping the edge of the sink.

She moved toward him in concern. "Matt?"

He didn't turn around.

"Matt, are you okay?"

He took a ragged breath. "I'm not sure I can handle this parenting stuff, Lana," he muttered. "Tonight almost killed me worrying about her."

Her heart softened. Oh, she so knew how he felt. It was a tough job at times.

"Too late," she said gently. "Once you're a parent there's no going back. She has our heart." Without thinking, she rested her hand on his shoulder and felt his muscles tighten.

"Don't touch me, Lana. Not right now. Not tonight."

The breath hitched in her throat. "Why?"

"I may not be responsible for my actions."

A knot rose in her throat. "Then don't be," she whispered, squeezing his shoulder.

He sucked in a sharp breath and slowly turned to face her, his eyes riveting on her face. "Are you sure?"

She nodded.

His hands slid onto her hips and held. "I've never wanted a woman like I want you."

Oh God, he was turning her into mush.

"If we make love, I'm going to share your bed from now on, Lana."

She swallowed. "You are?"

"It's no use us pretending we don't want each other."

Her heart thudded. Did he mean...

"But I make no promises."

Her heart hit the floor, then picked itself up.

Her eyes clung to his. "I don't want any promises, Matt. I don't want anything but for you to make love to me over and over."

He groaned and pulled her into his arms, his mouth capturing hers, her lips opening in invitation. He took slow sips from her mouth, drugging her with his taste and his velvety tongue.

And then he stepped back and held out his hand, his eyes glittering in the dark. "Shall we make ourselves more comfortable?"

Without hesitation she slipped her hand in his, happy to follow him wherever he led.

They stopped briefly to check on their daughter, who thankfully continued to sleep peacefully, and they smiled at each other with deep connection.

Then they went into his room and shut the door behind them, tucking themselves away, fully aware there was no need to hurry their lovemaking this time.

He held her in front of him. "You're gorgeous," he said huskily, his eyes going over her from the top of her head, down over her satiny bathrobe, to her bare feet. Then his eyes rose upward. "God. I almost don't want to take your clothes off you."

She became fascinated by the vein that pulsed in his neck. "You don't?"

"I'm lying."

She moistened her lips. "I'm glad."

"So am I," he murmured, undoing the sash at her

waist and peeling the robe off her shoulders, leaving her standing there in her pearl-colored chemise. "Oh yeah, sweetheart. I'm…so…glad."

He pulled her close and started kissing her again.

Deeply, this time.

Deeper than any other time, not so much in touch but in intensity.

And intimacy.

This time it wasn't about two people making love together, but about two people being intimate.

And then he reached down to her hem and lifted the nightgown over her head, leaving her naked.

She gasped as his hands slow-traced her hips… her derriere…brushing over the bare skin of her back…exploring her body from behind.

And then those wonderful hands moved up and around to her front, touching her breasts, circling the sensitive skin before cupping them as he weighed and measured them in his palms, before lowering his head and fitting one of the brown nubs in his mouth.

"Oh my heaven," was all she could manage, her mind reeling as he gently nipped and licked her body to life…a life that had her clutching his bare shoulders, wanting to touch him as he was touching her.

She was almost ready to sink to the floor by the time he moved back, but she somehow managed to speak. "Please, Matt. My turn."

A light smoldered in his eyes. "Go ahead."

A flash of heat washed over her and suddenly her hands shook, but that didn't stop her from sliding her palms over his hair-roughened chest, reveling in the hot feel of him beneath her palms.

He shuddered and her head spun and she grew more daring, her hands sliding down over the tight muscles of his stomach, over the front of his pajama pants to where he felt hard and demanding.

"Stop," he rasped.

She stood her ground. "No." She pushed his pants down until they reached his feet.

Swearing softly, he stepped out of them and kicked them aside and she made her way up his naked flesh, running her hands up along his flanks, across to his powerful erection, where she fondled him, loving the sound of his groan and the shudder of his body before she stood back to fully admire him for the first time ever.

He was fully exposed.

There was nothing left but *him*.

The utterly perfect male.

She reached for him again, but he put his hand over hers. "No." His gaze dropped down to her thighs, then shot back up. "Do you realize I've never tasted you? Not once."

His words sent electrifying shivers down her spine. "Then don't let me stop you."

Growling satisfaction, he dropped to his knees.

Her legs shook as he began kissing her in a more intimate way. She was acutely aware of his dark head at the junction of her thighs, doing marvelous things to her, his tongue warm and smooth, enticingly so.

She trembled, verging on the edge of discovery.
She was almost ready to topple.

"Not yet," he muttered, and the next thing she
knew he was lowering her onto the bed, her body
still one big ache, craving that joyous feeling just
out of reach.

He opened the bedside drawer and took out a foil
packet, and instantly her mind cleared even as her
body still hungered for release.

"Matt, stop."

He paused, looking at her with a question in his
eyes.

"You don't need those."

"I don't?"

"I'm protected." She saw him wince and the past
came back to haunt her. At the Christmas party it
had been over before they knew it, and afterward
she'd lied about protection so he wouldn't worry
about her becoming pregnant. "I'm telling the truth
this time, Matt."

She held his gaze.

If he didn't believe her she couldn't proceed.

He stared hard for a couple of loaded seconds,
then dropped the foil back in the drawer. The
mattress lurched as he joined her, just as her heart
was lurching in her chest. He stretched out on top
of her, his arms pure steel, holding him up to look
down at her from above.

His eyes trapped hers for a heart-stopping moment.

And he grew rigid between her legs.

"Thank you for trusting me," she said sincerely.

"No, thank *you* for giving me our daughter."

Her vision blurred as tender warmth entered her heart. Then she took a ragged breath. "I'm yours tonight, Matt," she murmured, and let her thighs fall open so that he could find his way.

He entered her and she moved to meet him. Soon after, she cried out his name, delicious contractions hitting her until she abandoned herself to a spine-tingling fusion to become one with him.

One body.

One heartbeat.

Her one true love.

"Are you okay?"

Lana heard the words in her ear but couldn't reply. How had it happened? How had she tumbled headlong into love with him? She was staggered by the revelation.

Oh Lord.

He stayed inside her and looked down into her eyes. "Lana?"

She thought fast.

"Just catching my breath," she said with a smile, her fingers itching to run lovingly along his jaw.

She daren't.

He studied her without giving anything away himself. "No regrets?"

Could she regret that she loved him?

She shook her head. "Not this time."

His face relaxed. "Me either." Leaning down, he gave her a long, soft kiss that made her want to stay in his arms for the rest of her life.

Eventually he lifted his head. "I've never made love to any other woman without a condom."

"I know. You told me that the first time we made love."

"I remember." His eyes darkened. "And you believed me."

"Of course," she said without hesitation.

His gaze searched her eyes. Then slid down to where the tips of her breasts pressed against his chest. "I want you again."

Her eyes widened as she felt him grow hard inside her. "So soon?"

"Yes."

She swallowed. He was looking at her as if he wanted her more than anything else in the world. The feeling was so new it made her blush.

"Don't you need to gather your strength?" she babbled, suddenly self-conscious that a man wanted her so much.

And not just any man.

Matt.

"I'm stronger than I look," he muttered.

She acknowledged something when she heard those words.

He *was* strong.

In every way.

And it wasn't just physical either. She'd known

men who were muscular but hollow. Others had been too strong for their own good and would never let a woman see their softer side as Matt had this evening over Megan.

But Matt, oh yes, he just seemed to fit her like a piece in a jigsaw puzzle. Everything he did, everything he was, seemed tailor-made for her.

It gave her a sense of rightness as Matt began to make love to her all over again. And afterward, when she rested her cheek drowsily on his chest, two thoughts crossed her mind before she fell into an exhausted slumber.

Yes, she loved this man.

But sometimes love wasn't enough.

Eight

Matt ignored the budget reports waiting on his desk and sat back in his chair for a moment. He was still reeling from seeing Megan sick yesterday. Thank God she was better now.

Lord, when she'd held out her little arms to him he thought his heart would explode with love and concern. He was learning that loving a child was a bittersweet pain. Lana was right. Once you saw your child and the love entered your heart, there was no going back.

Lana was an old hand at this now. She'd done this by herself for the last eleven months. Not to mention coping with being pregnant.

Something turned over in his chest at the thought

of her carrying his baby. To have been pregnant and alone with only an uncle a world away in France must have been terrifying.

He felt humble.

And could he really blame her now if she'd stolen that money to support her and her child?

If?

Yes, he had his doubts now and with each day they were growing stronger. But hell, he was still angry deep inside that she hadn't come to him about her pregnancy. He really didn't understand why she hadn't.

Yet she'd supported him yesterday over Megan and then again late in the night when she'd offered herself to him. If she didn't have some sort of feelings for him, would she have done either of those things?

Of course having *some* feelings was like having *some* money. A person could get by on a small amount, but it wasn't enough to build a house.

Or a marriage.

That's if a person wanted to build a house in the first place, which neither he nor Lana wanted. They were both only looking to put a roof over their daughter's head.

Dammit, Lana had come into his life with the greatest gift in her arms.

And he was now going to share her bed full-time until their divorce.

And *still* he couldn't figure her out.

Perhaps he shouldn't even try, he decided, accepting that some things were a mystery.

Just then the intercom buzzed.

"Matt, there's a gentleman on the line from France looking for Lana," Irene said. "He said he's her uncle."

Matt frowned. "Put him through, Irene." He waited a moment for the connection to go through. "Matt Valente here."

"Matt? I'm pleased to meet you. It's Dan Moore here. Lana's uncle. I've just got back from a trip to South Africa and I read the letter from Lana about her marriage. Congratulations. Lana's a wonderful girl."

"Thank you, Dan. Yes, she is."

"I'm sorry I missed the wedding. I would have been there if I'd known, but I understand the rush for little Megan's sake."

So he knew the reason for the marriage.

"Yes."

"I don't have your home number but if you could get Lana to give me a call that would be terrific. I need to tell her that now she's married to you, I want to deed the apartment over to Megan."

Matt's heart thudded. "The apartment?"

"Yes. Lana would have told you I bought it for her and Megan."

"Of course," he lied without missing a beat.

So *that's* where the money had come from.

"I want it to be my gift to my great-niece. I don't

ever want her to be alone like Lana was when her parents died." He took a breath. "Not that they were much use to her when they were living, God rest their souls. She would have told you about that, too, no doubt." He paused. "Unfortunately I was living in France and couldn't be there for her, but she always knew I was just a phone call away."

Matt felt a band of tightness in his chest. He should have read that report his father had ordered on Lana and her family. It would have explained a lot about the pieces that made up his wife.

"I won't let that happen to Megan, Dan. She will always have me and my family to look after her."

For all that, he suddenly realized he didn't like the thought of sharing his daughter with some unknown person. Not even one of Lana's relatives.

"That's good to know, Matt. Please give Lana my love and tell her Aimee and Julien send their love, too. I'll talk to her soon."

Matt was curious. "Is Julien your son?"

There was a moment's hesitation. "So Lana hasn't told you yet? I guess it's not an easy thing for her to say, but I'd appreciate if you could keep this in the family."

"Tell me what?"

"Julien is my lover."

Lana spent the day trying to come to terms with loving Matt, knowing she could never tell him.

If it had been only her and Matt, then she might

have given it a shot. She was strong enough to walk away if things turned bad.

She couldn't take such a chance when she had a responsibility to her daughter. Matt was great with Megan, but she couldn't stand back and let Matt's disdain for *her* become a part of their lives.

She wouldn't.

When Matt arrived home later that day, she hid her love from him and prayed to God she could keep doing it until the year was up. Their physical relationship would have to be enough.

So why hadn't he kissed her hello?

And why didn't he pull her into his arms and hold her close? she wondered throughout dinner. Was this the way it was going to be? Were they just going to be lovers in the bedroom and nothing else?

Her heart slumped against her rib cage as she realized something. He hadn't asked Ruth to move his things into the master bedroom. Or was he going to do it himself? Were they even going to share a bed now?

Oh God.

Was Matt having second thoughts?

She was tempted to come right out and ask him, once they'd put Megan to bed and were sitting in the living room watching television. At least they could talk without any interruption, Ruth having left a short while ago to spend the night at her sister's place.

She was working up the courage to speak when

without warning he grabbed the remote and turned the television off.

"I had a phone call today," he said. "From Dan Moore."

Her eyes went wide. "Uncle Dan?"

He nodded. "He received your letter but he didn't know the phone number for the house, so he called you at work. Irene put him through to me."

"And?"

"He'd just gotten back from South Africa. He wanted you to know he was delighted about your marriage and he sent his love." He watched her carefully. "He also said to tell you that Aimee and Julien send their love."

She blinked, then quickly pretended to brush some lint off her dress. "How nice."

Silence.

"Why didn't you tell me, Lana?"

She looked up. "What?"

"That your uncle is bisexual."

She gave a soft gasp. "How do you know that?"

"Dan told me Julien was his lover." He grimaced. "Did you expect me to be shocked? His sexual preferences don't matter to me."

"They do to the press. I owe Dan so much. I'd hate to repay him by having his private life dragged out in the open."

"I wouldn't tell the press. They'd be the last I'd tell anything."

She shook her head. "Matt, just being related to

a Valente is enough to send them into a media feeding frenzy. We were lucky that they romanticized our wedding because of Megan, but Dan's reputation wouldn't escape so easily."

He studied her. "He's the reason you let me believe you'd bought the apartment with the stolen money?"

Her eyes widened. "You know about that too?"

"Dan said he wanted to deed the apartment he bought you over to Megan."

"Oh, he's such a lovely man." Then she remembered something. "I'm surprised you didn't find all this when you did a background check on me. And I know you would have done one, Matt. I'm not naïve. It's a necessary evil for people with money."

"My father ordered the report on you. I didn't read it, but he gave me a brief rundown and that was all." He frowned. "I should have read it. It might have saved a lot of arguments between us."

"But it might not have said anything about Dan and Julien. I was just fearful in case that did come to light and someone somewhere leaked it to the papers."

He considered her for a long moment.

"Tell me about your parents, Lana."

She started in surprise, then groaned inwardly. If Matt had loved her she would have no hesitation in telling him about her background. People in love did that sort of thing, sharing their deepest thoughts and feelings.

But there was only one of them in love here.

Her.

Then she looked at him and saw a determined look in his eyes that said he wouldn't let her hold back.

"My parents' marriage was…abusive to say the least," she began, her throat croaky with words that had never been said before. "My father used to drink and he'd hit my mother, and my mother used to blame him for all her ills, and that in turn gave my father reason to drink. It was a vicious circle and I was caught in the middle." She drew a calming breath. "Thankfully Dan paid for me to go to boarding school when I turned twelve. Things were much better for me then."

A muscle knotted in his jaw. "I'm sorry."

She gave a strained smile. "Thank you, but there's no need."

Dear God, she hated thinking about those days. As a little girl her father had been remote and her mother had been loving and caring, but as the years passed it seemed that her mother had forgotten she had a daughter and had been hell-bent on making her husband's life a misery. Dan had tried to get his sister and brother-in-law some help, but they hadn't wanted it.

"From police reports they'd been arguing hours before the family home had burned to the ground with them in it."

"Bloody hell! I know they were dead but not how it happened."

"I know. It gives me nightmares sometimes."

There was a lengthy pause.

"Then I'm here to hold you." He held her eyes captive. "Come to me, Lana."

"Wh…what? There?" she said, looking at where he patted his lap. She was suddenly aware that they were alone.

"Yes, right here."

He waited.

She got to her feet and closed the gap between them, sinking down to sit on his lap. It felt strange sitting here like this with him.

"Look at me."

She lifted her head to look him in the eye.

He ran his palm up and down her shoulder in a comforting gesture. "I don't want you to feel alone anymore, Lana."

"I don't. I have Megan."

"You have me, too. Even after all this is over, I'll still be here for you."

Her heart rolled over. He didn't love her but he was showing her he cared about her. Oh, how she wished things could be different.

"Thank you, Matt," she said huskily.

He put his fingers under her chin. "Come here."

She frowned. "What do you mean?"

"Closer," he murmured, tugging her chin toward him. "I want your lips against mine. I want my body against yours. I want to be inside you."

Oh my.

"Yes." She wanted that, too.

Very much.

He cupped her face and silenced her with a kiss, and she realized that sex was his way of showing her comfort. Her heart swelled with the depth of her feelings for him.

He turned off the lamps, leaving the room bathed in shimmering light from the swimming pool outside. It gave a dreamlike quality to their togetherness as he lowered her to the thick living room rug and made slow, tender love to her.

It was so exquisite…so sweet…she cried afterward and he held her close. She'd never allowed another adult such free range of her heart before.

It stunned her.

He was truly a part of her now.

And no matter what happened in the future, no one could take this away from her.

Nine

Lana proceeded with caution over the next two weeks, her marriage to Matt having now deepened into a firm personal relationship. Yet she had to keep reminding herself it was only temporary.

And she fought herself constantly not to let him know that she loved him, especially when they made love every night, then slept, entwined together. It was wonderful waking up in his arms.

They watched television together after Megan went to bed, or they sat reading books, or sometimes Matt worked beside her in the living room rather than in his study. And they spent as much time as they could with their daughter.

As a family.

A temporary one, she needed to keep telling herself.

And Matt actually spent time with her checking over the accounts, and that meant more to her than anything. It signified that he fully believed she had nothing to do with the stolen money and had been set up to take the fall if something was discovered.

And if that were the case, *who* had used her in such a fashion? She still suspected Evan. The man seemed to be in her office more often than not on some pretext or other. Once she'd even found him at her desk looking through some paperwork. She'd challenged him, but he'd said he was looking for a report.

In any case, it made her burn to catch the real perpetrator, whether that was Evan or not. That person had put her very reputation on the line. He shouldn't be allowed to get away with it.

The night before Megan's first birthday, Lana got up from the sofa and went over to the sideboard.

"Matt, I have something for you," she said, coming back with a photograph album in her hands. "I thought you might like to see some pictures of our daughter's life so far."

Something emotional crossed his face.

"You've never asked about her birth, but I thought you might like to know anyway," she said, sliding onto the sofa next to him.

He swallowed hard. "I didn't ask before because it was too painful."

"I figured that." She handed him the album.

He looked down, almost in slow motion, and opened the heavy cover, staring at the first item. It was a commemorative birth certificate with his name as the father.

He darted her a look, turned the page. A picture of Megan just a few hours old stared up at them. She was still wrinkly and her eyes were shut.

"She was beautiful," he said huskily.

She smiled. "Every parent thinks their child is beautiful."

He arched a brow. "You think I'm biased?"

"Definitely," she teased.

He picked up her hand and brought it to his lips. "Then she takes after her mother."

She caught her breath. "No, she's like you."

His lips twitched. "Are you saying I'm gorgeous?"

He was.

She flushed and drew his attention back to the album. If she told him the truth, would she give herself away? Would he see that she loved him?

"Look at that mop of black hair on her," he said, interrupting her thoughts.

"She's a Valente. What do you expect?"

He grinned, then continued to turn the pages until he came to the one of Lana. He frowned. "You were crying?"

"They call it the baby blues." She didn't say but she'd been upset because Matt hadn't been able to share in the joy of Megan's birth.

He held her eyes a minute, then returned to the album. Page after page they went through together. At the end he closed the book carefully and went to hand it to her.

She pushed it back to him. "It's for you to keep."

He seemed to hold himself in check. "Thank you."

She cleared her throat. She couldn't tell him she loved him, but there was something else that very much needed to be said.

"I'm sorry, Matt."

"Sorry?"

"For keeping her from you. If I'd known how much you would love her—" She broke off, unable to finish the words.

He tenderly ran a finger down her cheek, turning her heart over. "That means more to me than you know."

"It does?"

He nodded.

"I'm glad you're here for her first birthday, Matt."

"Me, too." He leaned toward her and kissed her softly on the lips. Then without warning, he got up with the album in his hands and walked out of the room.

Lana's throat closed up. She'd wanted him to take her in his arms and make love to her, even as she understood why he hadn't. He needed to be alone right now.

If only she could feel less alone herself.

* * *

Lana was excited about Megan's party but tried not to let it get the better of her. She recollected only too well the last party her own parents had given her on her tenth birthday. Her father had come home drunk and caused a scene in front of her friends. And her childhood humiliation had been complete.

Oh, she knew no one would cause a scene at Megan's party the way her own father had done years ago. That wasn't the Valentes' style, and thank the Lord it wasn't. She wouldn't be here if it was.

But she didn't want to get too emotionally attached to this family when in years to come, possibly even Megan's next birthday, she would not be invited along. It would only end in heartache for herself, despite Megan's emotional attachment to them being a positive thing for her daughter.

"Lana, smile," Sasha said, holding up the camera.

Her sister-in-law took a picture of her and Matt crouching down to help Megan unwrap one of the myriads of presents on the living room floor.

And suddenly Lana was a part of them.

They were all just so thrilled to have Megan in the family that she couldn't be aloof. She tried…God knows she tried…but their joy was catching.

She smiled, then quickly looked down at her daughter's head, her eyes misting over, but not before she caught a gentle look in Matt's eyes. He knew how much this meant to her.

They continued opening the presents. Olivia and

Alex's son, Scott, was disgusted that no one had bought Megan any boy-type gifts, but their six-year-old daughter, Renee, thought the doll was great.

"It's bigger than Megan is," Nick scoffed when he saw what Cesare and Isabel had given her.

Cesare puffed up with full confidence. "It won't be long before she grows big enough to play with it."

They moved into the dining room, where the party carried on. Matt had decorated it with balloons and streamers and Ruth had made a selection of party foods for everyone. There was a birthday cake shaped like a teddy bear and they all sang "Happy Birthday" while Megan sat at the head of the table in her high chair.

For a moment Lana thought Megan might cry, but Matt waved a streamer in front of her face and that caught the little girl's attention.

The song finished and Isabel leaned toward Lana. "Doesn't she look cute?"

A soft curve touched Lana's lips. "Yes, she—"

"Da-Da."

Lana blinked. Had she just heard right?

"Da-Da."

There was a moment's silence.

"Did she just say Da-Da?" Alex asked.

Lana looked at Matt, who seemed to be rooted to the floor. She'd heard, but had Matt?

"Yeah, she did," Nick said. "Matt, did—"

"Oh my God," Matt muttered, "she called me Da-Da." A look of pride burst in his eyes, turning

Lana's heart over with love. Suddenly he whooped with joy and spun toward her. "Lana, did you hear her? She called me Da-Da."

Without warning, Lana was pulled into his arms. He kissed her hard and quick, before he eased away, their gazes locking and sharing the moment.

She blinked back tears of joy. "Yes, I heard her, Matt," she said huskily.

Matt kissed her again, then let her go and turned to Megan, scooping her out of her high chair. "Come on, you little darling. Come to Da-Da."

Lana watched the two of them together. Matt unashamedly kissed his daughter's cheek, then hugged her tight, and Lana's love for him…for them both… filled her until she thought she might die with the depth of it.

Everyone started to laugh and joke, but she couldn't have smiled to save her life.

The moment was too emotional.

And then she became conscious of Cesare watching her from across the room, the intensity in his eyes telling her he realized she loved his son.

She looked away. She couldn't admit it to the older man, not even in a look. Her love for Matt was something she never wanted anyone to know.

As if drawn by a magnet, her eyes found their way back to her father-in-law. She couldn't help herself. He inclined his head, telling her in his own way that he was pleased about it.

Her throat closed up and she turned and left

quietly to go to the living room, needing time to gather herself together. She didn't want anyone else reading her mind.

Or her emotions.

It was bad enough that Cesare had.

Okay, take a deep breath. It was her emotions she had to get under control right now. This was her daughter's first birthday. She needed to concentrate on that.

It would be the first of many, she prayed.

Many *happy* birthdays.

She would make sure of that. Her daughter would know only love and happiness from her parents.

Unlike her own childhood.

And when Megan was old enough, Lana knew she would make sure her daughter didn't feel any blame over her parents' marriage. To give Megan the Valente name may have been the reason for her and Matt's marriage, but only because they loved her enough to put her first, not because it was expected of them.

"Lana?"

The hint of Italian accent told her Cesare had followed her.

She planted a smile on her face and turned to face him. "Cesare, what are you doing here? You should be back there with your family."

"They're your family, too, Lana."

She said nothing. She wanted to believe that, but they both knew she was only here because of Megan.

"You love my son."

She gasped, then looked behind him in case anyone else had followed and heard. Luckily they hadn't.

"I don't know where you'd get that idea."

"I saw the love in your eyes, Lana."

She winced inwardly. "For Megan's sake, that's all. I'm thrilled Matt loves her so much. He's a wonderful father."

"Naturally," Cesare said, inclining his head in the Valente manner. "But it's more than that. I've been married three times, *cara*. I know that look of love in a woman."

She tried to act nonchalant. "You're wrong, Cesare."

"I'm never wrong."

"Cesare, look, even if it were true, don't get your hopes up. Matt will never fall in love with me. He doesn't want to fall in love with any woman. He likes his freedom too much."

Cesare held her gaze. "You've asked him that, have you?"

"He told me that before we were married."

"He didn't know you then. Now he does."

That was true. Matt had believed her a thief at first, but now he didn't.

Hope rose inside her for a moment.

Then died.

"Cesare, it isn't a matter of knowing me. It's a matter of Matt knowing himself. He's a playboy.

There's simply no possibility he would want to make this a permanent arrangement."

"Lana—"

"Cesare, please don't look for something on his part that's not there."

He drew himself up. "I don't need to look further than my *naso*." He tapped his nose. "But perhaps you do, *cara*," he said pointedly, then turned and left the room.

Lana released a slow breath. Cesare was a good man. He loved his wife and family and would always be there for them. Unlike her own father...

And then she realized something.

Matt was like his father.

He was a good man, too.

He wasn't in the least like her own father. Up until now, deep down she'd been judging Matt by her father's standards. And that was wrong. Matt was a far, far better man than her father had ever been.

Renewed hope filled Lana.

Hope that she and Matt would never be like her parents.

Hope that she and Matt might actually be able to make a go of their marriage.

And perhaps he might even come to love her one day?

Her heart fluttered and a feeling of warmth stayed with her for the rest of the evening. She couldn't shake it. She didn't *want* to shake it. The look in Cesare's eyes had given her hope for a future with Matt.

"Megan had a great time, didn't she?" Matt murmured, coming up behind her as she stood looking over the crib once the party was over.

She nodded. "Everyone did by the looks of them."

"Did *you*?"

She smiled softly at him. "Oh yes."

"But you didn't expect to, did you, Lana?" He didn't wait for an answer. "Did you have parties as a child?"

She felt herself freeze up. "Sometimes."

"I suspect they weren't fun."

"No." Maybe one day she'd tell him about them but not yet. She didn't want him staying with her out of pity.

If he stayed with her at all.

"Then this was an emotional day for you," he murmured.

"And you," she said, looking back down at Megan sleeping peacefully in her crib.

"Yes. I never thought I'd love her so much."

"I feel the same."

All at once she knew she wanted more children with Matt. Her heart expanded at the thought of carrying another baby of his, this time with him playing a major part. He'd be tender toward her for sure. She could see him in her mind's eye, running his hands over her expanding waistline, leaning forward to kiss their baby through her protruding stomach.

Buoyed by the warm feelings between them, she decided to test the waters. "I love being a mother. One day I'd love to have more children like Megan."

There was a moment of silence.

Then, "How many?" he said in a clipped tone that should have forewarned her but didn't.

"Three or four. I want a big family." She kept her eyes lowered to Megan. "Would you like to have more children, Matt?"

Another moment crept by.

"Eventually," he said, a coolness to him now that was hard to miss. It filled her with dismay. This discussion was obviously not to his liking.

He turned away, tension coming off him in waves. "I've got some work to do in the study."

Her heart broke in two as he left. It was clear he had no intention of falling in love with her or extending their marriage, or having more children with her.

With a sense of desolation she showered and went to bed. Matt joined her sometime in the early hours and she fully expected him to turn his back on her and go to sleep, but he pulled her into his arms and made love to her with an edge that stabbed at the pieces of her heart.

He brought her to climax, then reached his own climax, but there was none of the usual feeling of togetherness they shared.

One thing was apparent now.

They might be together in bed.

But they weren't—and never would be—together in their hearts.

Ten

Matt got through Sunday by keeping to himself, and then Monday at work was slower as he kept trying to keep his mind on the balance sheets, only it wasn't working.

He would never have believed how much he loved his daughter, and how great it had felt to share her first words with Lana. But did she have to go and spoil it all by saying she wanted more children one day in the future?

God, he hated the thought of another man in his daughter's life. Bloody hell, but he couldn't bear to think of Megan having stepsisters and stepbrothers, and calling another man "Da-Da."

And to think of Lana with another man…

He felt as if he'd been stabbed in the gut thinking about her marrying another man, making love to someone else, carrying that other man's child. Just the thought of it had him wanting to rip any man's throat out who came near her.

Yet she'd said it so calmly, as if it were nothing out of the ordinary. He hadn't needed to know she was already thinking of being with another man before she'd even left *him.*

"Matt?"

He spun his leather chair away from the window. The million-dollar view of Sydney Harbour was worth nothing to him right now.

"I'm leaving now for my three o'clock dental appointment," Irene reminded him. "I'll see you tomorrow. If you need anything just ask Evan."

"Fine. See you tomorrow." He doubted he'd get much work done this afternoon now. All he could think about was going home and seeing Megan and Lana, who was at home on her day off.

He missed them, dammit.

Maybe he should go home early?

He sighed and straightened in his chair. No, he'd better stay here and finish up this lot of accounts. They needed reviewing by tomorrow.

Half an hour later, Matt was sitting up much straighter in his chair. "Christ!"

He didn't believe it.

He couldn't believe it.

He hadn't been looking for any anomalies, but

fifty thousand dollars was missing from one of the
accounts. It was a brilliant piece of cover-up, but
even more brilliant was that the money had been
stolen at a time Lana wasn't working for them.

He knew who the thief was now.

Irene.

His PA.

He fell back against his chair stunned but greatly
relieved. It proved to him that Lana was innocent—
what he'd put her through with his accusations.
She'd be relieved to know he'd found the culprit.

He knew his longtime PA was the thief just by
something in the way she had fiddled the books. It
had her stamp all over it. He just hadn't been
looking beyond Lana before.

But what if Irene denied it? She was a personal
assistant, not an accountant. She could make a fairly
believable case that she couldn't possibly know how
to fix the books.

Would the authorities believe her?

He dared not risk it. He had to set up a trap. An
after-hours one because that's the only time Irene
could have accessed the accounts without anyone
getting suspicious.

But first he had to go and confess everything to
Alex and Nick. They weren't going to be pleased
that he'd kept the missing money from them, nor
that he'd blamed Lana. They'd understand that he'd
been trying to keep it quiet for their father's sake
after his heart attack, but now it really was time for
them to call in the police.

As for Lana, he'd sort all this out before telling her. It was the right thing to do.

After all his accusations, he owed her that much.

Lana's heart plummeted when Matt called to say he would be working late. He'd been aloof ever since Saturday night. Why had she mentioned having more children? She must have scared him off.

Sure, he was good with Megan but clearly he didn't want more children or a longer marriage to her. And clearly he wasn't about to fall in love with her. She should have kept quiet and been thankful he was a good father to Megan and a good, if temporary, husband to her.

He didn't come home until after ten that night. She'd given up and gone to bed, pretending to be asleep when he entered the bedroom and took a shower, then slid naked between the sheets, where he rolled over and went to sleep.

She wanted to say, "Hold me. Don't push me away like this," but what would be the use? She didn't want any man holding her against his will.

Somehow Lana managed to get through the next day at work without giving away her feelings. And then Matt took her home before saying he was going back to work. He kissed Megan goodbye, even gave *her* a quick kiss, but avoided looking at her and left.

Lana wanted to cry. It was obvious now what was going on. Her suggestion of more children had def-

initely driven him away—right into the arms of
another woman.

Oh God. How could she continue to live with a
man who was cheating on her? Would the next step
be that he didn't come home one night at all? How
long before it became a regular occurrence?

Like her father.

The thought panicked her, but somehow she held
herself together. At least she knew she was prepared
for the worst, and that gave her an inner strength.

He didn't make love to her that night either, not
that she expected he would try. And if he *had* tried
she certainly would have told him what she
thought of him.

After the third night of his dropping her at home
and saying he had to go back to work, Lana's heartache was overtaken by an escalating anger. So, he was
working, was he? Perhaps she'd just go down there
after Megan was in bed and check if that was true.

And if it was?

One step at a time.

At seven-thirty she asked Ruth to babysit Megan,
then hopped into her own car and drove back to the
office.

She parked in the underground car park, which
was well lit but deserted, rather than drive around to
the front entrance where the security guard would be.

With a shaky hand she punched in the code to
access the gate to the car park, her heart trembling
a minute later when she saw that Matt's car wasn't

there. She should go home right now, yet something forced her to go upstairs and check for sure that he wasn't working. She wanted no doubts about any of this.

All seemed quiet as she rode the elevator to the eighth floor. She was vaguely aware of its being eerie here, but her thoughts were on Matt and what she would find.

Or *not* find.

The door opened with a ping. And Lana's eyes widened at the scene before her. There seemed to be people everywhere, some men in suits and a couple of policemen. Alex and Nick were there and had turned to look at her, but she couldn't see—

"Matt!" she said, rushing forward with intense relief when one of the men moved and she saw Matt standing there.

He suddenly saw her and he scowled. "Lana! What are you doing here?"

She rushed up to him, putting her hands on his arm, needing to touch him. "I thought…" It didn't matter now. "Matt, what's going on? Are you okay? Is someone hurt? What happened?" She fired the questions at him, unable to stop herself from babbling.

"It's Irene. She—"

"She's been hurt? Oh my God!"

His mouth flattened in a grim line. "No, she's not hurt, Lana. She's our thief. The police are here to arrest her. She's in my office, but they'll soon be taking her down to the police station."

Lana tried to take in what he was saying. "*Irene* stole the money?"

He nodded. "I discovered another amount missing on Monday and decided to set a trap for her."

Just then Irene came out of Matt's office in handcuffs with a policeman. "You've got no proof I did anything, Matt."

Matt pointed to the potted plant on the filing cabinet. "It's all on tape, Irene. I'm not stupid, you know. I put a camera behind the plant."

She lifted her head. "I'll see you in court, *Mr. Valente*," she spat as they took her to one of the elevators.

Lana watched the exchange, stunned by Irene's changed demeanor, even as she registered one fact. Matt knew all this on Monday and hadn't told her. He'd kept it to himself.

For a few minutes she just stood there as the elevator doors closed with Irene inside.

"Lana, why—"

She rounded on him. "How *could* you, Matt?"

He frowned. "What's the matter?"

She lifted her chin. "Why didn't you tell me?"

He opened his mouth to speak, then suddenly seemed to realize they had an audience. He took her by the arm and marched her into his office, where he shut the door behind him and stood in front of it.

"Now listen to me, Lana. I was trying to protect you."

"From what?" she scoffed. "Irene?"

His mouth tightened. "Yes. You have to admit she isn't the person we knew her to be. She has a gambling problem."

That wasn't good enough.

"I would have been right there beside you helping to trap her. I don't know what she could have done to me."

"She could have lured you away on some pretext or other. She could have hurt you." Something flared in his eyes. "I didn't know what she was capable of. I couldn't take that chance."

Okay, so he had a point but...

"The thing is you didn't trust me enough to tell me. You trusted Alex and Nick but not me."

"Alex and Nick are—"

"Family?" she snapped.

"No, I was going to say they are management. I had to let my brothers know what was going on."

She understood that, too, but...

"You're missing the point, Matt. You accused me of stealing a great deal of money, yet you couldn't even ask me to help you trap the real thief? And then you let me believe that..." She trailed away.

"What?"

She swallowed past her dry throat. "That you were having an affair."

"What!"

She stiffened. "What did you expect me to think, Matt? You've been working late every evening this week. Wasn't it reasonable to think you were having an affair?"

"No. And I *was* working late. I was trying to catch Irene in the act."

Lana winced as they came back full circle. Whether it was about him not trusting her enough to tell her about Irene, or shutting her out until she thought he was having an affair, they were clearly lacking in trust.

And if they couldn't trust each other, how could their marriage survive?

He scowled. "Where's all this coming from? I promised you I wouldn't have any affairs while we were married, and I haven't."

"You said that, but—"

Someone knocked on the door. "Mr. Valente, I need to get a statement from you," one of the policemen interrupted.

"In a minute," Matt growled loudly. "Lana we need to talk. I—"

She pulled her shoulders back. "No more talk. Just leave me alone, Matt."

"No, you—"

There was another knock on the door, and frustration and anger swept over his features as he glanced back at it, then back at her. "Fine. You've got it." He spun away and stalked out of the room.

Lana stood there for a moment then left the room, too. She didn't look at anyone as she walked to the elevator, not even relaxing once the doors closed. Her mind was too full of her emotions. There was so much anger and hurt between her and Matt now. So much mistrust. How long before the raised voices started between them?

Like her parents.

She'd lie in bed and listen to their arguments and flinch at every word until her father stormed out to spend the night with some other woman.

She flinched now. Up until this evening she had fooled herself into believing she could get through the year without upsetting Megan.

But this was the moment where she knew what she had to do. She would never let Megan go through what she had gone through growing up. She'd made that promise to her daughter when she'd been born.

She would keep that promise now.

Eleven

Megan was awake and fretful when Lana got home, and Ruth was nursing her back to sleep.

"That's okay, Ruth. I'll take care of her now."

"If you're sure."

Lana nodded, desperate to get some time alone before she fell apart. She needed time to think, had to put one foot in front of the other. She'd have to find a new job and another place to live, her apartment having already been rented out. The thought of it all swamped her like a tidal wave. There was so much to do.

She wasn't sure how long it was before she looked up from rocking Megan in her arms and saw Matt in the bedroom doorway.

He'd followed her.

"Is she okay?" he asked quietly, his brown eyes dark and unreadable.

Lana rocked her. "She will be."

"Come into the living room when you've finished."

"It might be awhile."

"I'll wait."

That sounded ominous.

Fifteen minutes later, with Megan settled in her crib. Lana straightened her shoulders and walked toward the living room. As she got closer, she heard Matt's voice.

"You were the one who told me to marry her, Dad," he was saying into his cell phone, his back to her.

There was a pause.

"Yeah, like you forced Alex and Nick to marry, as well."

There was another pause.

"I'm not sure what I'll do yet."

Lana felt like her breath had been cut off. He was talking about *her*.

And what was this about Alex and Nick? Cesare had forced them to marry their wives? He'd forced Matt to marry her, too?

God, how many lives were the Valentes prepared to wreck for the sake of the family name? They'd certainly ruined hers.

She must have made a noise, because Matt spun around and saw her. "Dad, I have to go." He switched off his phone.

Lana swallowed with anguish. "Don't worry, Matt. I'll make it easy for you. Megan and I will be gone by the time you get home tomorrow."

Matt looked at his wife standing there in the doorway and something erupted inside him. He jumped to his feet. "The hell you will!"

Her chin rose in the air. "Matt, you can't stop me."

He strode toward her and put his hand on her arm, not tight but enough to bring her fully into the living room. "Right, let's talk." He slammed her with his eyes. "And I mean let's *really* talk this time."

She fixed him with a piercing gaze, then took a few steps away, forcing him to let her go. "Don't pretend, Matt. We both know you married me for Megan's sake."

He frowned. "That's right. So what's the problem?"

"But I didn't know your father had pressured you into it."

"He didn't."

She shot him a withering look. "Now who's lying? I heard you a moment ago. You reminded Cesare how he'd told you to marry me."

He waved a dismissive hand. "I was being sarcastic. He did tell me to marry you, but *I* made the decision to marry you, not him. There's a difference."

Her brow rose. "Different to Alex and Nick? How pleased you must feel to be one step ahead of them all," she said, sneering. "The youngest brother jumping in and sacrificing himself on the marriage altar would definitely make you a big man in their eyes."

What on earth…

He swore. "It wasn't like that."

"Then what was it like?"

"You already know all there is to know, Lana. I don't have an agenda."

She held his gaze and he held hers, then her shoulders suddenly drooped as all the puff seemed to leave her. "Matt, our marriage isn't working. Megan has your name now, so there's no further need for us to stay together. She's a Valente. I'll make sure she's proud of it."

Jealousy stabbed at him. "Even when you marry someone else?" he said in a harsh voice.

She looked baffled. "What do you mean?"

His muscles bunched at the thought of her with someone else. "You said you wanted more children."

"I do."

"I'm assuming you have someone in mind to father those children."

The air seemed to suddenly suspend itself.

"Of course."

Matt saw red. "The poor bastard."

Her forehead creased. "Matt, do you think—" She broke off. "It's *you* I wanted to father my children."

The blood rushed to his head. "Me?"

She met his eyes without flinching. "I wanted to have more children with you, only, you turned all cold on me and I knew I was grasping at straws to think you'd feel the same."

Matt was trying to take it all in. "You said 'wanted.' Is that feeling in the past?"

She swallowed hard. "No."

Hope began to rise inside his chest. "Then—"

"No, Matt. It can't be."

"Why not?"

She shrugged and looked away uncomfortably. "Because."

He took some steps toward her and put his hand under her chin, turning her to look at him. He wasn't going to let up. "Because?"

She lowered her eyelids, then slowly lifted them open, her feelings clear to see. "Because I love you, Matt."

A wave rolled inside Matt's chest. "You love me?" he rasped.

"Yes," she whispered. Then she stepped back, breaking away from his touch. "But it's not enough. I can't let Megan suffer in the future at our lack of trust for each other. I suffered growing up because my mother was pregnant and because my father did the right thing in marrying her, but I can't do that to Megan. My parents ended up hating each other. My father was always cheating on my mother."

He quelled a squeezing pain inside himself. "Your father married your mother because she was pregnant with you?"

She nodded. "Yes. I told you."

"No, you told me they had an abusive marriage. You didn't say why."

"Oh." Her expression clouded over, clearly with unhappy thoughts. "Well, that's why. I was always in the middle. It wasn't a pleasant feeling."

"That wouldn't happen with us."

"It happened tonight. We've already argued about Irene and about your affairs and—"

"I haven't had any affairs. Anyway, who said we would be arguing in years to come?"

"If we don't trust each other now, we certainly won't trust each other in the future."

Everything fell into place and Matt finally understood why she hadn't told him about Megan, and why she hadn't wanted to trap him. It wasn't wholly about him not being ready to be a father, as she'd stated. That had been only an excuse.

No, the problem was that her parents had left her a legacy of trust issues. Her father's adultery was the main offender, and he could only imagine what other mental scars she had. It came down to the fact that she couldn't trust *anyone* not to hurt her or her daughter—including himself.

As he looked into her pain-filled eyes he finally understood something else. It hurt like hell when you loved someone and they were in pain.

As he loved Lana.

He knew that in one blinding moment, but amazingly he somehow held himself in check. He had to tread carefully here or he could lose her.

For good.

"Did your parents love each other, Lana?"

Her expression clouded. "My mother loved my father, but it was never reciprocated."

Relief launched through his body. This was something concrete he could use. "Our situation is different."

She shook her head. "I've just told you I love you, Matt. It's not different. It's the same situation all over again."

Love swelled inside him. "It isn't, you know. You see, your father didn't love your mother…not like I love you."

"Matt, listen. I—" Her eyes widened. "Wh…what?"

"I love you, Lana."

Hope flashed in her eyes, then died. "You're only saying that. It's not possible."

"Believe me, it's very possible. It happened. It's true." He slid his arms around her waist and brought her close. "It took the threat of you leaving me to make me realize it."

She swallowed hard. "But you don't want to stay married to me, Matt."

"I don't?"

Her eyes searched his. "What about your other women? You were going to return to them after a year, remember?"

"Darling, I didn't have nearly as many affairs before I married you as you think."

Her forehead creased. "What about those nights

you stayed out late when we were first married? I
didn't want to believe you were with anyone else
but—"

"I went to stay at my old apartment each night
for a few hours. Alone. I admit it gave me some
space. I wasn't used to being married, but there
were never any other women involved."

"Oh God, that's the truth, isn't it?"

"Absolutely." His hands tightened on her waist.
"I married you for Megan's sake, Lana, but I want
to stay married to you for *our* sake."

Moisture glittered in her eyes. "Oh Matt."

"Stay with me, Lana. Have more children with
me to share our love. Be happy and make me happy,
too."

"I never let myself believe in forever, Matt." She
blinked rapidly. "This time I know I can."

His heart overflowed with love as he lowered
his head toward her. "Yes, darling, this time you
can. Trust me."

"I do."

Epilogue

Fireworks lit up the night sky over the Valente mansion for Cesare's sixtieth birthday, and family and friends oohed and aahed over the stunning display.

Isabel Valente looked at her husband of thirty-three years, her heart swelling with love and pride. He'd come to Australia from Italy with his parents when he was twelve, made his fortune and turned the Valente name into something he was proud to pass on to his sons.

And his sons were equally as proud of their father, she knew, gazing at those three sons of her heart, despite only giving birth to one of them. They were all now happily married to wonderful, caring women and starting to raise families of their own.

Alex and Olivia had adopted Scott and Renee and would adopt more children as time moved on.

Nick and Sasha had a glow about them that made her think there might be a baby on the way soon.

And Matt and Lana had adorable little Megan, who was the apple of her youngest son's eye.

"Well, Izzie," Cesare said, slipping his arm around her waist. "I'm a very happy man now. The Valente name will carry on for a long time to come."

She smiled. The Valente men could be proud, arrogant and exasperating to the women who loved them, but when it came down to it, none of the Valente women would have it any other way.

Isabel held up her glass to her husband. "Viva Valente, darling!"

And life, glorious as it was, went on.

* * * * *

MILLS & BOON
Desire 2-in-1
On sale 20th August 2010

More Than a Millionaire *by Emilie Rose*

The wrong woman is carrying his baby! A medical mix-up
means he may have to seduce the mother-to-be.

The Untamed Sheikh *by Tessa Radley*

Whisking a suspected temptress to his desert palace seems the
only way to stop her...until unexpected attraction flares...

Texan's Wedding-Night Wager *by Charlene Sands*

This Texan won't sign the divorce papers. He wants a sexy
revenge on his estranged wife. But his plan backfires...

The Oilman's Baby Bargain *by Michelle Celmer*

Falling for the heiress was unexpected – but so was her pregnancy!
Though the marriage would be business, their bedroom deals
soon became purely pleasure.

The Tycoon's Rebel Bride *by Maya Banks*

She arrives in town determined to get her man at any cost.
But suddenly it isn't clear any more who is seducing whom...

The Billionaire's Unexpected Heir *by Kathie DeNosky*

The terms of his inheritance bring this sexy playboy attorney a
whole new set of responsibilities...including fatherhood!

INTRODUCED BY BESTSELLING AUTHOR KATIE FFORDE

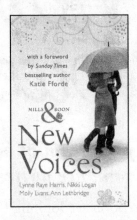

with a foreword by *Sunday Times* bestselling author Katie Fforde

MILLS & BOON

New Voices

Lynne Raye Harris, Nikki Logan
Molly Evans, Ann Lethbridge

Four fabulous new writers

Lynn Raye Harris
Kept for the Sheikh's Pleasure

Nikki Logan
Seven-Day Love Story

Molly Evans
Her No.1 Doctor

Ann Lethbridge
The Governess and the Earl

We know you're going to love them!

Available 20th August 2010

Discover Pure Reading Pleasure with

MILLS & BOON®

Visit the Mills & Boon website for all the latest in romance

Buy all the latest releases, backlist and eBooks

Find out more about our authors and their books

Join our community and chat to authors and other readers

Free online reads from your favourite authors

Win with our fantastic online competitions

Sign up for our free monthly eNewsletter

Tell us what you think by signing up to our reader panel

Rate and review books with our star system

www.millsandboon.co.uk

 Follow us at twitter.com/millsandboonuk

 Become a fan at facebook.com/romancehq

2 FREE BOOKS
AND A SURPRISE GIFT

We would like to take this opportunity to thank you for reading this Mills & Boon® book by offering you the chance to take TWO more specially selected books from the Desire™ 2-in-1 series absolutely FREE! We're also making this offer to introduce you to the benefits of the Mills & Boon® Book Club™—

- **FREE home delivery**
- **FREE gifts and competitions**
- **FREE monthly Newsletter**
- **Exclusive Mills & Boon Book Club offers**
- **Books available before they're in the shops**

Accepting these FREE books and gift places you under no obligation to buy, you may cancel at any time, even after receiving your free books. Simply complete your details below and return the entire page to the address below. You don't even need a stamp!

YES Please send me 2 free Desire stories in a 2-in-1 volume and a surprise gift. I understand that unless you hear from me, I will receive 2 superb new 2-in-1 books every month for just £5.25 each, postage and packing free. I am under no obligation to purchase any books and may cancel my subscription at any time. The free books and gift will be mine to keep in any case.

Ms/Mrs/Miss/Mr _____ Initials _____

Surname _____

Address _____

_____ Postcode _____

E-mail _____

Send this whole page to: Mills & Boon Book Club, Free Book Offer, FREEPOST NAT 10298, Richmond, TW9 1BR